**Also available from
Victoria Dahl
and Harlequin HQN**

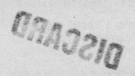

VICTORIA DAHL

LOOKING *FOR* TROUBLE

HARLEQUIN® HQN™

Recycling programs
for this product may
not exist in your area.

ISBN-13: 978-0-373-77861-4

LOOKING FOR TROUBLE

Printed in U.S.A.

This is for the women who helped with this book.
Jif, Tessa, Tonda, Kate,
and the Women Who Shall Not Be Named.
I'll meet all of you at the bar.

CHAPTER ONE

ALEX BISHOP WAS heading toward drunk at 11:00 a.m. on a Wednesday, and he didn't give a damn. The blond bartender didn't seem to give a damn either. She brought him another Scotch and pushed it toward him with a wink. Her hand lingered on the glass. "You sure about the burger? We're pretty famous for them around here."

"No, but thanks." He didn't return the wink. She was pretty, and there was something in her smile that told him she wouldn't mind a midday fuck against a wall with a man whose name she didn't know, but Alex might be hitting this bar a lot in the next few days. When two people were looking for nameless sex, neither wanted to hang out with a bar between them for days afterward.

She moved away and he stared into the tumbler of cheap Scotch until the whole world turned amber and bright, then he downed it without a wince. Number three or four, he couldn't remember, and he didn't feel even a twinge of shame when he pushed up from the stool and had to steady himself against the bar. He'd done this on purpose, after all. Drunk was the

best possible state of mind on his first day home in
sixteen years.

He'd hit the road in Idaho before dawn, hoping to
beat an afternoon storm rolling in over the Tetons,
but he'd skipped coffee, rejecting any more alert-
ness than was required to simply drive. He didn't
want to notice the landscape. Didn't want to deal
with memories triggered by his first taste of cen-
tral Wyoming since he'd turned eighteen and made
himself disappear.

But his willpower wasn't as strong as his memory, and the emotions had hit like a sledgehammer
when he'd made town. Hence the Scotch. The actual
people he'd come to see could wait.

Alex threw a generous amount of cash on the
bar and walked past the lunch patrons in a carefully
straight line. They glanced up from their plates as
he passed, but then looked quickly away. He wasn't
the type of guy that people started conversations
with. If he put out the right vibes, they avoided him
altogether.

But Jackson still greeted him when he opened the
door of the motel bar.

The sunlight blasted his weary eyes before he had
a chance to slip on shades. Jackson didn't give a shit
that he was drunk, and it didn't give a shit that he
didn't want to be there. It still threw itself at him, the
same old town, hardly changed at all during his long
escape. After all, that was its shtick. Old West charm.
Historical buildings. Though the no-tell motel he'd

chosen at the edge of town was less historical than just old.

He'd picked the place on purpose, eschewing cheer or comfort. He wanted temporary. He wanted an excuse not to unpack so he'd know every single moment he was here that he could grab his bag and ride away in a minute flat.

His lug-soled boots crunched against the gravel lot of the motel, and he remembered now that he'd stayed here once before. But that walk had been at night, in the snow, the moon shining brightly enough to highlight the gorgeous cleavage of the college girl he'd hooked up with at a spring-break house party. It had been her motel room, shared with three other girls, and he'd been thrilled to add to the crowded conditions for a night.

He'd partied a lot back then. Any excuse not to be home with his mom and brother. But he hadn't been this drunk in a good long while, and there were no spring-break flings awaiting him this time around.

There was only duty and misplaced obligation.

Fucking information age. A generation ago he could have vanished for good. But these days, one job in the wrong place and somebody had recognized him and volunteered family news that he didn't want.

Like the news that his dad was dead.

Of course, his dad had been dead for twenty-five years. Funny that it was still news.

He actually laughed at that thought, and an older woman getting bags from the trunk of her car shot him a glare of suspicion. He would've offered to help, but not only did he look menacing with his buzzed head and three days' growth of beard, he smelled like hard liquor and hostility, so he walked on.

He'd barely glanced at the room when he'd checked in an hour before, but it looked clean enough as he shucked his leather jacket and toed off his boots. A bed. An ugly bedspread. A dresser that had seen better days. At least it had a nice flat-screen TV. He traveled a lot for his job, and when he was holed up in some remote frontier town for a month, that was really his only requirement in a motel. A nice TV.

When he'd had an apartment for a couple of years, that had been all he'd added to the charm, too. Andrea had tried to bring some nice touches, but it had never become a home. For either of them.

Alex shrugged out of his T-shirt and tossed it on a chair, then headed for the shower. He'd scrub up, sleep off the Scotch for an hour or two, and then he'd finally do what he'd come here to do. He'd go see his family.

He didn't even know why he'd called his brother after sixteen years away. It'd been nearly two months since Alex had picked up that phone, and he still had no real idea of his motivation. Connection or reconciliation or even gloating over their father's corpse… All of those together or maybe none of them. But he'd called. And it had been a bad idea.

The first call had gone fine. Shane had sounded

relieved and even downright happy to hear from Alex, and Alex couldn't deny the way his heart had twisted at hearing his older brother's voice. They'd caught up a little, and Alex had finally heard the whole story about their dad, and that had been that. He'd promised to come by Jackson the next time he was near, but he hadn't meant it.

He'd decided by then that he was only being sentimental. His mentor had died the year before, and Oz had been the closest thing Alex had to family. Closer than Alex's actual family. But he wasn't going to let that loss change his mind about returning to Jackson. He'd learned early on to let things—and people—go, and he'd let his brother go a long time ago.

Then, a week later, Shane had called, and Alex had realized it wasn't going to go as smooth and easy as he'd hoped. "I'd like you to come back to Jackson for a couple of days," Shane had said.

Alex had shut him down cold, but Shane wasn't a kid anymore either, and he'd talked for thirty minutes straight. Somehow Alex had found himself saying he'd try, and then he'd straight-up promised that he'd come.

"Fuck," he said, stepping into the spray of hot water with a growl. A goddamn memorial service for a man who'd been dead twenty-five years. A way for his mom and brother to hold on to the man a little longer.

Sure, Shane had apologized. He'd sworn that things had changed. Even their mother was getting better, he'd claimed. In fact, this service would help her close the door on her obsession forever. This was the end of it, for everyone.

That was the only reason Alex had come. To end this. And if Shane was for real, maybe they could talk a couple of times a year. Meet up for a drink once a decade. And when someone asked if he had any family, Alex wouldn't have to say no.

He rolled his shoulders, trying to work out the tension that the Scotch and steam weren't touching, but they stayed as tight as ever. Six hours strangling the grips of his Triumph T140 couldn't be shrugged off that quickly, not when he was heading straight toward the source of his stress.

He scrubbed some soap across his head, cleaning the week's worth of hair and thinking he'd shave it again when he got settled somewhere else, then he soaped up his face and decided he couldn't be bothered shaving that either. Let his appearance match his mood. He didn't owe anyone more than that.

He was out of the shower in two minutes flat, but an hour later, he was still lying sleepless on the bed. The ceiling stared blankly at him, the white, textured anonymity of a thousand other places. He was used to the sight. Every once in a while he lucked into a place with faux-wood paneling and he could at least count the seams, but not today. He couldn't even summon the will to jerk off.

His buzz was already fading and he knew he wouldn't sleep, so Alex got up, dressed and headed out to grab a burger. After that, there was nothing to do but drive to his mother's house and see if anything had really changed.

HE DIDN'T KNOW he'd been hopeful. He would've denied it if anyone had asked. But the disappointment rolled over him in a cold, deep wave.

Things weren't better. Nothing had changed.

Actually, that was a lie. His mother had gotten older. Thirty years older, despite that it had only been sixteen. She was only sixty-five, but she was shrinking in on herself and had gone totally gray.

"Alex!" she said brightly, stretching up to give him a tight hug. "I missed you so much. But I knew you'd come back to us."

Yes. Of course she'd thought he'd be back. She'd always "known" that about his father, too. Lucky for Alex, she wasn't batting zero anymore. At least he hadn't been dead this whole time, even if his dad had.

He patted her awkwardly on the back.

She'd always been affectionate, and he'd always felt ungracious about it, but he knew why now. Her affection was too desperate, too overwhelming, as if she could will you to return her intensity. She'd been that way about her pain, too. She wanted you to share it or it wasn't real enough.

Alex let her go and stood straight to force her arms off.

When she'd opened the door he'd gotten a glimpse inside her house, and his first impression was confirmed when she let him in. The place was tiny, but it had looked only a little run-down from the curb. But inside? Inside it was packed with papers and smelled stale. If she wasn't obsessed with Alex's dad now, she was obsessed with something else.

Alex stepped reluctantly inside. He was going to kill his brother.

"Oh, honey," his mother gushed. "There's so much left to do. Your father deserves this honor so much and I want it to be perfect. We need to discuss your eulogy and what—"

"Eulogy?" he snapped.

"Of course, Shane will speak first since he's the oldest, and then you'll speak. I'll be the last to go. I have so much to—"

"You've got to be kidding."

She didn't seem to register his tone. She turned and moved in a stiff, awkward gait toward the far side of the little living room, then started digging through a pile of papers. "I've only gotten half of it written, and I still need to put together the program. I'd hoped to have that done last week."

Alex blew out a long breath. He'd been tricked. His mom hadn't gotten over her husband's disappearance at all. Oh, she'd had to accept that the man was dead, since Shane had found their father's remains himself, but that clearly hadn't stopped the madness.

What exactly did his mom think Alex had to say about the man? *From what I remember, he was a*

*decent father, but I must've been wrong since he got
himself killed while running off with some floozy.*

Alex watched his mother read frantically over
the papers in her hand, her lips moving. He recognized that bright-eyed fever. It had taken up half his
childhood.

He didn't even turn around when the door opened
behind him. "You said she was better," he said flatly.

"Alex."

Despite his anger, he didn't resist when Shane
spun him around and grabbed him in a hug. In fact,
Alex didn't even resist hugging him back. Shit.
Shane had taken care of him all those times when
their mom had shut herself in her room for days.
Shane might've tricked him, but the man was still
his big brother.

Though Alex might actually be the bigger one
now. That was a little disorienting. Shane had always
seemed huge to Alex.

"Jesus," Shane said, pulling back to hold Alex at
arm's length. "What the hell happened to your hair?
And your baby face?"

"The hair's still there somewhere. But I lost the
baby face a long time ago."

"I guess so." Shane slapped his shoulder. Hard.
"Christ. Look at you."

"Look at you," Alex said. "You look good." He
did. Shane had grown a couple of inches himself,
and he'd gotten a lot stronger, but there wasn't any
gray in his hair yet, and the lines around his eyes

seemed to be from smiling. He'd always been the charming one.

Still. "This isn't what you said it was, Shane."

Shane's eyes drifted past his shoulder and his smile faded. He lowered his voice. "She was getting better. I don't know what's going on."

"This is better?"

"No. Two months ago she seemed more stable... I mean it," he insisted when Alex shot him a disgusted look. "She's been seeing a psychiatrist for a while. She apparently has something called borderline personality disorder. It makes her...extreme. I don't know. The doctor thought this ceremony would be a good idea since Mom wasn't exactly stable when we interred Dad's remains last year. Closure and all that."

"Closure. For her? Or you?"

Shane shot him a hard look, but didn't take the bait. "For her. She's starting to accept that he's been dead this whole time and was never coming back."

"Yeah. Guess I had that pegged." The old anger was pushing through now, forcing his blood pressure up until Alex could feel his heart banging.

"As for me, I've spent the past sixteen years more worried about you than Dad."

"Yeah, well...I was doing fine until you dragged me back into this." Alex tipped his head toward their mother, who seemed oblivious to the quiet tension.

"She was better—" Shane started again, but Alex cut him off.

"Maybe you're just too damn used to the crazy to see it."

Shane's jaw stiffened with anger, but his voice stayed calm and low. "I didn't open myself back up to this until she started getting help. She's been good. I mean it. Maybe this is just… I don't know. Maybe it's just coming to a head, and once the ceremony is done…"

"Sounds like the same old wishful thinking, Shane."

Shane stared at him for a long moment, his eyes blazing with whatever he wasn't saying. But he just shook his head. "Maybe. But I'm not going to pretend I'm sorry you're here."

"Shane!" their mom suddenly yelped. "Tell your brother he needs to have his speech done by tomorrow night. It can't wait!"

Alex shook his head. "I guess I'll be sorry for the both of us. And if you think I'm participating in this dedication, you've got another think coming."

Shane started to reach one hand toward him, but Alex brushed past him and headed for the door. This family was as sick as ever. He shouldn't have come.

Shane followed him across the living room. "Don't run away again," he said quietly.

Alex paused, his hand on the doorknob. "I didn't run away the first time. I started a life, and I plan to get back to it."

"Fine. Just give me a few days. That's all."

"Okay," Alex agreed. "A few days. I just came

by to let you know I'm here, so you didn't have to worry I wouldn't show up. You've got my number if you need me."

"We're getting together tonight with my girl-friend, Merry, to figure out the logistics of the ded-ication. She's the one who runs the ghost town, so if you want to see where we'll be holding the dedica-tion, Merry will be out there until six. We're meeting for dinner at the Wagon Wheel at seven."

Alex shook his head, not sure if he was refus-ing or just exasperated as he stepped out and closed the door behind him. Shane didn't follow, but Alex only made it halfway to the sidewalk before he was stopped. Not by his brother or his conscience, but by the sight of a very pretty, very angry young woman heading straight toward him on his mother's front walkway. Her head was down, the sun glinting off her red hair, and her mouth held tight in a frown. The hands that clutched a crumpled pile of papers to her chest were white around the knuckles.

She was only two steps away when she looked up and stumbled to a stop. "Oh," her pink lips said, her anger falling away to surprise for a brief moment. She pushed up her little black glasses. The anger returned within a few heartbeats and her flushed cheeks got even redder as her eyes narrowed, first at him, then at the door behind him.

"Here." She shoved the papers at his chest, and Alex automatically caught them. Sticky tape grabbed at his fingers as he tried to catch the few sheets that slipped away. "Tell her to leave me the hell alone."

"What?" he asked.

"I have tried to be patient, but I won't tolerate harassment. I've reached my limit." Her finger poked at the papers and a few more fell away. "Tell her to stay off my property and out of my life."

"Who?" he started, but the wild bundle of female fury spun away from him and stalked off. Alex's eyes followed her as she turned left and marched down the street. The skirt of her green dress swayed with the movement of her hips, the black belt drawing his eye to her slim little waist. He lost sight of her when she reached some pine trees, but kept staring for a few seconds anyway. Who in the world had that been?

Remembering the papers, he juggled them until he could finally read one, and the murky confrontation became slightly clearer. They were all copies of the same flyer. Not a professional flyer, but something typed in all caps on a computer and printed in an obnoxiously large font. An announcement of the memorial service for his dad. Written in the sort of flowery language that could only have been conjured by an obsessed mind. His mother had printed these and taped them somewhere, apparently on that woman's property.

For a moment, Alex considered going back into his mom's house and asking who the woman was and why his mother had assaulted her with flyers, but curiosity wasn't a strong enough pull to force him back into that mess.

He stuffed all the flyers into his mom's mailbox and got on his bike, looking down the street in the hopes of spying the mystery woman as he buckled on his helmet. Apparently he wasn't the only one who was sick of his mother's madness. What a breath of fresh air.

CHAPTER TWO

THIS WAS SO humiliating.

Sophie Heyer slid a little lower in her seat, then considered continuing the slide until she was underneath the conference-room table and could crawl out of the library meeting room. But that might draw attention. After all, there were only four others in the room, and they each kept shooting side glances at her, as if waiting for her to break.

She suspected someone had purposefully scheduled this meeting on Sophie's day off, but she'd ruined the plan by picking up an afternoon shift from Betty, who had a sick baby at home. Well, Sophie was here now. She wasn't going to cower.

She made herself sit a little straighter and raised her chin, then ruined the confidence by nervously adjusting her reading glasses.

"I think that's about it!" Merry Kade, the curator of the Providence Ghost Town, finished her presentation with a big smile. "I can't thank you enough for providing space in the library to commemorate the dedication of the Wyatt Bishop Providence Trail. It means so much to the family."

Jean-Marie, the library director, nodded sternly. "We're honored. They've played such an important part in the history of Jackson." Her eyes cut briefly to Sophie, then she cleared her throat and forced a smile. "The display will be a great educational opportunity for people who've never made it out to Providence. Thank you for loaning us the items."

The curator gathered up her presentation papers and offered a friendly goodbye to everyone. She seemed to be the only person unaware of the tension her talk had caused.

Jean-Marie clasped her hands tightly together and cleared her throat one more time, looking solemnly over her employees. "I'd love to have the display done by tomorrow afternoon as the dedication is coming up this weekend. Lauren, would you be willing to—?"

"I'll do it," Sophie interrupted.

All eyes turned toward her. No one said a word. She willed her cheeks not to burn as she raised her eyebrows. "Is something wrong?"

"No," Jean-Marie said quickly. "Of course not. I just thought…"

Sophie tipped her head in what she hoped looked like innocent bewilderment.

"I mean…" Jean-Marie cleared her throat. "Of course. If you'd like to take on the project…"

"It only makes sense," Sophie said. "I'm working until seven and you know how quiet it's been. I should be able to get it finished before I leave."

They all sat in awkward silence for a few more beats before Jean-Marie stood. "Wonderful. As you know, the Providence Historical Trust is considering sponsoring a new local history section in the library. I'd like them to be pleased with this display, so let me know if you need anything from me or from the trust. I'll be happy to contact them for you. We don't need any drama."

Jean-Marie left the room, followed by her loyal administrative assistant, Yolanda. Sophie and Lauren stood, too. Lauren closed the door. "Are you okay?"

"I'm great," Sophie said, lying to her friend without any guilt at all.

"Are you sure? I was a little surprised you volunteered to work on it."

"It really doesn't have anything to do with me, so no big deal."

Lauren watched her for a long moment, doubt written in every line of her face, but she finally shrugged. "All right. It's your family scandal. As long as it doesn't affect our girls' night out tonight, you do whatever you want."

That actually made Sophie laugh, but she still made a quick escape, grabbing the box of artifacts and heading for the small lobby of the library.

Her family scandal. God, she'd thought it was finally behind her. But she should've known better. It had been part of her life for as long as she could remember and it always would be if she stayed in Jackson. But she knew how to deal with it. The same way she always had: by defying everyone's expectations. By being a good girl and not losing her cool. By not giving them anything to talk about.

She hadn't quite maintained that cool this afternoon, but Mrs. Bishop was pushing Sophie to the brink. The woman had made Sophie's childhood a nightmare, and now she'd picked it up again twenty-five years later like a returning plague of locusts.

When Sophie had moved into her uncle's vacant house on Fair Street a year ago, she'd had no idea that Rose Bishop lived a few houses away. She hadn't thought of the woman in years. That part of her life had seemed as far away as it could be.

The first time she'd caught sight of Mrs. Bishop coming out of her house, Sophie almost hadn't recognized her. She looked like a harmless old woman now instead of the threat she'd represented to Sophie as a child. But harmless old woman was just a disguise, apparently. Rose Bishop had lain in wait, pretending to only give Sophie the cold shoulder at first. But now it was full-out war. Sophie had awoken this morning to find two dozen flyers about the dedication ceremony taped to her front door. Unbelievable.

She finished adjusting the shelves of the glassed-in display nook, then carefully placed the artifacts that Merry Kade had brought over. An old rolling pin, some woodworking tools, metal toy soldiers a child had played with long ago. There were also pictures of the town and printed descriptions of each item. Sophie really wouldn't have to do much work at all, but the display would look too bare without more.

She stepped back and eyed the start of her work. She'd have to pull the shelves back out, but the display would look really nice with a big, faded picture of the town of Providence set behind it as a backdrop, along with some of the rusted barbed wire they'd used for an earlier historical display.

The door behind her opened, and Sophie glanced over her shoulder with a smile and said, "Good afternoon." For a moment the patron was silhouetted by the slanting sunlight and she was reminded of the man she'd nearly run right into an hour earlier, but when he got farther in and offered a cheery wave, she saw that it was only the postal carrier.

But too late. Her heart had already skipped a few beats, remembering that momentary panic. First, of looking up and finding someone in her path. Then of registering his height and the width of his shoulders and the menacing shadow of the stubble on his face that matched the stubble on his head. And then those bright blue eyes.

She'd realized who he was then. Mrs. Bishop wasn't the type of person who inspired people to visit, after all, so Sophie might've suspected anyway. But that angled jaw and those blue eyes looked like Shane Harcourt's. His long-lost little brother was home.

Not so little, though. Not little at all.

She'd never met him before. The brothers had

been too old for her to have known them in school, and she would've avoided them regardless. But living in the tiny town of Jackson, there'd been no way to avoid Shane Harcourt as an adult. Luckily, he'd never treated her with anything more than polite calm.

Alex Bishop didn't look like the calm, polite type.

She couldn't guess how he would've responded if he'd realized who Sophie was. After all, it wasn't every day you met the woman whose mother had disappeared with your father. That terrible and permanent connection had been made even more awkward by Rose Bishop's simmering hatred. For all Sophie knew, Alex Bishop shared the feeling.

She decided to go the long way around the block on her way home from work tonight, just in case. If the Providence dedication had inspired a Bishop family reunion, Sophie didn't want any part of it.

"Sophie?"

She jumped, too lost in thought to have noticed the door opening again, but she recognized the man's voice and was smiling even before she turned around. "Hi, Will."

"You look lovely today."

She touched the soft cotton skirt of her favorite green dress. "Thank you."

"I was wondering if you'd reconsidered my offer."

Her smile widened. He was awfully cute with his dimpled smile and curly blond hair. "I told you I don't date men I work with."

"But I don't work with you," he drawled, leaning against the wall and aiming that adorable smile at her again. His blue uniform shirt only added to the cuteness.

"The fire station is just on the other side of that wall. It's too close for comfort. It would be awkward when we stopped dating."

"Who says we'd stop?"

Sophie just shook her head in exasperation. *She* says they'd stop. First of all, while it was stimulating to work in the same building that housed the fire station, it really wasn't ideal for meaningless sexual flings. Way too close to home.

Second, Will was cute and all, and she enjoyed sitting outside watching him play shirtless basketball with the other firefighters during the summer, but he wasn't her type. Too local. Too young. And too gullible to her good-girl camouflage. She'd been working near Will for two years and he couldn't see past the librarian glasses and knee-length skirts to the secrets underneath.

But Will had too much confidence in his good looks to give up easily. "I'll ask again soon," he warned.

"So you've said."

He winked. "And don't I keep my promises?"

She shooed him out and he gave her a gracious wave and headed over to the fire station. She supposed she should feel flattered, but he wasn't truly invested. It felt like a game. Try to talk the shy librarian into a date.

Only she wasn't as shy as he thought. She was just circumspect. She had to be. Hopefully Will would never know anything about that.

Parents with kids in tow started passing by on the sidewalk, so Sophie packed up the artifacts and locked the glass cabinet. There'd be a rush of children in the library in a few minutes and she wanted to find a great photo for the display and fire up the poster printer while she still had time.

She pasted a smile on her face and walked past the other librarians.

You okay? Lauren mouthed from behind the circulation desk.

Sophie nodded. Why wouldn't she be? It wasn't as if she was helping to promote a ceremony that would remind everyone her dad was a cuckold and her mother had abandoned her small children and run off with someone else's husband.

Sophie forced her smile wider and walked through the library with a bounce in her step.

No, it wasn't like that at all.

CHAPTER THREE

HE SAW HER again, four hours later, walking down the sidewalk near the center of town as if she'd left his mother's front yard and never stopped moving. But it was late now and cooler as dusk set in, and she wore a black sweater over that modest green dress.

Alex slowed. He'd gone for a long ride to clear his head, but the clarity had only made him more reluctant to return to his mom's. She wanted to suck him back into her obsession, and he wanted nothing but distance. Relieved at the prospect of a delay, Alex pulled the bike up next to the redhead and put his boot on the curb.

She stopped and took one step back, uncertainty wrinkling her brow, but at least she didn't look furious anymore. Alex took off his helmet, just in case she didn't recognize him with his shaved head covered, but the uncertainty on her face didn't budge.

"Hey," he offered as he killed the motor.

"Hello," she said carefully, as if the weight of the word might change the energy of the air.

"The flyers," he reminded her. "This afternoon."

Her chin dipped to let him know that she remembered.

"I wanted to apologize. I gather she's been bothering you. I can't say I know anything about it, since I just got into town this morning, but I'm damn clear on how dogged she can be. Do you want me to talk to her?"

She relaxed a little, finally. And he could see more of the real her, now. A mouth that looked naturally happy on a sweet little pixie face. She tucked a stray strand of hair behind her ear, but the rest of her pretty red hair was still smooth, twisted into a roll at the base of her neck like something from the 1940s.

She shook her head. "I've talked to her plenty of times. Do you think she'd really listen to you?"

"Ha." He managed a quick smile at that. "No. She doesn't listen to anyone. Ever. I'm Alex, by the way." He kicked down the stand and dismounted. "Alex Bishop," he added, holding out a hand. "I assume you're a neighbor of my mom's?"

She blinked a couple of times. Maybe she'd heard of his long absence or maybe she was realizing that he was the crazy woman's *son*. But she took his hand and shook it. "I'm Sophie. It's nice to meet you."

She looked right up at him now, her brown eyes friendly behind the little black glasses. She was a slight thing, but not short. Five-six, he'd guess, in her delicate black heels, shorter without them. His eyes swept down to admire the little black straps over the arches of her feet. She had a style. He liked it.

"Have you been walking all day in those shoes? I could give you a lift."

"I've been working."

"The town museum?" he ventured. She certainly didn't work in one of the bike-rental places or T-shirt shops.

Her laugh skipped over his skin, and he realized he was still holding her hand.

"The museum, huh?" She slipped her hand from his grip, but she did it slowly.

Was this little thing flirting with him? The slide of her fingertips over his palm left him feeling decidedly inclined to flirt back.

"Do I look like I work at a museum, Mr. Bishop?"

He used her question as an excuse to look her up and down again. The little button-down dress kept her all covered up, but the black sweater hugged her narrow waist, emphasizing that there were hips beneath it. Very nice female hips that made the skirt flare out a little. "Yeah. You do. But a museum I'd really love to come visit."

Yes, she was definitely flirting. Her mouth stretched to a pleased smile. "Really? What about visiting the library? I try not to judge, but you don't look like the kind of guy who hangs out in libraries too often."

A librarian? Shit. An honest-to-goodness small-town librarian? Alex had to tamp down the wolfish grin that wanted to take over his face. This girl was adorable. And her gaze was now touching brightly on his bike. She'd probably never been on a motorcycle. Maybe she wanted to find out what it was like.

He quickly checked her ring finger and saw no evidence of commitment. "Want a ride?"

Her eyes sparkled as they moved over the bike again, but she shook her head. "I can't."

"Come on. The bike's nothing to be afraid of."

Her eyes still roamed over the gleaming chrome frame before they moved right over to him and all the way up his body. She studied his face for a moment, looking straight into his eyes without any shyness at all. Then she sighed with what sounded like genuine regret. "No. I can't. A strange man inviting me for a ride? What kind of girl do you think I am?"

Damn. Alex had no idea what kind of girl she was…except that she was the kind of girl who said something like that with a tiny smile on her face. Jesus.

"Sophie…" he started, but she shook her head.

"It was a pleasure to meet you." She slipped her hand into his again and shook it.

"Meet me somewhere for a drink? Dinner? I owe you something to make up for the rest of my family."

"Oh, you owe me?" One eyebrow arched in an enticing challenge.

"Obviously. I don't know what she's done, but you're clearly fed up. And if you meet me somewhere, you won't have to worry about getting on the back of a bike with a strange man."

Her eyes flickered to the bike again. She wanted a ride. Badly.

She closed her eyes and shook her head. "No. People will talk."

"People will *talk?*" This girl really was living in a time warp.

"Yes, they'll…" She seemed to catch herself and crossed her arms, shifting uncomfortably from foot to foot.

Alex ran a hand over his shaved head. "You mean because of how I look? The bike and the tattoos and—?"

"The tattoos?" She looked him over quickly, a flick of the eyes, as if she could see beneath his jacket if she looked hard enough. Hell, all she had to do was ask nicely. But she hadn't asked. Yet.

He watched her swallow as if her mouth had gone dry. Lust crawled down his belly.

He'd asked her to dinner out of curiosity, but now… Now he really wanted to take this girl out. "We'll go someplace quiet," he said, leaning a little closer. "And I promise not to tell."

She looked away, gazing down the street. He was sure she was about to offer a cool "No," but then she looked up the street, as well. She wasn't avoiding his gaze, she was checking to see who was watching.

"I'm meeting my girlfriends for dinner."

"And after?" he dared, hearing a hint of acquiescence in her voice.

"After," she murmured, then her eyes rose to meet

his. "There's a big tourist place up the block. The Bucking Bronco."

"I know it," he said quickly.

"I'll meet you for one drink. At the upstairs bar."

Alex raised an eyebrow. She was serious about not being seen. No local would ever set foot in that overpriced, mediocre tourist trap of a restaurant. "When?"

"Around ten-thirty?" she suggested.

"Sure," he said, thinking even as he said it that she wouldn't show. She'd chicken out. And that was fine. Because she couldn't take away the sight of her cute green skirt swinging around her ass as she walked away.

A little librarian to take his mind off his family and their bullshit. Sometimes life was damn surprising.

CHAPTER FOUR

SHE COULDN'T MEET him. She'd made a terrible mistake agreeing to do it. Her dark, reckless side had pushed her into a stupid impulse. It wanted a ride on that bike, but he was one guy she could never play with, even for a night.

Sophie told herself this even as she smoothed up a nude stocking and clipped it to her garter belt. She'd showered and shaved her legs and picked out a sleeveless black dress with an A-line skirt, all the while assuring herself she wouldn't see him after dinner. She couldn't. Alex Bishop obviously didn't know who she was. If he knew she was Dorothy Heyer's daughter, he'd never have asked her out.

Then again... He had a glint in his eyes that Sophie recognized. It was familiar because she saw it in the mirror every day. It was a glint that said she wanted to do things. Things she knew she shouldn't.

She smoothed up the other stocking and clipped it in place before letting the skirt fall.

The black dress was modest. The neckline didn't show even a hint of cleavage. Everything about her was modest. Everything except the truth.

She brushed her hair out until it shone, then twisted it back into her favorite chignon. She would've left it down, but if she went for a ride on his bike, it would stay neat under her helmet this way.

Not that she was going for a ride. She wasn't even going to see him.

But she kept getting ready, her heart beating hard. This was the real her. The woman who wanted things she shouldn't have. Things like a big stranger with a shaved head and tattoos she wanted to uncover. A man whose smile was almost as hard as those thighs encased by well-worn denim. Exactly the man she could not be seen with.

"No," Sophie told herself as her heart beat even harder. No. She couldn't do it. Yes, he was a virtual stranger. Yes, he was only in town for a few days. Yes, he looked dark and dangerous and he'd seen right away that she wasn't exactly what she appeared to be.

But no. His identity overruled all of her usual guidelines. There would be nothing logical about a fling with Alex.

She slipped on her black heels with the little bows on the back, then slid bright red lipstick over her lips, loving the way the color bloomed and transformed her average mouth into something wicked and wanton. She pressed her lips together and marveled at the bright shock of color that reappeared when she pouted.

She slipped on her black glasses.

God. It had been so long since she'd been bad. Months since she'd even tried, and that last guy had been so boring once she'd finally gotten him alone.

Alex wouldn't be boring.

But she couldn't go.

Then again… She didn't have his number. It would be rude to simply not show up. She should at least go to the bar after dinner to tell him that this was a mistake.

Of course, if she only told him that, he'd press, just like he had earlier. *Come on. It'll be fun.* He'd seen what she really wanted and pushed her to give in to it. *Come on. I promise not to tell.*

Pleasure shot through her belly at the memory of those wicked words. A few seconds with the guy and he'd already tapped into that naughty streak that had haunted her since high school.

Back then, she'd never indulged it, so it had been easier to ignore. It wasn't easy to ignore anymore.

So she couldn't just see him and play coy. She'd have to tell him the truth about who she was. That was the right thing to do.

Nodding to herself, Sophie shrugged on a little black sweater with pearl buttons, then slipped in matching pearl earrings.

Maybe a little too Audrey Hepburn, but with the red lipstick and the bows at the back of her heels, she hoped she'd added a hint of suggestion.

Sophie locked up the tiny house she was staying in and headed down the street. Dinner with the

girls was just what she needed. They tried to get together every other Sunday for girls' night out, but
this was an extra treat. Lauren had wanted to try
the new French restaurant in town and Isabelle had
just finished up a big project that had kept her working late for weeks, so they had a good excuse for a
weekday night out.

The restaurant was only four blocks away, so she'd
decided not to drive. If she walked, she'd have the
perfect excuse to accept a ride later.

Even if—*when,* she ordered herself—even *when*
she told him who she was, he still might offer a ride
home. It'd be very late, after all. And a ride would
be a pleasant consolation prize, pressed against his
broad back with that black-and-chrome machine between her thighs. That was a hell of a lot more than
nothing.

Her heels clicked against the wooden boardwalk
when she reached the first touristy block of town.
It was cool tonight, but she never minded that. She
loved the breeze sneaking over her silk-clad legs. She
loved the cool air in her lungs and the scent of turning aspen on the breeze. Fall was her favorite time
of year. It felt like the world was holding its breath
for something exciting.

She tried to tell herself she wasn't doing the same
thing as she reached the restaurant and glanced up
the block to the loud touristy restaurant she'd visit
later.

Lauren and Isabelle were already enjoying wine

by the time she spotted them and hurried to the table. "Sorry I had to work so late."

"We're sorry we had to start without you," Lauren said with a grin. "You look adorable as usual," she added as she stood to give Sophie a big hug.

"You, too. And you!" Sophie said as she hugged Isabelle. "You're alive!"

"Barely," Isabelle said drily. "Just don't look at my nails." She held up her hands to show off her paint-stained cuticles. Sophie didn't mention the streak of green oil paint on her collarbone. It clashed with the silky red shirt she wore.

She and Lauren had gotten to know Isabelle at the library where she often arranged to borrow expensive books from state universities. Her painting demanded very specific types of research, so she came in fairly often, distracted and color-streaked. She normally wore old jeans and sweaters, so Sophie was surprised to see the deep red flowy blouse she wore tonight. "You look so pretty. Are you wearing heels?" she gasped.

Isabelle stuck out her foot to show off cute black wedge boots. "Ugh. Yes. I'm considering getting laid sometime this decade. My neighbor talked me into ordering these online."

Lauren rolled her eyes. "You wouldn't have any trouble getting laid if you left the house more often than once a month."

"I don't want to leave the house. I don't know why a man can't be delivered along with my art supplies."

Sophie grinned. "Maybe you could advertise for models."

"That probably wouldn't go over well once they realized my specialty. Anatomical paintings sound fun until you realize it's not a euphemism."

"It could be," Lauren insisted, with a tip of her glass. "These snowboarding bums are always looking for a few dollars. And they're in very, very nice shape."

Isabelle's normally serious face got even more serious for a moment. "Hmm."

Sophie snorted. "Oh, my God, she's actually thinking about it. Let's just make clear that Lauren and I would be happy to pose as art students to make this happen."

"Oh, yeah," Lauren agreed. "We'd do it for you, Isabelle. Goodness of our hearts and all that."

"Screw you," Isabelle said. "You've got a naked man to look at any time you want."

"Hey!" Sophie interrupted, bumping Lauren's arm. "Didn't you say your mom was here to visit? Why didn't you bring her along?"

"She's in bed already. She said she was tired, but I think she wanted a few hours of alone time to read. She just got an e-reader. She doesn't want me to tell any of her old librarian associates."

"Oh, I forgot your mom was a librarian, too. You're a legacy family!"

Lauren laughed. "I spent half my childhood in the stacks. I couldn't break free from my fate."

"Does your mom like Jake?" Sophie asked.

"What's not to like? He's a wholesome fire captain!"

"Wholesome, huh?"

Lauren's wide smile told them everything they needed to know about her new relationship with the fire captain. Sophie tried not to sigh. She didn't need a serious relationship, but the steady sex would be really nice. She'd never had that. She didn't know when she ever would. Yeah, she was much more comfortable with sordid, hidden affairs. Funny how those traits could be inherited.

She spent the rest of dinner trying not to think of having a sordid affair with Alex Bishop. The knowledge that she absolutely couldn't do it made the thought harder to force out of her mind. She was so distracted that her friends didn't even blink when she made an excuse about being tired and wrapped up their dinner a few minutes earlier than they'd normally have broken up. It was a weeknight, after all.

"Do you want a ride, Sophie?" Lauren asked. "Jake's coming to pick me up."

"No, it's a beautiful night. I want to enjoy as much walking as I can before winter sets in."

She said her goodbyes, her heart speeding a little at the small deception. Or maybe it was speeding with excitement, because it only beat faster as she stepped onto the boardwalk. If her friends were paying attention, they'd notice that she wasn't heading toward her house, but she glanced through the window and saw that they were still chatting as they gathered purses and jackets. Sophie rushed up the block, not bothering to hide her smile.

Even during the slow season, a cacophony sounded from the Bucking Bronco when the door opened a few feet ahead of her. Country music played and people spoke loudly to be heard over it. The outdoor tables were abandoned for the evening, but past the windows, families with tired children ate ribs and steak and took the opportunity to get a little drunk.

When she stepped inside, she noticed the younger crowd at the bar, but she knew from experience that the music was even louder back there. Sophie ducked to the left and headed up the wide staircase.

The bar upstairs was smaller. They only served beer and wine and margaritas, but there were small tables around the bar here, and she and Alex would disappear from view behind the larger dining tables at the front.

Though Alex might have a hard time disappearing anywhere, she realized as she caught sight of his shaved head and walked toward him. He stood at the bar, looming over the few other people there. Sophie glanced around, but there was no one she knew here. There was better steak and cheaper beer to be had a few streets out of town.

Alex saw her and straightened. He didn't smile, but the slight rise of his eyebrows as he looked her up and down conveyed approval. Sophie did smile. That man was a pleasure to look at. He'd shaved his

face, and now his jaw and cheekbones were emphasized, giving him a lean and deadly look. He'd also
shucked his leather jacket at some point, and there
they were. Tattoos.

One arm was covered all the way down to his
wrist with the vivid colors of a design she couldn't
make out from ten feet away. She did her best not to
lunge at him like she was bringing down prey.

"Hi," he said. "I didn't know if you wanted to
get a table."

"That'd be great."

He gestured toward the closest empty table, then
reached past her to pull out the chair before she could
sit. A gentleman. With tattoos.

He grabbed his jacket from a bar stool and slipped
it over the back of the other chair. "What are you
drinking?"

"White wine, please."

He nodded as if he'd expected that and stepped
back to the bar without another word. The order only
took a moment to place, but she used that short time
to study him from behind. His gray T-shirt hugged
thick shoulders and revealed the delicious taper of his
back down to his waist. Those ancient jeans showed
off thick thighs and a delicious-looking ass. It all
ended in lug-soled black boots that made her heart
skip a little.

He was just so…masculine.

She looked away before he turned around with

her wine and a bottle of beer, and Sophie folded her hands demurely on the table.

He still looked big when he sat down. She knew she couldn't hide her stare, so she didn't even bother. "I like your tattoos."

His head drew back a little in surprise. "Yeah?"

"Yeah. Can I see this one?" She gestured toward his left arm.

He helpfully pulled his sleeve up to his shoulder.

"Wow," she breathed.

Sophie wanted to reach out and touch, despite that she knew there'd be no texture. But the reds and blues and greens were so vivid, she imagined she'd feel *something*. It wasn't just passive art. His arm was alive with it.

She'd never seen such deep colors on skin. Dark green pine trees rose up his biceps in stylized spikes outlined in black, but the tips disappeared into wisps of clouds. A bright blue river wound through the green and then down his thickly muscled forearm. It splashed between angled boulders of red and yellow and gray before the river tightened to a bright red ribbon that finally wound around his wrist.

"It's really beautiful. It's honestly the most beautiful tattoo I've ever seen."

"Thanks. An artist in California did it. He's really amazing. He's the only one I go to now."

"And that?" she asked, tipping her head toward his right arm, where a raven was drawn in stark black lines that looked like slashes.

"An earlier work."

"I like it, too. You've got nice taste."

A small smile, finally. "Not as nice as you. You like pretty dresses."

That surprised a laugh out of her. "I do. I like pretty things."

"Like me," he said drily.

"Oh, sure. You're my pretty treat for the night." *Stop,* she told herself as she watched his nostrils flare a little. *Stop flirting.* Just tell him the truth and leave.

But her mouth refused to obey. Instead of speaking up, it quirked a secret little smile at the way his gaze had intensified. Sophie reached for her wine. "How long are you in town, Alex?"

"Through the weekend," he answered. "Not long."

"The dedication ceremony?"

He looked surprised for a moment, then he seemed to remember how small Jackson was and nodded. "Yeah. I'll ride on as soon as the damn thing is over."

Now it was her turn to be surprised, but she wasn't going to press him on this issue, that was certain. It wasn't a topic she wanted to intrude on. "Where do you live?"

One of his big shoulders rose in a shrug. "Here and there. I'm on my way to Alaska next month."

"Alaska?" she gasped. "In *October?* Isn't it already freezing there by then?"

"Not quite, but the work doesn't stop during the winter."

"What sort of work?" Her pulse quickened at the thought of Alaska. She wanted to see it, so badly.

"I'm a groundwater engineer. I work as a contractor for oil companies. Making sure they're not fucking things up."

"Is that the official engineering term?"

Now his mouth relaxed into a real smile, and she was shocked at how sweet he looked. "Pretty much. It's a rough-and-tumble engineering field. Not a lot of scientists stationed in the places I go."

"Is it always Alaska?"

"Not always. I travel a lot."

Sophie's thoughts were swirling almost too fast to catch one. She had a thousand questions about Alaska and a thousand more about where else he went and the things he'd seen. She took a drink of wine and grabbed hold of one question. "Tell me what it's like. Alaska. Is it…is it amazing?"

"It's pretty amazing. What do you want to know?"

"Everything," she breathed before she realized how odd and greedy it sounded. "I mean… Where do you go? Are there polar bears? Is it dangerous? Is it cold?"

He chuckled. "You look like a little girl right now, wide-eyed and sparkling."

A blush hit her hard and fast, and she reached for her wine again, trying to think of a way to backtrack.

"It's cold, at least where I go. And barren, if you can use that word for something usually covered in snow and ice. I've been to the fields in the summer, and it's different then. Like a savanna, I guess. Mile after mile of grass and sun and flies. You see caribou everywhere then. Foxes. Even some wolves. It's beautiful and quiet."

"Wow," she breathed, her skin tingling at the idea. Or maybe it was the wine.

"You want another?" he asked, gesturing toward the glass she realized she'd drained.

"Yes," she answered quickly. He'd barely touched his beer, but she didn't care. Her buzz was pushed on by her excited pulse, and she felt deliciously alive.

Alex rose to get her another glass, and she realized her mistake then and almost grabbed his wrist to make him sit and keep talking. Thankfully, he was back within moments.

"And in the winter?" she pressed before he'd even sat down.

"In the winter, it's cold and dark. It's eerie, knowing you're so far from anyone or anything. And it's not so quiet. The wind blows day and night when it kicks up. When you're inside, it sounds like you're on a ship, and not a steady one."

"Can you see the northern lights?"

"They're pretty bright there in the winter."

"That is so cool," she murmured, not realizing she'd touched his arm until he looked down. She looked down, too. Her fingertips rested on a swirl of red ink. She let them linger for a moment, then let them whisper over the bright color until her touch slipped off his wrist.

"So it's out on the tundra?" she asked, her voice slightly fainter than before. A heartbeat passed before he spoke.

"It is. Nothing but wild animals and crazy men out there."

"You help drill for oil?"

"No, I'm there to piss people off. I do testing and make sure they're obeying regulations."

"And do they?"

He smiled. "They try. When there are eyes on them, at least."

He looked like he'd fit in perfectly out there in a harsh land with rough men. "How long will you stay there?"

"For this gig, only three weeks. Sometimes I go for a week, sometimes six months."

"Six months," she murmured, trying to imagine that. Of living somewhere entirely new and knowing you'd be moving on soon. Everyone you saw would be a new person, a stranger. Every drive or hike or walk a new experience. Her skin prickled and she licked her lips. Physical and emotional desire twisted inside her and swelled.

She'd only ever lived in Jackson, really. She'd done most of her college work online, then gone to Laramie for her senior year to complete the courses she couldn't take long-distance. Aside from a two-year monthly commute to Salt Lake City to get her MS in Library Science, she'd been at home. She had obligations here. People she couldn't leave behind.

She was connected. To her father and her brother. Even to her great-uncle, who'd asked her to rent his house until he could get out of the convalescent home. He didn't want strangers living in his place, and no one had the heart to tell him that he wasn't ever going to be able to live on his own again.

No, she had too many ties here. She couldn't do it. Yet. But Alex was oozing adventure out of his pores.

"You should go sometime," he said, as if he'd read her thoughts.

"Maybe." Maybe she would. Maybe she'd drive up all the way through Canada. Or fly to Seattle and then work her way up the coastline on ferries, only staying in each town for a few days.

"Not very many single women up there. Assuming you're single."

She smiled and glanced up at him. "Would I be here with you if I weren't?"

"I'm not sure. You did want to keep it quiet."

"I did." This was her chance. Thank him for the drinks. Tell him the truth. Apologize for any misunderstanding on his part. But she wanted more of his deep voice dragging along her nerve endings. More of his stories. She even wanted more of his painted skin under her fingertips. Just a tiny bit more. A touch.

"Am I still a stranger?" he asked.

Sophie's skin prickled again and her nipples slowly tightened. That question promised something. Some dark and dangerous prize if she answered it correctly. She let her hand move closer to his arm and then followed that same swirl of red back up his wrist. This time she let her fingers climb just a little bit higher.

"Oh," she said as she touched him, "you're definitely a stranger."

"Does that mean I can't talk you into a ride?"

She dragged the pads of her fingers across a yellow stroke of ink. "I don't know."

When she looked up, she found him staring at her. Hard. His brows heavy and serious. "You'd like it," he said. No question in that tone, and no dominance either. It was just fact. He knew she'd like it. They both did.

The wickedness inside her stretched with pleasure. The power of it overwhelmed her.

"It's not safe," she countered, but even she could hear the breathless approval in her voice. It wasn't safe and she wanted it that way. God. Her body was shameless, and her dangerous heart was even worse.

She waited for him to reassure her. *I'll take care of you. It'll be fine.* But he just watched her face as her fingers pressed harder into his ink, her nails against his skin now. She watched him, too, waiting, her pulse so quick she had to part her lips to get enough air.

This was wrong. So wrong.

Finally, his arm turned under her touch and he slid his hand around hers. He stood, and Sophie followed.

CHRIST, THERE WAS something incredibly sexy about this woman. Something that couldn't be summed up by the slim waist and cute face and black heels. It was that smile, small and secret, and the way she watched him with a challenge in her eyes, wanting him to do…something.

If she were timid, he wasn't sure he'd ever have noticed her. If she'd hidden behind her glasses and sweaters, his eyes would have skipped right over her, letting her red hair and brown eyes blend into the crowd. But she wasn't hiding, she was…waiting.

And Alex was perfectly willing to step up to the plate.

He touched the small of her back when they reached the stairway, gesturing her to go ahead. The feel of the warm, thin fabric of her sweater reminded him that she wasn't quite dressed for a bike ride.

"Here," he offered when they got to the front door of the loud restaurant. He eased his jacket over her slim shoulders. He'd be more than warm enough with her hot little body pressed to his back. It was still warm for fall. Sixty-five or so.

"Thank you," she said softly, slipping her arms into the sleeves, then laughing when her hands failed to emerge.

"That should keep your hands warm. Have you ever been on a bike?"

"No." He walked her toward the bike and watched her eyes roam over it again, greedy with excitement. Shit. Alex wondered if she'd look at his body that way, if he stripped down and offered a ride. A man could hope.

"It's a 1980 Triumph. A T140. I've had it almost fifteen years now."

"It's big," she said.

He flashed her a smile. "Not as big as a hog."

"But less common?" she asked.

"Bingo."

Alex unlatched the pannier at the back of the bike and got out his helmet, then grabbed another one he kept for the occasional passenger. "All you have to do is hang on to me. Stay with my movements."

"I think I can handle that."

"And watch your legs. Keep your feet on the rests. You don't want to burn yourself on the exhaust."

"Okay." She slipped her glasses into her purse, then eased the helmet over her hair and clipped the chin strap.

Alex had to stop himself from smiling at her little face framed by the big helmet. She had the most innocent face. And then that wicked red mouth... He took her purse and stored it in the pannier. "Are you ready, Sophie?"

The brightness in her eyes answered the question. Alex mounted the bike and hit the throttle. She licked her lips as the engine roared to life. He tried to ignore the way his cock stirred at the sight. Yeah, she was damn ready.

He waved her closer, and Sophie held her skirt in the primmest little gesture he'd ever seen a woman manage as she swung her leg over the bike and slid into place behind his hips. He waited a moment for her to arrange herself. Her front pressed to him, her arms came around his waist and her hands finally emerged from the leather sleeves to clasp each other.

"Ready?" he asked over his shoulder. He felt her head bob in a nod.

"Hold on."

He eased away from the curb and her arms tightened. If it were daylight, he would have headed north, but since there were no sights to see, he took the road that went south from town. It was a little more wide-open for her first ride.

The moon was just rising above the hills, a view that Alex never got tired of on night rides. You forgot how much light it cast until you had to ride without it. Being swallowed up by darkness had its own beauty, but it was nothing compared to this, the silver light shimmering off the aspen trees that peeked out between the towering pines.

The road was a blank strip ahead of them, defined only by the middle line and the pale shoulders on either side. They slipped free of the town limits, passed a few trucks, and then there was a long straight path as they roared toward the Snake River Canyon.

After the first few minutes, he felt Sophie begin to relax against him, her body fitting tighter to his. Alex began to relax, too. She felt nice against him, soft and sweet. He hadn't had a woman on his bike in a while. There'd been women since Andrea, but mostly one-night stands at whatever uninspiring motel he was sleeping in.

When he'd been younger, that had been one of the great advantages of traveling. New women. New possibilities. No commitments. But he'd gotten grumpier since then, older, and often his hand offered more relaxation with way less hassle.

But this? Flirting and anticipation and just enjoying someone's presence? That hadn't happened in a while.

Alex eased the bike around a long, wide curve and felt her go taut against him. He settled a hand on her leg, and the silkiness of her stocking was a tiny pleasure under his fingers. Such funny retro quirks, her full skirts and panty hose and little black glasses. Her thigh flexed, muscles moving against his palm, and Alex found himself suddenly struck with the startling idea that her outfit might be even more retro than he thought.

He was frozen for a moment, the heat of her leg radiating through the silk and straight into him. But she relaxed again. She relaxed enough that her legs parted a tiny bit farther and her hips slipped closer. Now he could feel her body all the way from his shoulder blades down to his ass. All of her, pressed against him, her shape molding into him.

Alex kept his eyes straight on the road, but all his concentration was focused on one small place. He took a deep breath and let it out, then slowly spread his fingers out on her thigh, edging an inch under the hem of her skirt.

She didn't tense. She didn't stiffen against him or clear her throat or nudge him with her clasped hands.

Alex slowed around another curve, then, as he straightened the bike out again, he slipped his hand a centimeter higher on her thigh. Then another.

His fingertips tingled from the intensity, the anticipation. And finally, he felt it. The smooth seam at the top of the stocking. The slightest rise of the edge. Then…bare skin. Bare hot skin.

She was wearing stockings. And a garter belt.

Holy shit. Something feral inside him roused itself.

His hand brushed the clasp holding the silk in place. He wondered if he'd know how to unhook it if he were given the opportunity, then realized he wouldn't want to. He'd want the stockings on. He'd want to fuck her that way.

Alex let out the breath he'd been holding. She melted more fully against him. He left his hand just where it was. The clouds turned silver above the trees.

At first, he didn't feel the change, but when Sophie's hand flattened against his stomach, he realized she'd unclasped her hands. Now her fingers spread wider, feeling his body through the cotton of his shirt. Her other hand slipped up to trace over his chest. Nerve endings all the way from his neck down to his dick woke up and paid attention.

Adrenaline rushed into his veins, and if he'd managed to catch a chill on this ride, it vanished in an instant. His brain worked quickly, helpfully pointing out that there was a scenic turnout just ahead, in case he wanted to pull over and kiss her. *And don't you want to kiss her?* his mind yelled.

Yeah. Hell, yeah, he wanted to kiss her. At least.

Alex slowed and cut across the highway, driving into a small dirt lot that overlooked the river. He cut the engine and toed down the stand, but he didn't move. Her arms were still wrapped around him, her fingers still sliding slowly along his chest, mapping the shape of him. The only sound now was the water below them and a few crickets waiting for the first freeze.

He slid his hand back to her leg and heard a soft sigh. The sound made him close his eyes. Her other hand pressed tighter against his belly.

Jesus, this was insane. Locked like this with a woman he hardly knew and had never kissed, his fingers tracing the top of her stocking. He pushed her skirt a little higher and looked down to see her. The garter was pale in the moonlight. Not white, but the same color as her skin. The stocking just a shade darker.

He'd never seen them like that. Anytime he'd been lucky enough to be this close, the lingerie had been black. This was a subtler form of sexy, just like the rest of her. A nudge that dared you to find out more, if you were man enough to take the hint. He slipped his thumb beneath the strap of the garter belt and stroked the top of her thigh.

Yes. Another sigh. Alex took off his helmet, then felt her do the same. When he reached back, she handed over the helmet and slipped off the bike. His back was like ice without her.

He followed her slow walk to the railing and stopped behind her, keeping a few inches of space between them so she wouldn't feel stalked. Her neck curved so delicately up from where his jacket hung loose around her. Two pale inches of skin between her shoulder and the sweep of her pretty red hair. She watched the water below them, dark and dangerous until it turned white against rocks. But he only watched her.

Finally, her head turned and she smiled at him. A demure tip of her lips. A coy glance. Alex stepped closer. His heart sped as he slipped his hands beneath the leather jacket and framed her hips. Then he slowly, slowly dipped his head and watched her face tip away, giving him access, letting him close until he could press a kiss to that soft skin just behind her ear.

Oh, she sighed again. A tiny, sweet sound. Alex opened his mouth on her. Just a little. Just enough to let her feel the heat, and this time her neck arched until he could brush his lips all the way down to the line of her shoulder and back up. As a reward, he scraped his teeth against her skin.

That got more than a sigh. She shivered and

gasped and her hand came up to curl around his skull and pull him tighter. He sucked at her then, just below her ear, and Sophie's whole body arched, pushing her hips back.

Hell, he hadn't intended on pressing his erection against her ass that quickly, but he wasn't going to push her away. Even if he'd wanted to, his hands had other ideas. They gripped her hips tighter and held her right there. Right where she'd wanted to be. The brush of her ass against his cock was a shudder of pure pleasure. He closed his eyes and let it wash over him. The sweetness of her.

She smelled good and tasted even better, but he wanted more of her. More.

Alex clasped her chin, turning her toward him so he could taste her kiss. She turned eagerly, offering her mouth to him, moaning into him as he kissed her. When she twisted toward him, he let his hands slide around her waist, turning her until he was holding her hips again. He tugged her belly against his hard-on.

Her tongue met his and slipped tentatively into his mouth.

Jesus, she was hot. A ridiculous mix of primness and eagerness that made him want to own her, dominate her, but with a few "Yes, ma'ams" thrown in out of respect.

He kissed her, carefully at first, getting to know her mouth and her taste. He knew he was a big, rough guy, and he didn't want to scare her. But if he was trying to take care and go slow, Sophie didn't have the same compulsion. Her hands freely explored him, sliding up his arms and over his shoulders. His ego swelled along with his cock when she made little noises of approval in her throat. He tugged her hips tighter to him and kissed her more deeply.

God, the pressure against his cock felt good. And her hands felt good as her fingers dug a little into his muscles, making him aware of his body. Of his strength and size and the way that might turn her on.

He backed her up to the flat wood planks of the railing. He could let go of her hips now and stay pressed to her. Her waist was a slight curve under his hands, and then her long, delicate back, and that arching neck. Then, finally, he cupped the back of her head and held her for a deeper kiss, his tongue working slowly against hers, letting her know exactly how he'd fuck her.

Her moan let him know she might like it.

But not tonight.

He was startled by the thought. He didn't know where it came from. Not from her, but from some dark part of his brain. *Not tonight*. Not even if she'd let him. He felt…deviant, touching this woman, making her moan. He felt perverted and he liked it. He wanted to draw it out. Expose her secrets like layers of hidden need. They were there. He could feel it in the way she stretched up to take more of his tongue. More of him.

He'd give her more if that would make her happy.

Alex raised his head, pulling back from the kiss even as she tried to follow. He kept his hand cupped to her neck, holding her still as he feathered a kiss over her top lip. Then her bottom one. Then the crease of her mouth. The tip of her tongue licked at him, and he chuckled and tasted her again. He couldn't resist it, but the kiss was quick this time, then he raised his head to look down at her.

Her face was silver in the moonlight, her pupils black as the sky when she opened her eyes.

"You shouldn't be doing this with a stranger," he said.

"This is a small town. You're not really a stranger."

Alex shook his head, knowing that wasn't true. "No one here knows me anymore."

She closed her eyes and raised her mouth, and when Alex kissed her again, she whispered against him, "No one knows me either."

He could believe that. He understood that. She was a secret, right here among people she'd known all her life.

Alex bunched her skirt in his hand and raised one side of it, sliding it up her leg, waiting for her to stop him. She didn't. His hand touched bare skin, then the warm strap of her garter belt. Jesus.

"Do you wear these to drive men crazy?" he growled.

He felt her smile against his jaw. "I wear them to drive me crazy."

Damn. He'd thought he was hard before, but now

he was in pain. Yes, she was a secret, and his hand was on the hot skin of her thigh.

He gripped her there, and her knee rose, just a few inches, just enough for her to curl her foot behind his calf and make space between her legs for him. His cock notched into place. He groaned against her neck and felt her throaty laugh vibrate through him.

"But…" she murmured, "I'm glad they drive you a little crazy, too."

"A little," he rasped, sliding his hand over the back of her thigh. The slippery fabric of her panties teased his thumb. He slid his hand low again, dragging it over the stocking, memorizing the wicked feel of bare flesh above silky material. His rough hand caught at the delicate threads. "Sorry," he whispered, trying to make himself feel that, but he couldn't. Her hips tipped up a little, like she liked it. Did she? That his hands were rough against her perfection? Did she want that?

He let his fingers curl all the way behind her knee, then up again, up. Over silk stocking, and the bump of the fastener and then sweet bare skin. And then…

"Oh," she whimpered as the edge of his hand grazed between her legs, slipping along the fabric of her panties. His thumb edged beneath them as he cupped the bottom of her ass and hauled her tighter to his cock.

Her hips rocked against him. Alex closed his eyes and tried not to moan like a boy dry-humping his first girlfriend. But it felt that good, and his heart pounded with the shocking pleasure of it, just as it had in junior high.

Maybe it was something in the air. A perk of returning to the same sights and smells he'd hit puberty with. Or maybe it was that his whole hand was under her panties now, cupping her naked ass while she slowly, slowly worked herself against his torturously covered shaft.

For a moment, he imagined it. Unzipping his jeans, setting his cock free, pulling her underwear to the side, then just plunging deep, feeling her pussy drag hot and wet over him as he sank into her body. She'd love it. She'd arch up and ride him and come all over him, screaming and bucking.

And then they'd be done.

Somehow he knew that, and he didn't want this done. Not that quickly.

So instead of setting his throbbing cock free, Alex edged back and eased her leg down. Her eyes opened slowly as a confused and nearly grumpy frown took her mouth, but when he slipped his hand down the front of her panties, her lips parted on a sigh.

His did, too. There was nothing but bare skin under that little triangle of satin fabric. Bare skin, and plump lips, and sweet, hot wetness that led his fingers right where they wanted to go.

Taking it slow or not, Alex now wished they were inside. In his sad, anonymous hotel room, in the dreary light of that bedside lamp, on worn white sheets, so he could strip off this dress and these panties and fucking *see* her. God. The stockings and garter belt and perfect, parting legs and the pinkness of her, shining with wetness, begging for his mouth, his hands, his cock.

This was torture, sliding his fingers along her, feeling the way her hips jumped as he grazed her clit, and all of her was hidden by the modest skirt of her dress. He grazed her clit again, and the hand that had been clutching his biceps let him go and curved around the top of the railing to hold tight.

"Oh, God," she groaned.

Power flooded his veins. He was going to make her come right here. Right now. A truck roared by, the pale edge of light skimming down her neck and body and highlighting the way his arm disappeared beneath her skirt. She didn't even glance toward the road, though she did murmur, "We shouldn't be doing this." But it wasn't an admonition. It was encouragement. He could hear the eager edge of it in her voice and feel it in the way her thighs eased the tiniest bit farther apart.

We shouldn't be doing this and that's why it's so good.

Her eyes opened. "We really shouldn't," she whispered, sounding almost sad this time, but then her free hand slipped up his neck and pulled him down.

God. *Yes.* Now his tongue was in her hot, wet mouth and his fingers were in her hot, wet pussy and she whimpered into him as he took her both ways.

He pushed two fingers deep inside her and swallowed her wild cry.

Her nails bit into his neck, and when he thrust again, her second cry was just as rough as the first. He would've paused, would've gentled his touch, but her hips rocked up for more.

Goose bumps broke out over his neck and down his arm as he realized that if he was hurting her... she liked it. His heart beat harder. So hard he could feel it in his throat as he fucked her with his fingers and she whimpered and sucked at his tongue.

She wanted this. She fucking *needed* it.

When her cries finally quieted to desperate whimpers, Alex slipped his fingers back to her clit and stroked her there.

Her mouth broke free then as she threw back her head with a gasp, but he couldn't stop thinking of the way she'd sucked at his tongue. Like that was part of her need, part of what she wanted. A girl like her deserved everything.

He kept stroking her clit, listening to her breath grow rougher and faster, and he slid his other hand up her shoulder, up her neck, then spread his fingers over her jaw. Her neck arched higher, as she stretched under his touch. Her mouth was still red, lipstick perfect. He imagined that she bought lipstick with staying power just so she could look like this while she fucked.

Alex slid his thumb between her parted lips, into her heat, and she sucked.

The sensation punched him in the gut and made his desperate cock throb in pain.

"Fuck," he growled, sliding his thumb deeper as he circled her clit faster.

She moaned and sucked harder, her hips working against his touch in tiny little thrusts, as if she couldn't stop herself from fucking his hand.

"That's it," he murmured, leaning in until his mouth was near her ear. "That's what you like." Her groan vibrated through the bones of his thumb and straight into his entire nervous system. Fuck, he wanted that pretty little red mouth around his cock. He wanted her moaning for him, sucking at him, trying to make him come, because that was what she fucking *needed*.

The heat of her mouth slid away as she pulled back with a cry. The pain of her nails in his skin brightened as she clutched tighter. "Oh, God," she sobbed as her hips jumped. Then her words dissolved on a sob of pleasure as he felt the spasms take her over. Her scream echoed down the river as he pressed her tighter to the railing and made her ride every wave of her orgasm.

"Please," she finally begged, and he stilled his hand. Her clit jumped under his fingers as she shivered one last time.

His thumb was pressed to her bottom lip. Her mouth glistened with moisture. She was calming now, but his breath shuddered from his throat as he tried to control his need. He finally managed to ease back, slipping his hand free from her soaked panties. His fingers felt too cold without the heat of her pussy around them.

She finally opened her eyes. "Oh," she breathed. He was trying to grab some control, but her hands ventured up his chest and then behind his neck. She tried to pull him down. Alex shook his head.

"Give me a second." If he kissed her now, he'd lose it. He'd fuck her. He would fall to his knees and beg her for it, and nobody wanted that. So Alex let his head tip back and he breathed the cool night air and watched stars wink in and out of the traveling clouds.

He could do this. He could wait. Because if he didn't, she'd call it a good date and keep it secret and go back to her life. He knew it from how she'd said no to a ride at first, and then how she'd hidden him away in a tourist trap, and used him for a little night adventure that no one else would see.

If they fucked, the adventure would be complete. Where was the fun in that?

His dick protested that there'd be loads of fun in that, but he managed to ignore it.

"Let me," Sophie murmured, her hands sliding down now. Down his chest to his belly, then to his belt. His heart twisted so hard he thought it might have torn free of something important.

Let me...let me touch your cock, set it free, get my pretty little hot mouth around it until I suck you dry.

Oh, fuck.

He stepped back with a pained laugh. She frowned in complete confusion.

"Next time," he said hoarsely, shaking his head at his own strained patience.

"What next time?"

"The next time I see you." He knew by the way she winced that he'd been right.

"No," she said. "This time." Her fingers hooked into his belt and tugged him closer. His feet took a step before he could convince his body that he really meant to say no.

He huffed another half-tortured laugh and closed a hand over both of hers. "You're trying to tell me there won't be a next time, aren't you?"

Her gaze slipped away from him. She cleared her throat.

Alex smiled. "And I'm telling you there will be."

"I can't. You don't understand. This isn't…a thing. It *can't* be. And you're leaving in a few days. So…"

"So. There's tomorrow. Unless you have other plans."

She opened her mouth, but he cut her off.

"Even if you *have* other plans."

That narrowed her eyes. He wanted to smile, but he suspected there might be a temper under those mild manners. Sophie raised her chin. "You can be as bossy as you want, but there's no reason for me to see you again. I already got what I needed."

Oh, he smiled now. A wide smile full of every filthy thought he was thinking. He stepped closer again, backing her into the railing, just as she'd been earlier when she was coming.

"Oh, Sophie," he whispered. Her fingers tightened around his belt as he raised a hand to brush his knuckles over her jaw. "I can tell by how hard you sucked my thumb before you came that you didn't get half of what you really need."

When his thumb touched her lip, her eyes fluttered closed for a brief moment as her breath whispered over him. Then she jerked her chin away and shoved him.

Alex stepped back, but he was still smiling. "Come on, darlin'. I'll give you a ride home."

"I won't invite you in."

"I didn't ask to come in."

She stared at him for a moment, then raised her chin and brushed past him. Alex watched her walk. Her hips swayed as enticingly as ever, but he could see she wasn't quite steady. Next time, she'd be too weak to move. He'd make sure of it.

CHAPTER FIVE

"Hi, Dad," she called out as the screen door slammed behind her.

"Hey, princess," his deep voice called from the back of the ranch house.

Sophie headed toward the bright yellow kitchen and the scent of coffee. He was there, of course, hands warming around a steaming mug and eyes on the cattle prices in the newspaper. He could get more current figures online, which she'd explained a million times. She'd even bookmarked it on his laptop for him, but he hated the computer. Which was why she was here.

"Everything good?" she asked, leaning down to kiss his cheek.

He patted her arm and nodded. "Things are fine."

She grabbed a cup of coffee and headed for the small office tucked between the kitchen and his bedroom. The ancient office chair creaked ominously when she took a seat, but the sound made her smile. She'd loved this chair when she was little and would sit in the corner and color while her dad worked. The casters and base were made of steel, the seat itself upholstered in thick, ugly green leather. It would never wear out. It was steady. Like her dad.

"Did you get the new bank statement?" Sophie asked.

He still banked with a local ranching bank that sent paper statements. There was no talking him out of this. She'd tried.

"Honey, I've told you you don't need to do this." He edged into the little office and slipped the statement onto the ledger.

"Dad." She didn't want to have this conversation for the thousandth time.

"We're fine out here. There's no reason for you to spend almost an hour driving out here to be holed up in this office. A young woman like you should be enjoying life in town."

She'd been opening her mouth to protest, but she closed it now. Oh, she was enjoying life in town plenty. Thank God she was facing the desk, because she could feel the red-hot blush that flashed over her face. She heard her father walk back into the kitchen.

Last night had been her best adventure yet. It had been hot and naughty and satisfying and perfect. And so completely wrong. One hundred percent wrong. Not because she'd let a near stranger on a motorcycle get her off on a highway pull-off in full view of anyone who might have decided to pull in. No. That she could definitely live with. But because Alex didn't know who she was. More importantly, because Sophie knew *exactly* who she was.

The daughter of Dorothy Heyer. The heir of all the heartbreak and scandal her mother had caused. For Sophie. For her stepfather and brother. And for Alex's family, too.

Not that Alex's father was somehow absolved from the affair. Sophie was no believer in boys will be boys. The idea disgusted her. Both of them had been married. Both had had families. And both had ruined lives with their reckless choices. But in a small town twenty-five years ago, no one else had seen it that way.

If they'd run off, if they'd abandoned children and spouses... Well, sometimes men did things like that. But women? That just wasn't natural. It wasn't right. Dorothy Heyer hadn't been right. And Sophie wasn't right either. She just made sure that no one else knew that.

Especially not Alex Bishop.

"God," she whispered, dropping her face into her hands. That had been such a bad idea. But he'd seduced her. With his bike and his tattoos and that hard smile and then *Alaska*. How was she supposed to have resisted that?

With your legs closed, a little voice inside her admonished. Sophie clenched her teeth and wished she could slap that little voice. All of those things were the perfect invitation to open her legs, not close them. And he'd been so confident, too. So in control.

The nerves between her legs twitched at that thought. Of his hands on her, so steady and strong and calloused, of the way he'd kissed her, fingers cupped to the back of her head to position her just the way he wanted.

Oh, God, that had been hot. It was exactly what she always wanted. He was the perfect temporary adventure, the man she was hoping for every time she flirted with a stranger at a bar. And he was Rose Bishop's son.

"Damn it," she whispered.

"Something wrong?" her dad called.

"No! It's fine." She needed to concentrate. An hour or two of work, and then she could enjoy her day off. Spend some time in the garden. Do some work around the house.

Sophie crossed her legs, smoothed down her skirt and opened the statement. Everything looked good. She took good care of the books. There'd been a hiccup when her brother had dropped out of college and played at being in charge for a few months. A hiccup that had taken years to straighten out, but everything was right as rain now. Her dad was still scraping by with his small cattle ranch, but just barely.

It had been a much larger ranch twenty-five years ago. Thousands of acres leased and deeded. Not a lot of the acreage had been flat, but the hills had been good summer grazing. Then Greg Heyer's wife had disappeared. His kids had needed tending. He'd let things go that summer. The next year, beef prices had plummeted. He'd sold off land and leases and cattle. The year after that, a drought had hit hard. It hadn't let up for three years. He'd sold off more. Now he was down to a tenth of what he'd owned before, and he was almost seventy years old and hired out some of the rougher work.

Sophie finished balancing the account and reached for the basket that held the bills. This part always made her chest tight, but it was okay. Her dad was fine. With her help, he could keep this place going for another decade if he wanted to. He didn't seem to want to sell, and she wasn't going to try to talk him into it. As hardscrabble as it was, this place was his life.

"Before I forget," her dad said, his voice just behind her in the doorway, "your mail is in the bedroom."

"Thanks."

"You should really change your address."

"I'm not going to stay in Uncle Orville's house forever, Dad. I don't want to bother changing my address just to have to change everything back again."

"It's been a year, Sophie. I think you're plenty settled into town now. Why in the world would you want to come back out here?"

Because this was her home. Because he was her family. Because she took care of things for him and she always would.

But living in town did have its advantages. Privacy, namely. Granted, on those occasions when she met a man who seemed to push her buttons, she preferred going back to his hotel room. It was less conspicuous that way. No neighbors to notice and comment. No lifelong acquaintances to realize who Sophie really was. Only tourists and seasonal men. Just the way she wanted it.

Sophie opened the credit-card bill and noticed that her brother had been making a lot of ebook purchases again. It felt strange to resent the way he spent money on books. She was a librarian, after all. But it wasn't that her brother was overspending on books, it was that he spent his time getting obsessed with learning some new skill he was convinced would make him successful. Gaming online auctions or selling Western crap on websites or starting his own sales lead business for web courses or a hundred other things that he'd purchased books about and then lost interest in. God knew what it was this time. Two years ago, he'd decided to sell mail-order tumbleweeds for people in the East throwing cowboy-themed parties. Then he'd realized he'd actually have to go out in the heat or cold and search for tumbleweeds. They were never around when you wanted them.

"Where's David?" she asked, thinking if he was around she'd at least ask what he was up to.

She glanced back to see her dad's mouth flatten. "Sleeping."

Still asleep at 10:00 a.m. That was practically blasphemy on a ranch. But even their dad was starting to realize that David was never going to take over the ranch. It was hard for him to accept that the remaining land would be sold someday, but there it was. David could do all the work, but he didn't love the land. Sophie loved the place and she could stumble along well enough, but she was too indoorsy for ranching. Dresses and kitten heels had no place in a corral. Not unless a big, rough man had her pinned up against a fence and—

Damn. Alex was going to haunt her for a long time.

"You want me to wake him?" her dad grumbled.

Sophie flashed him a smile. "Only if you want an excuse to get his butt out of bed."

He laughed. "I need his help later with the yearlings. I'd better let him get his beauty sleep or he'll be grouching around here all day." He leaned a hip against the counter and sipped his coffee.

"You know, you don't have to keep me company. I'm not a guest."

He shrugged one lean shoulder, and Sophie wondered if he was getting thinner. "It's nice to talk to you. Gets a little lonely out here these days."

"I'm off today. Why don't I stay and make a big lunch?"

Her dad huffed. "That's not what I meant. Go shopping. Go have lunch with your girlfriends. Don't spend your day off with an old man, Sophie."

"I like being here."

"Well, I'm afraid I've got a busy day later. I can't hang around all day for lunch."

She narrowed her eyes and watched him for a long while, trying to read his face. Was he lying just to stop her from staying around? But he gave away nothing. He just looked back at her with those pale blue eyes framed by familiar wrinkles from spending too many years in the sun.

"Okay," she finally conceded. "But I'll make something good for dinner before I leave. I'll throw it in the Crock-Pot and it'll be ready by five-thirty."

"Thanks, pumpkin. You take good care of me." He came over to give her a kiss on the crown of her head, then headed for the back door. "I'll see you next week."

"Bye, Daddy."

Sophie tried to ignore the embarrassing amount of pride she felt at his words. She did take good care of him. She'd been doing it since she was five, and she'd be doing it until she was sixty. He needed her. She was never going to walk away from that.

With the house quiet now, Sophie was done with the bookkeeping in no time. Next week it'd be time to take stock of supplies and order in anything they needed for winter, but today's work was pretty simple. She tidied up the desk and headed to the kitchen to throw some meat and veggies into the slow cooker. She wouldn't be around to make gravy, but she set out a jar of premade. That man loved gravy. Hopefully, he'd clean up the leftovers with a few slices of buttered bread while no one was looking and put a few pounds on his skinny frame by next week.

Once she'd tidied up, Sophie went to her dad's room, gathered up his dirty clothes and started a load of wash. She ignored her brother's closed door. He'd have to learn to fend for himself if he was ever going to live on his own someday. But he probably never would. He'd gotten too used to being taken care of, and Sophie knew she had to take a lot of the blame for that. Something else to feel guilty about.

Speaking of…even the thought of the word *guilt* led her back to Alex Bishop.

Would she see him again? He'd seemed awfully sure that she would. And he'd been right about one thing. She did want more. A lot more.

She wanted to be near him, wanted to feel the way her skin prickled at the very sight of him. And the way she felt small and submissive when his big hands touched her. God, the man had gorgeous hands. And arms. And tattoos.

She wanted to lick him. Wanted to fuck him. She wanted to call and keep lying about who she was so she could see him again and do everything they hadn't done yet.

She was a terrible person, but she tried her best to keep it to herself. It didn't matter as long as no one knew, as long as no one was hurt. But this had the potential to hurt Alex, herself and both of their families.

Not worth the hot sex, she scolded herself. But the terrible person inside her disagreed. Strongly.

She checked over the house one more time before leaving, slamming the door in the hopes that her brother would get his lazy butt out of bed. But by the time she got into her car and started for home, she wasn't thinking about her brother. She was thinking about Alex. Again.

With her car window rolled down, the wind reminded her of the cool air against her body the night before. Just the ride on his bike had been a turn-on. The feel of his body guiding the beast beneath them, the way he'd fitted between her knees, the scent of his leather coat, the rumble of the engine. Then the speed. The power. The wind. The shimmering, sizzling knowledge that the ride was dangerous. Even deadly. It had all added up to the most arousing experience she'd had in years.

And then he'd slipped his hand over her thigh. The same bolt of pure animal lust she'd felt at that touch speared through her right now.

Sophie squirmed, then squeezed her thighs together, catching the pleasure between her legs and squeezing it tighter.

That first touch had been a rush, but then an even larger pleasure had pulsed through her, growing bigger and bigger as his hand slid higher and higher. The knowledge that he'd touch bare skin, that he'd know, that he'd find out. She wasn't what people thought she was. She wasn't a shy, modest local girl afraid to venture far from home. She was naughty. She was wicked. And she loved it.

His hand had finally found the top of her stocking. He'd discovered that secret. And unlike most men, he hadn't missed a beat. One touch of her wickedly bare thigh, and Alex had pulled the bike over to discover whether or not she meant it. She did. She always did.

Sophie squeezed her thighs together again, gasping at the shock of that sweet pleasure.

God.

She could deny anything she wanted, but he saw the truth.

Sophie bit her lip, trying to bite back her need, but it didn't work. She wanted to see him again. He'd touched her exactly the way she needed to be touched. He was right. She needed more.

She slowed the car to a stop at the side of the road and calmly withdrew a tube of lip balm from her purse. She smoothed it over her abused bottom lip, then stared at herself in the mirror. Her face looked calm, but her cheeks were flushed and her eyes bright with an excitement she recognized.

She had to tell Alex the truth, but as she slipped her sunglasses on and pulled back onto the narrow dirt road, she could no longer pretend that she regretted the lie.

CHAPTER SIX

ALEX TURNED HIS phone on, confirmed that only his brother had called—four times—then switched it off. The only calls he was interested in taking were about work or a certain naughty librarian. But she hadn't called. Not that he was surprised. He'd seen that in the stubborn way she'd said "Good evening," when she'd gotten off his bike. He'd watched until she got inside her house. She hadn't looked back once.

Fuck, she was hot.

He knew he'd have to see his family today. He'd considered meeting them for dinner the night before, but then he'd seen Sophie, and he'd decided not to screw up a good evening. He'd see them on his terms, on his time, and first he wanted another glimpse of Sophie.

She only lived a few doors down from his mother, so he parked his bike in front of his mom's and walked toward Sophie's little place. She might not be home. She might not want to see him. But Alex still felt a smile try to tug at his mouth as he approached.

The smile finally won out when he spotted Sophie before he even got to her house. She was working in the flower beds along the front of her house, and looked even more prim than she usually did. Instead of a dress, today she wore khaki capris and little white sneakers and a flowered button-down shirt that almost hid her slim curves. But he knew them now. There was no hiding them. Especially when she bent over and he caught sight of the perfect rounds of her ass.

Damn. He wanted to see her just like that, except naked and begging.

But for now he stepped onto her front walk, avoiding her carefully tended lawn because he thought she wouldn't like him grinding it down with his big boots. Even in September, her grass was just starting to lose its green.

Her head rose when his boot caught a rock and kicked it toward the front stairs.

"Oh!" The trowel dropped from her hands as she stood. "Alex."

He liked the pink that rushed to her cheeks. "Sophie," he said softly, and her cheeks turned crimson, as if her name was something intimate.

"Um, hi," she stammered. Her eyes darted toward his mother's house, then back to him. "Did you come to talk?"

He leaned against the front porch banister and looked her up and down from behind his sunglasses. No one would guess in a million years that this innocent-looking woman had come like an animal last night.

She swallowed hard. "You're intimidating with those glasses on."

"Am I?" he asked.

"Yes. I can't see your eyes, and your mouth always looks so serious."

He liked making her nervous, but he still slipped off his glasses. "Better?"

"Yes," she said, but she still licked her lips and glanced down the street again. "Alex, I'm so sorry."

"You don't need to apologize. Unless you're about to pretend you can't see me again."

"I can't."

"Come on. It'll be fun." He lowered his voice and raised an eyebrow. "Don't you think it'll be fun, Sophie?"

The color had begun to fade from her cheeks, but they blazed red again. Alex let his gaze sweep down her body and let her see him do it. Her pretty mouth parted as she drew in a quick breath. But she still shook her head.

"I really can't. There's something I didn't tell you."

He cocked an eyebrow. "This is a little early for 'We need to talk,' isn't it?"

But the way she worried her bottom lip let him know she was serious. And just like that, he knew what it was. Why she played so coy. Why she'd met him in secret. Why she didn't want to go out again.

She was seeing someone else. She was taken.

Alex didn't particularly care.

"Okay," he said. "I think I know what you're going to say."

"I don't think you do."

He shrugged. "Fine. We'll talk. Go out with me, or invite me in, or I'll take you for a ride. I'll let you choose."

That snapped her eyes up to his. "Oh, you'll *let* me?"

He laughed. "Definitely. Whatever you want. You want things, don't you?"

She shrugged and slipped off her gardening gloves. "You're handsome when you smile," she grumbled.

"But not when I don't?"

"No. *Handsome* isn't the word I'd use then."

He tipped his head a little closer as if she were revealing a secret. "What word would you use?"

He'd expected a flip answer, but she seemed to take his question seriously. Her brow furrowed as she looked up at him, and a dozen heartbeats passed before she answered. "I'd say you're…"

During her pause, he watched closely, studying her eyes, waiting for her answer. But it never came.

"Get away from her!" a woman yelled from a distance.

A strangled gasp tore from Sophie's throat as she straightened and took two steps away from Alex. He was a little slower, checking idly over his shoulder to see what neighborhood drama was going down. An old woman was storming up the street. It took him several seconds to realize that old woman was his mom. He still wasn't used to the change in her.

"Alex!" she screamed.

Jesus. Alex shook his head. "Whatever's about to go down, I apologize for it."

"Alex, I'm sorry. I meant to tell you. I swear."

"Tell me what?" he asked. When she didn't answer, he looked away from his charging mother to see Sophie twisting her hands together, her face tight with something like fear. "Hey. Don't let her scare you. She's just—"

"You get away from that whore!"

"Hey!" Alex barked, swinging toward his mother as she stormed across the lawn. "Watch your mouth."

"I should say the same to you," she sneered, skidding to a stop only a few feet away. Her slippers were damp and muddy around the edges. "Watch your mouth and every other part of yourself around her."

"Jesus." He glanced over his shoulder. "I'm sorry, Sophie."

His mom snorted. "Don't apologize to her."

"I will and so will you."

Sophie's whisper broke through his building anger. "No. I'll go inside. It's fine. Just…"

"It's not fine," he insisted. His mom's insanity was spilling out all over her neighbors now. "She can't try to pull innocent people into her deranged world."

"Innocent?" his mother scoffed. "Oh, my God. *Innocent?*" She barked out a laugh as Alex stepped forward, herding her toward the street. He was sick of this shit. He'd been sick of it his whole life.

"Let's go," he ordered.

She shook off the hand he put on her elbow. "She's not innocent. She's just like her mother!"

"For God's sake, if you think I give a damn about your neighborhood gossip, you're even crazier than I thought." When she froze, Alex got a grip on her arm.

Her crazed gaze tore free from Sophie and rose to him. Her mouth gaped. "You don't know," she breathed.

"No, I don't, and I don't care to."

"Ha!" She shot a grim smile at Sophie. "You're even more devious than I thought."

"Mrs. Bishop…" Sophie said, but then seemed at a loss for how to address the manic senior citizen in her yard.

"She's Dorothy Heyer's daughter," his mom said, the words thrown out with the same tone one would declare a man guilty of murder. *She's a murderer. She's a child abuser. She's the daughter of…*

Whoa.

His mom pointed at Sophie. "Don't you recognize her? She looks just like her slut of a mother."

Alex shook his head in shock. Sophie was the daughter of Dorothy Heyer. His dad's mistress. The woman who'd disappeared with him twenty-five years ago.

Shit.

But he kept his mouth shut and his surprise to himself and tightened his hold on his mom's elbow. "I don't give a damn who her mother is, and who I talk to is none of your business. Let's go."

This time when he tugged her toward the street, his mom actually came along with him.

He glanced back toward Sophie to find her watching them, but her gaze fell before he could think what to say. The situation was way too fucked up for any kind of intelligent response, so he just led his mother down the sidewalk to her house.

"You think you can manage not to embarrass yourself for a few more feet?" he growled. When she nodded, he let her go and stalked toward her house. Shane stood in the doorway, looking nearly as unhappy as Alex felt.

"Where the hell were you last night?" Shane asked.

"Somewhere sane," Alex snapped back. "I came for the dedication, not to be on the planning committee. By the way, Mom just called one of her neighbors a whore."

Shane winced. "Who? Sophie?"

Alex was apparently the only one not in on this joke. "Yes, Sophie. You know who she is?"

"Sure. Everyone knows. I mean…most people don't care, but you know how it is here. Small town. Long memories."

"Yeah. I'm sure it doesn't help anything that the woman down the street treats Sophie like crap."

His mom brushed past him and Shane. "She should know better than to show her face around me."

He followed her inside, his surprise and outrage hardening into true anger. "Are you kidding me? She was standing in her own yard! And she seems like a perfectly nice woman."

"Ha. Until you find out who she really is."

Alex couldn't believe this. "This can't be all about her mother. Sophie was a kid when that happened. Even younger than Shane and I were. What the hell is wrong with you?"

"She's the one who moved onto *my* street and threw the past in my face like the hussy she is. Do you know how much it hurts to see her every day? With that red hair just like her mama? And now she's putting the moves on my son? No, sir. I won't stand for it."

"Putting the *moves* on me? Are you kidding me? We were having a conversation in her garden."

"You can't fool me. I saw the way you were looking at her. She's just like her mother and apparently you're no different than your father!"

Alex laughed instead of yelling what he really wanted to yell. "Am I supposed to be sorry about that? You're the one who made him into a saint."

"He was a saint compared to that home wrecker who lured him away!"

He ground his teeth together. He fisted his hands. The old familiar fury flooded his veins. The wish that she would disappear as thoroughly as his dad had just so they could have some damn peace.

"Nobody needed to lure Dad," he ground out. "Anyone with a thought in his head would run as far and fast from you as possible."

She gasped, her hand flying up to cover her mouth in horror. "Don't say that," she cried past her fingers. "You were always so cruel to me. Always."

"Alex," Shane said quietly. "Come on. Let's get outside for a few minutes."

Shane. Always the peacemaker. Always trying to calm them both down. He was her accomplice just as he'd been all those years ago.

"I don't need to get outside. I need to get out of town. She's abusing the neighbors! This is insanity and you've been living in it so long you can't see it anymore."

Shane ignored that and walked toward the back door. "Come on."

He almost didn't follow. He almost spun on his heel and walked out the front door. He knew he'd keep on walking forever. This was it. Whether he left now or stayed for a few more days, this was the end.

He was right back where he'd been as a kid. Frustrated, furious, helpless. And now even more resentful that he'd been forced to deal with her irrational delusions for ten years of his childhood. Even adults couldn't deal with her, and he'd had to live with her every single day.

It was the end of his family. So he figured he

could humor Shane one more time. Then Alex could at least say he'd tried.

"Alex," his mom started, tears thick in her voice. "You don't understand. She looks just like her. And she's a whore just like her. Everyone knows it."

"Everyone knows because you tell them!" he shouted.

"If I have to!" She broke down into sobs.

Alex shook his head and headed toward the kitchen and the back door. He tried to ignore the piles of boxes leaking papers everywhere. Printouts of every half-assed lead she'd ever pursued. Newspaper articles. Police reports. Scraps with her familiar, frantic handwriting scrawled in different colors. Her life's work was a swamp of meaningless words and pictures and she was going to drown in it someday.

He stepped out onto the back deck and took a deep breath. The backyard was overgrown and unkempt, but it was relatively clutter-free. Shane leaned against the deck rail and crossed his arms.

"Better?" he asked.

"No."

Shane blew out a long breath and looked up at the blue sky. "Okay. Everything you said in there was true. This is insanity. She's out of control. All that. But it's not true that I can't see it. Not anymore. That hasn't been true for a long time."

Alex walked to the far side of the deck and looked out at the lodgepole pines that towered over the neighbor's house.

"I know you don't believe me," Shane said, stating the obvious. "You don't have any reason to, but the minute you left, I saw how bad it had gotten. I saw what *I'd* done, Alex. Not just her, but me. I just…" He blew out another long breath. "Jesus. I wanted it all to be true. That Dad was still around. That he'd come back. That we could find him. I *needed* it to be true."

"Yeah. I know." He did know. Even as a kid, he'd seen it, but that had only made him feel more enraged.

"What I wanted blinded me to what you needed. I should've taken care of you, and I didn't. If I—"

"I get it," Alex snapped.

"No, you don't. You think I've been playing this game with Mom the whole time, but I haven't. I distanced myself. I changed my name. I moved on."

Alex finally met his eyes. "Why'd you do that?" he asked, even though he told himself he didn't care.

"I was done with it. The fantasy of Dad coming back. Mom's obsession. Dad's whole damn family and how they treated us after Dad disappeared. As soon as you left, I saw what really mattered. But it was too late to get you back, so my only option was to cut them off."

Alex nodded, shocked that his brother had changed so dramatically that long ago.

"Alex," he sighed, "I swear I wouldn't have brought you back for this if she hadn't improved. I wouldn't have gone along with this dedication at all. But now…I think we just have to get through it. Fuck, I don't know."

Alex ran a hand over his head, scrubbing at the rough stubble until he could think. "Fine. But what the hell do you want from me?"

Shane distractedly went through the same motion, rubbing both hands through his hair. "Her psychiatrist thought this would help. It's obviously making it worse, but if we call the whole thing off, God only knows what will happen. She'll go off. Concoct some giant conspiracy theory. Raise hell."

Alex grimaced. Yeah. She'd definitely do that. And considering her feral reaction to Sophie, that poor woman was likely to bear the brunt of it.

"Just help, all right?" Shane asked. "You left. I get why. You needed to. But you left me here to deal with her, and I've done it. I've dealt with her for sixteen years alone, and I'd like a little damn help now, Alex. She's sick."

The old resentments were back in full force at that. His brother pretending things weren't as bad as they were, trying to explain away their mom's behavior. As a kid, it had made Alex feel like the crazy one. "Is that why you got me back here? To take over carrying her shit?"

"No," Shane snapped. "This isn't a fucking trick. I'm asking you for help. You can run away and live your life like you've never had a family, but we still exist. You still have a brother. I'm right here and I'm asking you to help me, even if you think I don't deserve it. Even if you hate my guts."

They glared at each other for a long time. Both of them through their father's eyes. Pale blue and distant and hard to read. Alex finally felt some of his anger leave. "I don't hate you."

Shane shrugged, but Alex could see the relief on his face. "Maybe you should. But I'm glad if you don't."

Alex rolled his own shoulders and tried to let go of the tension bunching his muscles into knots.

"It's only a few more days. Just put in a little time. Ignore Mom if you can. And that'll be the end of it."

He nodded and paced back to the far corner of the deck. It was what he'd told himself he'd do. He could handle it. He wasn't a kid anymore, even if being around her filled him with those same old emotions.

"Okay." He nudged a pot full of dirt and one dead plant with his boot. A gray kitten darted out. Alex blinked in shock, but the cat disappeared beneath the deck. "Is Mom working or anything?"

"No. She started on disability this year."

"Maybe that's bad for her."

"Maybe. She's certainly gone downhill in the past few weeks."

Alex nodded. "What was she doing before that?"

"Cashier, clerk, bowling alley attendant, cleaning crew. Same things she always did. Her bosses always liked her fine until she'd skip town to chase after Dad's ghost. That died down a few years ago when she couldn't afford a car anymore."

"How'd she get this place?"

"It's one of Jackson's affordable housing rentals."

Alex stared at the trees and let out a deep breath. Shane had been dealing with the reality of this for a long time, and Alex had never let it worry him for a second. "All right," he finally said, "I'll try to help."

"Great. Can we sit down for a little while? Figure out the logistics?"

The trees were too thick to see any farther than the house next door. Even if they weren't there, he probably wouldn't be able to see Sophie's place. Considering his mom's vitriol, that was a good thing.

"Sure. Let's get this over with." He shrugged off his jacket and followed Shane inside. He could check on Sophie later. Or maybe he should just stay away. That's what she'd been trying to tell him, after all. That's why it was bad for both of them. But somehow he wanted to make her say it.

CHAPTER SEVEN

SHE'D WAITED AN hour, pacing and sweating and be-
rating herself for what she'd done. She'd jumped at
every small sound, expecting that it was Alex's boot
on her front step or his hand opening the storm door
so he could knock.

Eventually she'd worn herself down into exhaus-
tion and given up the vigil to make herself a cup of
tea. He wasn't coming back. He'd learned the truth
and he'd decided Sophie wasn't worth speaking to
again.

Because she wasn't.

With the history between their two families, he'd
never have gone out with her if he'd known whose
daughter she was. But Sophie had taken that choice
from him. She was awful, and she hadn't even been
able to hide it this time. His mother had gotten it
right for once.

"First time for everything," Sophie murmured
into her tea.

God. At first Rose Bishop hadn't been part of the
story for Sophie. The only story had been that Sophie's mother was gone. Missing. Kidnapped. An ac-

cident victim. Nobody knew. She was just gone. The biggest void in the longest night that Sophie could ever have imagined.

That night had gone on endlessly. It had stretched out over weeks. Her mother had disappeared in the summertime. No school. No friends nearby. Just her father, wandering the house like a ghost when he wasn't working himself to the bone. And her brother, too young to know anything except that he needed taking care of. And the neighbors, eventually.

If her mom had died, they would've been there in droves with warm arms open for a scared little girl. But instead, they'd come awkwardly, in whispering pairs, not sure if they should help or disapprove.

Was it a tragedy or just something someone had done wrong? Eventually, they'd settled on the latter. Everyone had.

Especially Rose Bishop.

Not at first, though. At first she hadn't been involved. The story of Sophie's mother had sustained itself. Long through those first months back at school. Long past the point when Sophie had finally figured out the threads of the story. It had taken a full year for interest to die down, and that was when Rose had risen to the challenge. No one was allowed to forget her husband. And no one was allowed to forget that Dorothy Heyer had been the cause of the trouble. Whatever Wyatt Bishop had done—run off, disappeared, been injured, been killed—it had been at Dorothy's instigation. Her jezebel temptations. Her lies and whoring ways.

It had never been Wyatt's fault. Always Dorothy's. Dorothy was a devil in female form. And Sophie had looked just like her.

Not that the good folks of Jackson were that gullible. They understood that it took two to tango. But really...men ran off. It happened. But what kind of woman walked away from her little babies?

So they tutted. And whispered. Their eyes had gleamed with excitement over the tragedy that had infiltrated every single second of her childhood. And they all watched Sophie like she might show signs of becoming her mother any day. Rose had made sure they did.

Sophie pressed a hand to her turning stomach. The tea wasn't helping.

It was only 2:00 p.m., yet she couldn't imagine doing anything productive for the rest of the day. But if she gave in to her desire to crawl into bed and comfort herself with a terrible movie, that would hardly be penance for what she'd done to Alex, would it?

Then again, she hadn't really harmed him. Nobody knew about it, and he'd had a good time.

"Well," she muttered into her tea, "*I* had a good time." He hadn't even gotten off. God, she was the worst kind of lying slut there was. No movie and cozy bed for her. Maybe she should drive out to her dad's house and wash her brother's laundry. *That* would be punishment.

She was still staring into her teacup when the doorbell rang. The sound startled her so much it took her a moment to realize who it probably was.

"Oh, God," she groaned. Despite that she'd been waiting for him, she'd decided he wasn't coming and now the idea of talking to him terrified her. But maybe if she got up and answered the door and faced his justified anger, she could call that punishment enough. The thought of hiding in bed for the rest of the day was exactly the incentive she needed to push to her feet. But she still jumped like a little chicken when his fist hit her door in a booming knock.

She tiptoed over, but then made herself take a deep breath and stand tall before she answered. She hoped he didn't notice the way she stepped back when she caught sight of his angry face.

She'd meant what she'd said earlier. That he wasn't handsome until he smiled. He wasn't. He was stark and masculine and intimidating. And right now? With his jaw tight and his brow low and that almost-sneer on his mouth? He was gorgeous.

"Damn it, Sophie," he snarled.

"I'm sorry."

He did notice when she stepped back that time, and he apparently took it as an invitation to come in, because he slipped past her arm and closed the door behind him. "Why didn't you tell me?"

God, his voice was a rumbling menace. Her skin prickled with nervousness, but despite her alarm—or maybe because of it—her nipples went tight, too.

"I meant to," she said. "Last night."

"Jesus." He scrubbed both hands over his head, his bare arms flexing with the movement. He looked dangerous inside her small living room. Dangerous and strong, the deep colors of the tattoos rippling as he moved. And those big hands.

Sophie could no longer separate fear from arousal. She swallowed hard and tried not to think of those blunt fingers shoving into her.

"Sophie," he finally sighed. "You should have told me."

"I know. I'm so sorry. I didn't know how to say it. And then I'd waited too long. You must be so angry—"

"You're damn right I am. That's why you didn't want to be seen with me, right?"

"Yes," she admitted. "People would talk. It's all bad enough right now with the memorial and your mom and…"

"If you'd told me, I never would've exposed you to that."

"You…" Sophie paused and blinked several times to try to clear her thoughts. "What?"

"I'm sorry. She's obviously made your life difficult. I wouldn't have pursued you that way if I'd known. I wouldn't have teased you."

Sophie pressed a hand to her thundering heart and tried to think past her shock. "You don't need to apologize. I'm the one who let you take that risk. Of people talking. Of dredging everything up."

He flashed the briefest of smiles. "Sophie, do I look like the kind of guy who cares what people say? You're the one who has to live here. And my mom never wants anyone to forget."

"Yeah. She's a real sucker for nostalgia."

"Ha." His bark of laughter startled her. "Christ, Sophie. I'll try to talk some sense into her while I'm here. But…"

"I know. She honestly hasn't been that bad until recently. But if I'd known she lived here…"

"You wouldn't have bought the place?"

She shrugged. "It's my great-uncle's. I'm taking care of it for him while he's in the nursing home. It won't be forever. It's just been tough lately with everything being back in the spotlight."

He ducked his head for a moment, then his eyes rose to meet her. "So why'd you meet me at that bar? Seems a little risky."

His voice had dropped. Sophie's heart skipped. "It was risky," she whispered.

He nodded. "Almost as risky as accepting a ride with a stranger."

"Yes." Her voice cracked a little.

His gaze went hot, as if he knew exactly the effect he was having on her. Fuck, he looked eight feet tall inside her house. She was barefoot and out of sorts and he was so *big*.

"I won't take you out again," he said.

Her fantasy froze to ice. "Oh. Right. Of course not."

"It's not fair. I'm leaving town. You're staying here. You're the one at risk."

She nodded. She understood. Of course she did, but… "It's not that big of a deal. Once this week is past, people will go back to not caring. Especially now that the mystery is dead." As dead as her mom and his dad.

"Yeah." He glanced around the room as if noticing it for the first time. The couch and television were new. Her uncle's had been moved to his room so he could feel more at home. Still, very few of the things here were hers. It was a house, but not her home.

"But I still owe you," Alex suddenly said.

She snapped her gaze back to him. "What?"

"I promised you more."

"I'm not…" she stammered. "I mean, I thought you'd… Once you realized who I was."

"It's risky," he said, using her own words to seduce her. "Probably a terrible idea."

"Yes. It is."

"And you fucking turn me on like crazy."

Oh, God. Her heart twisted and then set off running, the pulse of it echoing to her throat, her stomach, her pussy.

That was what she wanted. To make a man like him crazy for her. Desperate to put those big strong hands on her and show her exactly what he wanted from her body.

She licked her lips, trying to wet her mouth

enough to speak, but when Alex's hooded gaze dropped to her parted lips, her throat went even drier.

"But you really shouldn't have kept it from me, Sophie."

"I know," she rasped.

His gaze dropped to her throat when she swallowed, then his eyes fell lower. "Take off your shirt."

She drew in a quick breath, as stunned by his words as she was by the lust that stabbed through her. She stared at him in shock, wondering if he was just teasing or if she'd misunderstood him, but he didn't say it again. He just watched and waited.

Her hands trembled. She tried to quiet her breath.

"No one will know," he murmured. "I promise." And oh, God, that was all she wanted. For no one else to know anything about her. To be hidden. To disappear in darkness and animal lust and anonymity.

Sophie reached for the top button of her shirt. She fumbled with it. His eyes narrowed as she finally slipped the button free. "The next one," he said. This time she didn't hesitate. She unfastened the second button, and the third, then all the way down until she could shrug her blouse off her shoulders and let it fall to the floor.

She felt more confident now. She was wearing one of her favorite bras. A simple little ivory number made of such delicate fabric that the pink of her nipples was clearly visible. And the matching panties were nearly sheer, too.

"Keep going," he said.

Sophie unfastened her pants and slipped them down, too. She stepped out of them and raised her head to watch him. He looked even more dangerous now, fierce and aroused, but somehow she only felt calmer. She lifted her chin and set her shoulders and let him look at her until she could hear that his breathing came almost as fast as hers.

His gaze fell to her panties, and she shifted. Cool air touched between her legs, and she knew she was wet already. So wet that she'd soaked through the thin material. She wondered if he could see that, and the idea embarrassed and thrilled her. She squeezed her thighs together. Alex seemed done with ordering her around. Instead of speaking, he stepped closer, moving slowly as if wanting to give her a chance to say no.

But she wasn't even close to objecting. She watched his big hand reach toward her, and when it slipped over her hip, pleasure flashed through her and then settled deep in her belly.

"Look at you," he murmured, his hand sliding up her ribs and then back down to her hip again.

Yes, she wanted to say, *look at me.* She kept this side of herself so hidden, but not with him. With him she wanted to stretch her body out and demand every ounce of his attention.

But she didn't need to. He watched his own hand as his fingers spread over her curves. She looked down, too, and God, it was beautiful. Her pale, smooth skin under his tanned and tattooed flesh.

She could feel the slight rasp of his fingertips and see the long stretch of muscles flexing beneath his inked skin.

Jesus, she wanted to lick every inch of him. Bite his most sensitive spots. Make him suck in his breath and tighten his hold and get too rough.

His big hand slid beneath her panties to grasp her ass and pull her to him. He ducked his head and kissed her.

He wasn't so careful this time. If there'd been any question about her willingness, she'd already answered it, so his mouth slanted over hers and took her hard. He reached behind her and then her bra was sliding down.

Thank God. She was ready. She needed this. She moved both hands up to his head to clutch his skull and pull him tighter, and now his hands were gripping her ass, pulling her tight to him, kneading her flesh.

There'd be no more waiting. He meant to fuck her today, and she meant to take him.

His hand slid farther down and stroked between her legs. Sophie tore her mouth free to gulp enough air to feed her racing heart.

"Damn," he cursed, apparently shocked at how wet she was, but she wasn't shocked. She felt so tight and swollen that she could come within seconds if she wanted to.

Alex backed her up a few feet, and she went blindly with him until her back touched the wall.

Then he went to his knees. His mouth was on her before she could brace herself, the heat of him startling through the fabric of her panties.

"Oh, God," she gasped as his tongue pressed against her, then his teeth scraped against her flesh and she cried out. If he'd meant to tease her, he quickly lost patience and tugged her panties down until they fell to her ankles. If she'd thought his mouth was hot before, she'd been wrong. Now it was liquid fire against her pussy, and his tongue a firm, stroking touch as he tasted her.

He grunted against her, his tongue pushing deeper before it settled against her clit.

Sophie moaned, sliding her feet farther apart to make it easier for him to please her. And God, he did. His tongue flicked her clit, almost too lightly until he grunted again and sucked at it, the scruff of his face scraping her sensitive flesh. His fingers dug into her ass. He sucked and she groaned, then felt him chuckle against her, the vibration of it singing over her taut nerves. She thought she'd come right then, but his tongue was light against her again, teasing, nearly breaking her with the nearness of her orgasm.

Sophie grasped his head in her hands, the prickle of his stubble against her palms almost too much for her mind to process. Yet another wicked sensation to take in. Her palms sizzled with the feel of it as her whole body trembled. His tongue was so light, so torturous, so perfect and maddening.

She gripped his head harder, pressed him tight,

and when he sucked at her this time, she finally got what she wanted. Her entire body was that one spot, all heat and pressure and tightness. She pressed her head back against the wall, and let everything spiral tight.

"Yes," she urged. And then she broke apart, shaking, screaming, pressing herself to the sweet heat of his mouth.

He didn't let up, he didn't miss a beat, he just opened his mouth wider and sucked harder and rode the wild spasms of her hips as she came. When the pleasure finally shook its way out of her, she felt drugged. Spent. Her knees trembled with such weakness she would've felt embarrassed by it if she'd had the capacity. But she didn't. All she could think was *Oh, fuck.*

He was good. So good.

When he rose up, Sophie had to press herself to the wall to stay upright. Then he reached for the buckle of his belt, and she wasn't sure the wall would be enough. Her mouth went dry and her heart gave up its new languid pace and thumped to eager life again.

Right here. While she was naked, her clothes strewn across the living room floor. With him still fully dressed. He was going to take her right here, against the wall, like she was a toy to be enjoyed whenever he felt like it.

He unzipped his jeans and reached into his briefs and then, good Lord, he fisted his cock in his hand

and eased it out. Sophie made a noise. She couldn't help it. He was thick and beautiful, the head a perfect plum she wanted to taste. And when he reached for her hand and wrapped it around the base, she moaned. She couldn't help that either, because he was even thicker now with her small hand wrapped around him. So thick and hard and heavy that she felt faint with lust. She wanted all of that.

He tugged his wallet from his back pocket. He must have been getting out a condom, but Sophie couldn't bother to look. She was too busy watching her hand squeeze him. Then stroke. All the way up to that gorgeous head and then back down. He hissed in a breath, so she did it again. More firmly this time. She was rewarded with a tiny bead of liquid at the tip. Sophie slicked her thumb over it and swirled it around.

"Jesus," he groaned. She heard the tear of the condom wrapper and let him go so he could put it on.

There was clearly no need for more foreplay, and she was glad he didn't pretend. Alex simply bent his knees and lifted one of her legs to his hip. He notched his cock to her opening and he penetrated her. Slowly. Patiently. But without a hint of hesitation. He pushed in, forced her open, and Sophie groaned at the way her body stretched for him.

"Oh, God," she whispered. "God. Yes."

He pulled back a little, then thrust hard, burying himself deep and tight inside her. She couldn't breathe for a moment, so stunned by the brutal invasion. But she loved it. She was so wet that it didn't matter how big he was, her body let him in.

Alex pulled her other leg up, wrapped her ankles around him, and began to fuck her. Her shoulders were pressed to the wall, but his big hands held her ass in a steady grip as he thrust hard and slow, looking down to watch as his cock disappeared into her. Sophie twined her arms around his neck and took him.

"God, you're hot," he growled. "So hot and wet for me."

"Yes."

"You're perfect. Fucking beautiful."

"Yes," she repeated. She was. Shoved against the wall and fucked like an animal. She was wild and amazing.

He kissed her and she tasted herself on his mouth and loved it. She wanted more, so she wrapped her arms tighter around his neck and began to move with him. Alex groaned into her mouth. His hands got a better grip on her ass and he moved her like she belonged to him. Like she weighed nothing. Like she was just an extension of his body and he could use her any way he liked.

His cock filled her over and over, shoving out thoughts of anything except him. His thick, hard flesh. His need to be inside her, as deep as anyone could get. Sweat made his neck slick beneath her hands, and she liked making him work hard for it.

He shifted his hold, hooking his arms under her

thighs and lifting her higher against the wall. Now she was spread wide and vulnerable. Alex thrust hard. Sophie screamed.

"Is that how you like it, Sophie?"

She shut her eyes and nodded. He slammed his hips into her, his cock sinking deep and true.

"You like to be fucked hard? Tell me."

"Yes," she whispered.

"Look at me." His voice was a snarled order. "Look at me and tell me what you want."

She didn't want to. It was too much. She'd already shown him just who she was. But his hips slammed into her again. "Look at me," he growled.

She opened her eyes. Alex looked like someone's deepest fears. His shaved head and stubbled face and wide, muscled shoulders and the vivid threat of his tattoos as his biceps flexed to hold her still for his pleasure. His face offered no reassurance. He looked furious and desperate as he fucked her. An animal bent on violence. Like he wanted to hurt her with his cock.

Sophie's stomach clenched inside her. Her heart tripped over fear and lust and danger. "Fuck me, Alex," she said.

He snarled and fucked her faster.

"Fuck me," she repeated. "Hard. Please, just… *Please*."

He lifted her hips, tipping them up, pressing her shoulders harder against the wall. His motorcycle boots provided the perfect traction on her wood floor. Sophie whimpered as he pistoned into her.

"Are you going to come again?" he asked.

She shook her head. She couldn't. Not even for him.

"Yes, you are," he growled. "Touch yourself."

"I can't—"

"Touch yourself."

There was no saying no to him. Not when his voice was as hard as a fist. She unlaced her clutching fingers from behind his neck and carefully slid a hand between their bodies. Her bare sex was slippery wet. Her fingers brushed his cock as it slid out of her, and his shaft was slick and hot from her cunt.

"Oh, God," she whispered, then said it again when she brushed her clit and jerked against his thrust.

"That's it," he murmured.

She pressed her fingers to her clit and felt the way his cock dragged against her flesh. He was so thick, so big. "Yes," she urged.

"I want to feel it," he said. "I want to feel you come around my cock. Do that for me, Sophie."

She shook her head again, but she wasn't sure she meant it. Just the way his voice ordered her so roughly was pushing her closer.

"Yes," he insisted, his hands pulling her hips even higher. "That's it," he murmured when she circled her clit faster. "Show me how much you love it."

Oh, fuck, she did love it. She did. "Harder," she demanded.

Alex cursed and wrapped a hand behind her shoulders to pull her toward him. He knelt and lowered her back carefully to the floor, but that was the last hint of restraint. Once she was on her back, he drove hard into her, forcing a cry from her throat.

"Harder?" he growled, his hips slapping into hers.

"Yes," she rasped. "Yes, yes," as she took him deep and deeper and she finally felt that sweet tension building, tightening around his thick cock. He curved over her, fisting a hand into her hair.

"Come for me," he ordered. And she did. She came, head thrown back, clenching her teeth to hold back a scream, hips lifting to take him deeper as she climaxed.

He stilled within her. For a moment, all she could feel was her own body, tight and pulsing, the spasms just starting to fade. But as her awareness returned, she realized he was still hard, his muscles still taut.

The fist in her hair loosened. He slid his hand to her jaw and tipped her head toward him. "That was good, Sophie," he murmured against her mouth. "So good." Then he kissed her and moved slowly inside her. His cock pushed deep, then slid out so slowly that she hummed with pleasure.

She curved her arms around him and dug her fingers into his ass. He still wore his jeans. And she was still so naked. But she felt powerful as his muscles clenched under her hands. Alex grunted and went taut as his heart thundered against hers and he thrust one last time. She held him there and wished it wasn't over.

CHAPTER EIGHT

"Hɪ, Mᴀɴɴʏ!" Sᴏᴘʜɪᴇ called as she walked down her driveway into the crisp morning.

Her sixty-year-old neighbor popped up from the open door of his taxi and tipped his porkpie hat. "Hey! Beautiful day, ain't it?"

"It's perfect," she responded, meaning it wholeheartedly.

Manny got back to cleaning the inside of his windshield. "You know, my nonny always said 'Autumn days come quickly like a running hound.'"

"That's a lovely saying, Manny. You must miss her."

"She was a good woman. Real traditional-like."

Sophie shook her head once she was past his lot. Manny didn't have a nonny. His family had come to Wyoming by way of Utah in the nineteenth century, and his name was Michael. But Manny had gone to New York once in his youth and he'd fallen in love. He'd retired from his job teaching high school shop class five years ago, and he was finally living his dream of being a New York cabdriver. In Jackson Hole.

He'd somehow acquired a trace of a New York accent along with his yellow-checker-painted Ford Taurus and old-fashioned cap. The tourists bought into the shtick and she was pretty sure Manny had bought into it, too. But it made him happy, so even the locals played along.

Everyone deserved something to make them happy.

Sophie ducked her head and tried to hide her smile as she walked up her block. It wasn't easy to hide. It was a big smile. She had a lot to be happy about.

It was a gorgeous September day, even warmer than the last. She knew she'd only have a few more weeks of weather suitable for walking to work in a skirt and heels, so she reveled in the sun on her face and the swish of her blue cotton dress around her thighs. She also reveled in the slight twinge of soreness as she walked. Her muscles were still tired, her hips a little sore, and between her legs she felt bruised in the most satisfying way.

A soft breeze swept over her as she turned a corner, air slipping over her bare thighs. She'd worn her favorite pale pink garter today. The silk fabric was embroidered with taupe swirls that perfectly matched the color of her nude stockings. The bra was the same pale pink, with taupe straps that matched the swirls on the garter. Beyond that…she wore nothing at all.

The smile snuck up on her again, because that felt most wicked of all. The air caressing her bare sex as she walked. The most secret of secrets and no one would ever know. Unless she happened to see Alex later.

She patted the royal-blue skirt of her shirtwaist dress. She looked like Mrs. Cleaver in this dress. Like a woman who should be home cooking a nutritious meal for her loving family. But the truth was that all she wanted to do in the kitchen was be shoved over a counter and taken hard, her pretty little dress bunched around her waist. And she knew just who should be doing the taking.

She still couldn't believe he hadn't been angry. She'd lied to him, or at least withheld the truth, and he hadn't seemed the least bit affected.

Then again, maybe he had been affected. Maybe when he'd realized who she was, the wrongness of it had turned him on. Because it was wrong. Their parents had been lovers. Cheaters. Liars. They'd run away together.

Sophie's heel scuffed the sidewalk and interrupted her stride. She kept walking, but she'd lost her smile.

That was the truth she'd lived with her whole life. That her mother had run off with Wyatt Bishop. That they'd both abandoned their children for lust and illicit love and disappeared together forever. The shame of it had clung to Sophie her whole life, and to her father and brother, too. It had felt like a stain on her skin. A marking that everyone could see. Your mother didn't love you. Your mother was a slut. Your mother left her children.

Sophie was only just starting to get used to the fact that it wasn't true.

A year ago, Alex's brother, Shane, had accidentally solved the twenty-five-year-old mystery. While exploring Bishop property near the Providence ghost town, he'd found a washed-out camp road and then, far below it, hidden in a ravine, he'd found their father's truck and camper.

The news about Alex's father had been immediate. But the confirmation that the second set of skeletal remains had been Sophie's mother…that had taken weeks.

Dorothy Heyer hadn't left her family. She may have cheated, but she hadn't left Sophie motherless. Not on purpose. There'd been an accident, and she'd died.

Sophie took a deep breath and tried to ignore the shaking of her heart. She'd grieved for her mother too many years ago. She couldn't do it again. The knowledge of her death didn't change anything. Not really.

A horn honked behind her and Sophie jumped. By the time Manny pulled up next to her, Sophie had caught her breath and turned toward the street.

"Hey again, Miss Sophie!" he called.

"Manny, you scared me."

"Sorry! I'm on my way to pick up a fare at the airport. Need a ride somewhere?"

She pointed at the library. "Just headed to work. But thank you." She started to wave, but he didn't pull away.

"All right. But I just thought I'd warn you that Mrs. Bishop is looking for you."

"What?" Again?

"She just came by your house, all bothered about something. I told her you were long gone."

"Thanks, Manny. I appreciate it."

Crap. Had she somehow found out about Alex's visit yesterday? Maybe she had a camera set up to point down the street. But it didn't matter. Sophie couldn't worry about it. Alex would be leaving soon enough.

"Hello, Sophie," one of the firefighters called from the doorway of the station. He was with two of the other guys, all of them young and built for playing hero.

"Hi, guys," she called with a wave.

They all smiled at her, and Sophie blushed, feeling more than a little scandalous after what she'd done yesterday. They thought she was shy, of course. One of them called out, "That's a pretty dress, Sophie!"

She laughed and let them have their fun. She liked that they thought she was a bashful, conservative girl who was fun to tease but definitely wouldn't be much fun to take home. It contrasted perfectly with the fact that she was so close to naked in very important ways.

If she ever actually needed rescuing by the fire squad, they'd all be in for a serious shock, especially if it involved hauling her down a ladder.

She was still giggling when she stepped into the

library. Compared to her mood the last time she'd worked, today was going to be like a party. She hadn't made plans to see Alex tonight, but she had a feeling he might text her. This time, he'd had as good a time as she had.

She was smiling at the thought when she spotted Lauren behind the circulation desk and waved. But instead of responding in kind, the smile Lauren had been wearing fell away. She took the books that a young boy was handing her, and she shot a pointed look toward the director's office. When she looked back to Sophie, Lauren widened her eyes and shook her head. She was obviously trying to convey some sort of alarm, but Sophie couldn't imagine what. She hadn't even worked yesterday. What could she possibly have screwed up?

Lauren jerked her head toward the small office they shared behind the circulation desk, so Sophie headed that way to hide out until she could get the scoop. But she hadn't moved quickly enough. She'd hesitated out of confusion and before she could make it past the director's office, the door opened and Jean-Marie stepped out.

"Sophie," she said coolly. "Could I speak with you a moment?"

"Of course!" she answered cheerfully, but she shot Lauren a look of horror over her shoulder. Lauren winced but couldn't offer any clue. She had to turn back to her patron. Oh, well. Sophie was about to find out what she'd done to inspire a Serious Talk.

Her day had suddenly lost its background music of singing birds and tinkling piano notes.

"Sophie," her director said in a mournful voice. She sounded as if she were personally pained by just the sound of Sophie's name.

"Yes?"

"In light of the new circumstances, when Merry Kade stops in today I'm going to tell her that I assembled the Providence display in the lobby."

"The new circumstances?" Sophie asked blankly.

"I know you did the work, but I'm sure you understand why it would be better not to attach your name to it."

"No, I don't understand," she insisted, but as the words left her mouth, a terrible thought struck her. People knew. People knew that she and Alex were sleeping together and it had created a new scandal. Maybe his mother really had put up cameras on the street. Maybe she—

"Don't you think Merry might take offense?" Jean-Marie had dropped any semblance of concern and now looked only impatient.

"I'm sorry," Sophie stammered. "I…I honestly don't know what you're talking about."

"Your brother," Jean-Marie said, her mouth as flat as her words. "Now…" She turned back to her computer, obviously dismissing Sophie. "If you'll—"

"My brother? I have no idea what you're talking about. What does he have to do with anything?"

"Honestly, Sophie, if you can't keep up with your

family's peccadillos, then I don't know what to say. Your brother filed a wrongful death lawsuit against the Bishops this morning. I'm sure they're understandably distraught, and I don't want the library thrown in with your pile of dirty laundry. You know how important the support of the historical trust is to us. Now if you'll excuse me, I've got work to do."

Sophie would've liked to excuse her, but she couldn't move. Her brother had filed a lawsuit? Against the *Bishops?* She just sat there, staring at her boss, mouth agape in undignified shock. The calm part of her brain told her to get up, close her mouth and leave. The shocked part was running around in mad circles, squealing like a panicked mouse.

Jean-Marie aimed a long-suffering look in her direction. It was the look she assumed anytime she had to do more than show dignitaries around the library or play solitaire on her computer. Sophie had seen it a hundred times, but it still snapped her out of her state of shock. The mouse stopped running in circles, Sophie closed her mouth with a snap, and she made her escape.

Lauren grabbed her arm and led her into their office. "You didn't know," she sighed.

Sophie shook her head.

"It only happened fifteen minutes ago, I think. You know Betty's sister works in the county clerk's office, and she called…. Well, never mind. Anyway, I was just about to text you, but I didn't know if I should stick my nose into your personal business."

"It's not my business," Sophie said numbly, but she knew it wasn't true. It was her business now. Her awful, insane business. "I need to call my brother."

"Yeah, go on. Jean-Marie won't be out of her office again until lunchtime."

That brought an automatic smile to Sophie's mouth, but it felt stretched and unnatural. Lauren left and closed the door behind her, giving Sophie some privacy. She dialed her brother's phone immediately, only realizing her hand was trembling when the phone shook against her glasses. He didn't answer. She could barely find the words to leave a message.

"David, what did you do?" was all she said.

Sophie hung up and called her dad's home phone number. When there was no answer, she called his cell, but it went to voice mail right away. He was out of range. He almost always was.

She didn't leave a message for him. She couldn't. She had no idea what was going on.

Shaking her head, she stared down at her phone. This couldn't be happening. It *couldn't*. The entire twenty-five-year scandal had been over, just one more weekend, one little dedication, and it would be done.

Now what was she supposed to do? Just put her phone in her purse and go to work?

She sent a text to David, repeating What did you do? He didn't respond after thirty seconds. Or sixty. Or ninety.

Five minutes later she was still staring at the phone, waiting to hear anything. For one terrible moment, she considered calling Alex to ask if he'd heard something, but she recoiled from the idea. If he hadn't heard yet, how would she explain it?

Oh, God. David had mentioned something about a lawsuit a few months ago, but she'd blown him off. She'd said no. She'd considered that the end of it.

She tried her brother's cell again, then squeezed her eyes shut. This had to be a misunderstanding.

Still shaking, she slipped her phone into her purse and stood up to smooth down her hair and take a deep breath. She had work to do. She couldn't break down now.

Sophie sneaked behind Lauren's back and grabbed a cart. She hadn't planned on weeding books today, but she needed to hide in the stacks, for a little while at least.

She made it halfway through one shelf, feeling a surge of satisfaction when she found an obsolete children's book about the future of the space race and dropped it onto the cart. That book was definitely heading for the trash. There'd been a lot of progress in the space program since 1976. She hoped nobody had checked it out for research in the past two decades.

But Sophie's brief interlude of peace was over when Lauren sneaked around a corner and grabbed her in a hug. "What did you find out?"

"Nothing," she said into Lauren's shoulder. "He didn't answer."

"Crap. So you didn't have a clue?"

"No, and I doubt my dad did either." She pulled back. "Neither of us would've supported this. It's outrageous."

Lauren grimaced. "Maybe it's not that bad. You haven't seen the suit yet."

"It's a wrongful death suit over a car accident that happened twenty-five years ago! There's nothing reasonable about that! They're both long dead. No one even knows what happened."

Lauren put a finger up to her mouth to shush her, and Sophie realized she'd been speaking well above a whisper. "I'm sorry. I just can't..." Tears sprang to her eyes, and she tried to blink them away.

"Sophie, you need to figure this out. Take a personal day."

"I can't! I'm going to need all the personal days I can get when I go to trial for murdering my little brother."

"Ha. Don't murder him. Just rough him up a little. Either way, you can't do that from here."

"No. I may as well stay. At least I'm slightly distracted here, and unfortunately this whole mess will be waiting for me whenever I get off work."

Lauren glanced at the clock. "Are you here until six?"

Sophie nodded.

"I've only got a half shift until two. We'll switch.

You leave at two, and I'll stay until six. You need to talk to your brother."

"No. I need to talk to my dad. He's going to be so…" She waved a frantic hand. "But I can't do that to you."

"Of course you can. I owe you. If it weren't for you, I'd never have hooked up with Jake."

That actually cheered Sophie up enough to snort. "You're joking, right? With the way you stared longingly at the fire station all the time? He was bound to notice."

"I wasn't staring longingly at the station. I was staring longingly at his body every time he jogged to work."

"Regardless, it was only a matter of time before you two fell on each other like hungry beasts."

Lauren blushed and nudged her. "I still owe you. So get out of here at two if you won't leave now. Okay?"

Sophie thought of her dad. And then of Alex and what he would think about all of this. "Okay."

She got back to work weeding and somehow managed to keep distracted until the busy lunch hours. Those went quickly at least. And thank God for that, because she caught several people studying her as if they wanted to ask a question about the long-ago scandal. None of them did, though, and after a very long half hour of reading to preschoolers for story time, it was finally two o'clock. Lauren waved her out the door.

Sophie glared out the windshield as she drove. She'd tried her brother two more times, but he wasn't answering. Of course he wasn't. He knew exactly how pissed she was going to be.

Well, he *thought* he knew. He couldn't have any idea that her day had started off so sweet and perfect, and that she'd been looking forward to an even sweeter evening with a man who probably wouldn't be too keen on her anymore. Did the lawsuit involve him? It must. He would have inherited part of his grandfather's estate.

"David, you little shit," Sophie muttered to herself as she took the highway south toward her dad's ranch. It was supposed to have been a perfect day and now she was driving to her family's house wearing no panties and a scowl on her face. She passed by the pull-off from the other night and growled, "Unbelievable."

At least she still had some clothes at the ranch. She wasn't going to argue with her brother while the mountain breeze caressed her naked ass. "God," she groaned out loud. She'd never be free of these stupid family nightmares. It was like her family was living out a Wyoming version of *The Thorn Birds*. At least there wasn't a wayward priest involved. Yet.

She tried her brother one more time and then threw the phone onto the passenger seat hard enough to make it bounce. It was possible he wasn't at home, but she doubted it. He never went anywhere except to weekly karaoke with the same people he'd hung

out with since high school. Though he'd apparently
added "trips to the county recorder's office" to his
habits.

The drive seemed to take forever, and when she finally skidded to a halt in the gravel yard that fronted
the house, her heart fell. The house looked locked
up tight. Her dad's truck was gone. But maybe her
brother was locked in his room, trying to hide from
her wrath. Best of luck to him, the little shit.

Sophie walked through the silent living room and
kitchen and headed straight down the hallway to her
brother's door. She pounded hard on it, hoping he
was in there, hoping she would scare him half to
death. But there was no gasp of shock and no response. When she tried the knob it was unlocked.
Only her anger made her open it. She'd never have
invaded his privacy otherwise, and when she saw
that he wasn't in the room, she closed the door immediately. She had too many of her own secrets to
tempt fate by poking her nose into others'.

Speaking of… She grimaced and hurried to her
own room. She dug through her top dresser drawer
until she found a pair of pale pink panties and slipped
them on. Even she wasn't perverted enough to have
a family meeting in this state.

Once that little housekeeping task was taken care
of, she lost her momentum. She didn't know what to
do. She was standing alone in an empty house with
too many feelings whipping through her, and Sophie

was suddenly exhausted. Her knees began to shake and she finally gave up and sat down on her bed.

The springs squeaked and slumped under her weight. Amazing how old your childhood bedroom could make you feel. It was strange, because she'd lived here only a year ago, yet it felt like something from her girlhood. Probably because she still had high school pictures on the wall.

"That could have something to do with it," she muttered before collapsing back on the bed. Dust motes burst up and danced through the slanting rays of sunshine that sneaked past the blinds.

She should've transformed this room long before, but she'd somehow never managed it. It was her childhood room, after all. She didn't plan to stay here *permanently*. She'd leave it behind. She knew that was true because aside from the photos from high school and a gigantic map of the world, all the other decorations were posters of faraway sights. Sandy deserts and ocean glaciers and African savannas. She'd once collected postcards from friends traveling closer to home, too. Washington, D.C., and New York City and San Francisco. But all those postcards had been cut up and used in scrapbooks.

That was okay. She'd get out there soon. She wouldn't need scrapbooks or posters or postcards from friends, because she'd travel herself someday. For now, she was patient. Her dad needed her. Clearly, her brother did, too.

Sophie sat up with a sigh, thinking she may as

well put dinner in the oven while she was waiting, but she didn't have the will to stand up. Instead, she just slumped and stared at her dresser and tried not to freak out about her brother. Her eye fell on a new stack of mail and she snagged that and started going through it. All junk. Except one letter.

She froze at the sight of the return address. With everything else going on, she didn't want to think about this right now. Or at any point.

It had taken the medical examiner's office quite a while to complete their final examination of the remains. There hadn't been much to work with, but with the vague possibility of a crime, they'd waited months for clearance from the sheriff's office.

The clearance had come, her mother's bones had been sent to a funeral home, and she'd been cremated. Sophie had taken care of all of that. But this part she couldn't seem to manage. This part she couldn't make herself do.

When she heard the rumble of an approaching engine, Sophie tucked the letter from the funeral home into a drawer and raced to the living room. A peek out the window revealed her brother and dad getting out of the truck, both of them dusty and sweat-soaked from whatever work they'd been doing.

Shit. She'd really wanted to speak to her brother alone, but she supposed her dad had to find out at some point.

David's head was down when he walked in, his mouth drawn into a scowl. He always looked like that after being forced to do real work. Sophie wanted to grab him by the hair and shake him just for that damn look.

He glanced at her, then headed straight toward his room, as if he really thought she'd let him walk right past her.

"What the hell did you do?" she asked.

He shrugged one shoulder and tried to brush past. She pushed him. "What did you do?" she yelled.

"Hey!" her dad said, startled by the sudden tension. "What's going on here?"

"Ask David!"

"Get over it," he mumbled.

"Are you kidding me? Did you think Dad and I would have nothing to say about this?"

"I didn't care what you had to say about this. It's my name on the lawsuit, not yours."

Her dad's chin drew in. "Lawsuit? What are you talking about, David?"

Her brother crossed his arms and frowned at her, seemingly unwilling to admit what he'd done.

Fine. She'd do the hard work. She always had. "He filed a wrongful death lawsuit against the Bishop estate," she finally said, the words dry and bitter and sticking to her throat as she said them. Tears rushed to her eyes. This time she couldn't stop them. "He's suing the Bishops because this all wasn't ugly enough without that!"

"David!" their father gasped.

Her brother shrugged again. "What? Whatever

happened in that accident was his fault. He was driving. People file lawsuits when that happens. Their insurance will pay for it."

Greg Heyer had never so much as spanked either one of them, and he rarely lost his temper. Even now, he didn't. But he did point at his son and shake his head in disgust. "No. *People* might file lawsuits, but we don't. She's been dead for twenty-five years. Let it lie."

David, face red and hands balling into fists, knocked their father's hand away. "My *mother* has been dead for twenty-five years!" he screamed. Sophie's heart nearly pounded out of her chest. She jumped in front of her dad and shoved her brother back before he could lash out further.

He barely noticed. "My mom is dead because of something Wyatt Bishop did. Someone has to pay for that!"

"His kids?" her dad yelled back. "That's what you want? To make his kids pay?"

"Why not? Everyone has been making us pay for decades! And now *they're* the ones getting all the sympathy, holding that bastard up like a fucking community hero."

"Watch your language," her dad snapped.

"Watch my *language?*" he shouted. "Are you kidding? Watch my language, keep my head down, keep my mouth shut, calm down. That's all you ever had to say about *any* of this. 'Ignore them, David. You give them more power if you respond.' Well, guess what? That's not fucking true. I should've fought all of them a long time ago!"

Her dad blew out a long breath behind her. "What are you talking about?" he asked wearily.

"I'm saying I'm not going to be weak anymore. I'm going to take what belongs to me."

"And what belongs to you is someone else's money?" he sighed.

"Fuck you!" David snarled.

Sophie pushed her finger into his chest. "Don't you speak to him that way. Ever."

He knocked her hand away, too, startling her so much that she stepped back.

"Fuck you, too, Sophie. You're not my mom and you never have been." He finally spun away and stalked to his room. The slam of his door shook the whole house.

Sophie stood frozen in shock. Her brother had always seemed sullen and childish, but this was a new low.

"Hey, don't cry, princess."

Her dad turned her into his arms and hugged her. She hadn't realized she was still crying, but as his arms closed around her, she sobbed.

"It's okay," he murmured. "It's all right. I'll talk to David once he's settled down and find out what's going on. Maybe he just needs to talk it out and then I can get him to drop this nonsense."

"But he's already done it. Everybody already knows."

He patted her back in that way he'd done since she could remember. He'd probably been doing it since she was a toddler and her mom had married him. "It doesn't matter what they think, Sophie. What matters is that we do the right thing. You know that."

Yes. She knew that. He'd always told her and David that. She hadn't believed it, and neither had David apparently, but Sophie had always appreciated it at least. Her brother clearly hadn't seen it the same way.

"Why would he do it?" she whispered, as if her dad could have any sort of answer.

He squeezed her hard again. "He was only one. He doesn't remember your mother at all, sweetheart. All he's ever known about her is anger and shame. You and I, we knew something more than that. We knew how funny she was. How quick to laugh. We knew the good things. He never got that. He's mixed up about it."

Well, Jesus, Sophie was mixed up, too, but she had some damn common sense. She did sometimes wonder if David would've been a better man if Mom had been around, but maybe he would've been just as weak and whiny. Maybe he would've been worse.

"I'm sorry," she said, pulling away to wipe her tears. Her dad pulled a handkerchief from his pocket. "This must all be tough for you. The memorial service and the memories, and now this…."

He shrugged. "It is what it is. I'm a grown man. I can handle a little gossip. Anyway, I've got this place, and a great daughter to take care of me. It's not so bad."

When she'd been young, she'd wondered if he'd even heard the rumors that had flown. After all, he lived way out here on his own. She and David hadn't had the choice to be isolated. They'd had to go to school. Had to face the taunting.

In fact, her dad had been so good at facing things stoically, she'd wondered whether he missed her mom at all. But sometimes when she'd been a little girl plagued by bad dreams and afraid to sleep, she would sneak down the hall toward the faint light of her dad's reading lamp. And every once in a while she'd find him sitting in his big easy chair, head in hands, and a bottle of Scotch open on the table next to him. The night when she'd finally realized he was quietly sobbing, she'd stopped sneaking out to the living room. It was too scary to know her big strong stepfather was just as hurt as she was.

But just like he always did, he assured her he'd be fine about this new blow. She didn't know how to figure out if he was really fine or not, so she mopped up her tears and did what she always did. She got to work.

"What were you doing today?" she asked as she moved to the kitchen to wash the few dishes that had been left in the sink.

"Looking for the last few strays. We're selling a little early this year."

"Any luck with the strays?"

"We found two. I suspect the last one made a good meal for something. He was that steer with the bad eye, remember? Anyway, I'll try one more time tomorrow."

She set a pot of coffee on to brew and opened the fridge. "I'll put a chicken in for you two, if that sounds good."

"I can make a chicken," he said, just as he always did, and she answered just as he knew she would.

"I know you can." But she rinsed one off and stuffed it with lemon and garlic all the same. Once she had it in the oven, she started sweeping the kitchen, ashamed to see the dust bunnies chasing across the floor ahead of her broom.

"You gonna stay for dinner?"

She glanced down the hall where her brother had disappeared. "No. I don't think so."

"It's probably best. He's not going to be pleasant." As if on cue, the muted sound of loud music started up from the other side of the house. He was twenty-six years old and still handling stress like a teenager.

"God," she muttered and got back to sweeping. When that was done, she bundled the tablecloth up and took it outside to shake out the crumbs.

"All right now," her dad said when she got back in. "We're fine. You don't need to take care of everything."

She ignored him and poured a cup of coffee, fixing it up with sugar and no cream just the way he liked. "Sit down and relax, Dad."

"I can't. I've got to drive over to the feed store."

She reversed course and took the cup of coffee to the counter instead of the table and poured the contents into a travel mug. It was a thirty-five minute drive. She didn't want him nodding off, and after that confrontation, he definitely looked tired.

"Dad," she started, but then she didn't know what she should say. She wanted to apologize again, for all of this, but none of it was her fault. Except the letter in her dresser. That was her fault. Her mother's ashes were ready to be picked up, they'd been ready for six weeks, and for some reason, she couldn't bring herself to go get them. It felt shameful and wrong, and she didn't want to tell him.

"I'm fine, Sophie," he said, squeezing her shoulder. "We'll all be fine."

Yes. They would. He'd always promised her that, and he'd always been right. They'd gotten through those first few days and weeks and months. And they'd gotten through school-yard cruelty and every new person whose eyes went a little wide when they realized who you were. They'd get through this, too. This was nothing.

But as soon as she was back in her car, Sophie was crying again. She had no idea why. This lawsuit was stupid and untimely and just plain wrong, but it wasn't the end of the world. So why did she have to pull her car over as soon as she was out of sight of the house?

She dug blindly through her purse for Kleenex,

but as soon as she wiped her eyes tears spilled out again. She finally gave up and laid her forehead on her steering wheel to cry.

It couldn't be that she was sexually involved with one of the Bishops. She wasn't that shallow, or at least she didn't think she was. This pain was deeper than that. It *hurt.* Her stomach ached with it. And she felt…terrified. Shaky.

That had nothing to do with Alex. How could it?

She just wanted this over. All of it. She wanted to have a normal family and a normal past.

And that was it, wasn't it? She'd thought it was finally over. The Bishops were having their dedication and then people would finally forget.

The welcome truth was that the story wasn't that interesting anymore. For so many years, the fates of Dorothy Heyer and Wyatt Bishop had been a mystery. Rumors had flown, every one of them pushed and plumped up by Rose. Where the pair had gone, what had happened, whether they were still together or ever had been, who had spotted someone fitting their descriptions.

No one had known what had happened, so *anything* could have happened. Any delicious, scandalous, awful thing.

But in the end…it had been almost boring. They'd been in Wyatt Bishop's truck together, hauling a camper up an ancient road to a campsite on Bishop land, and the dirt had given way. All those years their bodies had been lost in a narrow canyon near an abandoned town, and that was the end of it.

The story was finally done. Everyone could move on.

But not anymore. Thanks to her immature, thoughtless, aimless little brother, the story was delicious again. Scandal tinged with bad behavior. This was a small town. Everyone knew the players. There were sides and they would be taken. Rose Bishop might not be sympathetic, but she was good at propaganda. People didn't like Rose, but they sure loved her stories.

Sophie took a deep breath and then let the sobs fall from her throat. She was so sick of dealing with what her mother had done when Sophie was only five years old. She was so damn sick of that being her life. Maybe she should dye her hair. Maybe she could change her name. Alex's brother had done that. Shane had gotten so sick of being Shane Bishop that he'd changed his name to his mother's maiden name. Of course, that itself had been a scandal. There was no way to get away from it. Except to leave.

Sophie found another tissue and mopped up again. She had to stop crying; the tissue packet was empty.

Anyway, there was no point crying. She couldn't leave. Her dad needed her, and as tough as it was to be Dorothy Heyer's child, it was a blessing to be Greg Heyer's daughter. He hadn't turned his back on her all those years ago. She wouldn't turn her back on him now.

And the truth was they'd all be fine. Just like her dad always promised.

"It'll be all right," she whispered to herself. "It will go away." It would. Eventually. She just had to keep her chin up and pretend it didn't matter and keep her thoughts to herself.

She nodded and wiped one last stray tear away. The long drive back to town was a good thing today. She needed time for her swollen eyes and stuffed nose to recover. If she pulled up and found Rose Bishop waiting on her doorstep, Sophie didn't want to look like she was falling apart. If that woman sensed weakness, she'd go for Sophie's soft spots.

Unfortunately all of Sophie's spots were soft today, but she couldn't let people see that. She never could.

CHAPTER NINE

"WHAT THE HELL do I care?" Alex snapped, irritated that he even had to think about this.

"Because a lawsuit might affect the inheritance," Shane countered calmly.

"You got the inheritance, brother."

Shane winced and ran a hand through his hair. Sawdust filtered out and drifted past the sunlight that shone behind him.

Alex had driven out to see Shane's new place. It wasn't much, just a trailer set up on the land he'd inherited from their grandfather, but Shane was steadily making it into his. He was almost done with a small stable and had graded a spot for a house he planned to build next summer. He'd always been good with his hands. Alex wasn't surprised that he'd become a carpenter.

"I want to do something about that," Shane finally said. "This land belongs to you as much as it does to me. Which is to say not much at all." He winked. "But old man Bishop left it to me because Dad was his only kid. He should have split it between you and me."

"You're the oldest and I wasn't around."

"It doesn't matter. You should have half."

Alex shook his head at his brother's sentimentality. "And what would I do with land in a place I come visit once every twenty years? It's yours, Shane." He turned in a small circle, taking in the dried grass and sagebrush and the high slopes of the Tetons in the distance. "You belong here. You always have."

"Then I'll sell some off and send you the money."

"You might need that money to fight this lawsuit."

Shane shook his head and set down the two-by-four he'd been sizing. "If there's any settlement, it'll likely come out of the trust or be paid by insurance."

"You can't be sure of that. How much is he asking for?"

"A million dollars."

Alex sucked in a breath. "Wow."

Shane shrugged. "It's a lawsuit related to a car accident. My lawyer says if it goes any further, the insurance company will probably settle for a smaller amount. There's not a lot of evidence to prove anything either way."

"Yeah." Alex folded his arms and stared out at the mountains. The sight was beautiful, but it reminded him of too much. "Why's he doing it?"

"I don't know. Money hungry, I guess. He hasn't made much of himself."

"Do you know him?"

"Not really."

Alex glanced at Shane. "His sister seems nice."

"Yeah, they're not a lot alike as far as I can tell. She's always been a hard worker. Quiet type. Polite."

"Right," Alex muttered, then cleared his throat against a memory of her very politely saying *please, please*. "Anyway, you seem calm about it." Shane had been hot-tempered in his youth, quiet until you pissed him off.

"I let it all go last year."

"What do you mean? The money?"

"The money," Shane murmured, his eyes turning toward the jagged Tetons. "Yeah. But not really the money. When Gideon Bishop left me this little plot of land and gave everything else to that damn ghost town... Fuck, it was just another slap in the face. You remember how cold he was after Dad disappeared?"

"Well, he was right about Mom being unstable," Alex said.

"He was. But that should've been more reason to reach out to us. To help."

Alex grunted in agreement. One day they'd been a stable, nuclear family. Mom and dad and two rowdy boys. The next day they'd been free-falling. A dad who'd run off, a mom who could barely take care of herself, and grandparents who considered her nothing more than trash with two brats to support.

"When our grandfather died and thumbed his nose at us in the will... Shit. I thought I'd moved past a lot of it, but it came rushing back, and all my anger came down to that damn will. I wanted to make him pay. Maybe because I couldn't make Dad pay. Or Mom. Or this whole fucking town. I don't know."

Now instead of watching the mountains, Alex watched his brother. They'd been close in their early years, and less close as teenagers, but as adults? As an adult, Shane was a complete stranger to him. His face looked different, of course, harder and older and a little sadder. But it wasn't just that. Alex didn't know anything about who he'd loved and lost and what his struggles had been.

"So you sued them," he pressed.

"Yes. I didn't really care about the money, it was just the idea that that asshole would rather give it all to a tourist trap than leave it to you and me. I guess he felt closer to ancestors who'd been dead for a hundred years than he did to us."

That sounded about right. His grandfather had been a hard, intimidating man. He'd considered his own son a weak failure for marrying the woman he did and then getting mixed up with someone even worse. No doubt he thought Shane and Alex would end up just like their father. Or worse, turn out like their mom.

"But I figured it out," Shane finally said. "I got to know Merry, and suddenly all that anger felt as wrong as it was."

"That's good," Alex said, though he didn't understand it. He'd loved a woman, too, but he'd never felt any better about his family.

"I hope you can accept that I gave up the fight for the money."

Alex shot him a confused look.

"The money that went to the historical trust. If I'd kept fighting the will and won the lawsuit, part of it would've gone to you."

Alex shook his head. "I don't want that old man's money. I don't want any of this."

"Still," Shane murmured, his eyes roaming over the landscape. "It's a good place."

"It is." He'd meant what he'd said. His brother belonged here. Alex couldn't begrudge him that, even if he did feel a twinge of longing. Not for the place, but for the feeling of being home. He'd never had that anywhere. It was something missing in him, and it always would be.

Even in his earliest childhood, when things had been good, he'd had little in common with his dad. Ranching and handyman work hadn't held Alex's attention at all.

Shane cleared his throat and shifted, warning Alex that things were about to get awkward. "I hope it doesn't bother you that Merry is the curator for Providence."

Alex raised his eyebrows in question.

"I don't want you thinking I dropped the lawsuit just to support her work."

Alex finally realized what he was saying. Their grandfather's money had gone to the Providence Historical Trust, and Merry had her job thanks to that.

Alex kept his mouth shut for a few heartbeats just to make his brother squirm, but then he finally grinned. "Brother, if you'd pay millions of dollars to win her over, then I'd say that must be some awful sweet loving, and congratulations."

"Ha!" Shane slapped him on the back.

"Are you blushing?" Alex asked.

"Fuck you," Shane shot back, but he was definitely blushing. Not to mention grinning like a fool. "Speak of the devil," he said.

Alex turned to see a car driving up the long road. The brunette behind the wheel waved, and they both waved back. He'd only met Merry briefly at their mom's house yesterday, but her enthusiasm for life was contagious.

As soon as she'd skidded to a stop on the gravel drive, Merry jumped from her car and held up a bag. "I brought Chinese food!"

"Wow," Alex murmured. "She is pretty awesome."

"I know." Shane stepped forward to take the bag and give her a kiss.

"You'll stay for dinner, right?" she asked Alex, her eyes wide with encouragement.

He hadn't planned on it. He'd planned to talk to his brother and make a quick escape, just as he had in every interaction with his family since he'd returned. But he couldn't say no to Merry's hope. "How can I resist?" he asked, gesturing toward the picture on her bright pink T-shirt. "I love a girl who knows her *Dr. Who* references."

"You know *Dr. Who?*"

"I spend a lot of time in hotel rooms streaming old TV shows."

Merry squealed and jumped forward to give him a big hug. "You're awesome."

"You're easy."

She gave him a little shove and headed up the stairs of the trailer while Shane held the door open for her. "Uh-oh. Shane's been telling tales."

Alex followed her laughter up the stairs to Shane's temporary home. He was surprised to see that the place actually looked livable. The rust eating up the siding on the outside hadn't promised much, but the small living room was softened by a blue shag rug and a black leather couch piled high with gray and blue pillows. Merry had obviously helped him decorate. Alex might not know his brother well anymore, but he was damn sure Shane hadn't picked out the hip-looking lamp with the blue streaks in the glass.

Merry grabbed plates and napkins and set them on the coffee table along with a few beers. The Chinese food was surprisingly good. Alex had been spoiled by time spent in California and this was, after all, Wyoming, but even chefs liked to ski. Good food had made it to Jackson along with tourism money.

"You look funny," Merry suddenly said.

Alex looked up from his kung pao in surprise. "What?"

"You look like some kind of biker felon with your tattoos and your shaved head, but you use chopsticks like a pro."

"You've obviously never met any Chinese felons. Scary motherfuckers."

Merry burst into laughter and Shane looked at her with a smile of delight. Like just her happiness was enough to make his day. Jesus. Alex looked away, letting them have that moment to themselves.

"Have you been to China, Alex?" Merry asked.

"No, they've got damn good engineers there. No need to import me."

"So…" She glanced at Shane before continuing. "Where have you been?"

He thought about Alaska and all the stuff he'd told Sophie. For some reason, he didn't want to share that.

Shane leaned back into the couch with his beer. "Yeah, where'd you disappear to, brother?"

Alex grabbed his own beer and settled into the chair. "I went to Colorado first, meaning to go to Colorado State, but I couldn't afford the tuition."

Shane looked shocked. "You got in? You never told me."

"We weren't talking much by high school. Anyway, I knew I couldn't afford it, so I moved out there to work for a year. They held my spot and I went on in-state tuition for two years. Then I transferred to the School of Mines."

"Wow." Shane blinked a few times. "That's impressive."

Alex shrugged. "I did well there. I really liked my hydrology professor, so that's what I went with. He was a real mentor to me. Took an interest. He died last year."

Shane nodded, and Alex meant to keep talking, but for a moment he couldn't. Oz Thompson had been an amazing engineer with forty years of field-work under his belt, and for some reason, he'd singled Alex out. Maybe because Oz had been tattooed and scary-looking, too. For whatever reason, they'd clicked. He'd looked out for Alex, pushing him when he needed pushing. But now he was dead.

Maybe that was how Alex had ended up back here, looking for...something.

Alex cleared his throat. "Anyway, I worked with some natural gas companies while I was going for my master's, and now I'm a contractor. It keeps me from getting stuck in one place too long."

"Where have you worked?" Merry asked.

"Alaska, Canada, all over the continental U.S. A little bit in South America. The Netherlands."

"Whoa! The Netherlands! That's so cool."

"It was pretty damn cool."

They all settled in to talk about Texas, where Alex had worked and Merry had grown up. By the time he realized it was full dark outside, Alex had spent two hours catching up with his brother. It had been surprisingly good. Shane hadn't brought up their mother once, and when she'd called, Shane had let it go to voice mail.

Maybe Shane had been telling the truth. Maybe he really had distanced himself. Shane hadn't been a mama's boy or anything, but he'd let their mom get into his head when they were young. He'd let her give him hope and she'd poured her sickness in there with it. Shane had been desperate for their dad to return. Alex had only hated the man. Hated him for leaving. And hated him for being a decent dad before he'd left. If he'd been awful, it would have been so much easier to live without him.

"I'd better get going," Alex finally said.

"You can stay here if you want. The couch is damn comfortable."

"No, thanks." He wanted to be alone. He always did.

"Listen, I hate to ask, but could you do me a favor if you're headed back to town? I've got the paper samples for the program. Can you drop them at Mom's?"

"Shit," he cursed, but even he could see it wasn't a big favor to ask. He held out his hand for the samples and smiled at Shane. He wasn't too immature to stop by his mom's house for five minutes.

Plus, a trip to his mom's would get him close to Sophie again. He considered the idea as he drove toward town.

It wasn't a good idea to see her after what her brother had done today, but he couldn't exactly blame her for it. And good idea or not, he wanted to see her.

Alex tried to let the wind take his thoughts away,

but he couldn't shake them. Sophie Heyer inspired thoughts with some staying power, after all. He'd be remembering her for a long time. Especially when he jerked off like he had first thing this morning. He'd woken up thinking of her coming for him, nails biting into his skull while the taste of her wet his throat. God. That'd been fucking amazing. Almost as amazing as lifting her up and making her ride his cock.

Yeah. Fuck it. He was gonna see her.

Alex pulled into the lot of his motel and got out his phone. She hadn't gotten in touch, but he wasn't surprised. Things were even weirder than they had been before. But Alex liked weird just fine.

He pulled up her number and sent a text. Hey. I thought I might stop by. Are you decent?

I'm not sure how to answer that after last night.

He grinned from ear to ear before her next text came through.

But after today... I'm really sorry.

Did she mean she was sorry about her brother or sorry because she didn't want to see Alex? Wanna talk? he asked hopefully.

Maybe.

He let out a breath he didn't realize he'd been holding. Gimme 30?

Sure. I'll see you soon.

Alex wasn't the type to smile much, but fuck if he didn't smile his way through a quick shower and a change of clothes. This girl was the nicest thing in his world right now, by far. The nicest thing that had been in his world for a really long time. Not only the sex, but just the way she *was*. Sweet and hot and smart and secret. The best kind of mystery.

He really did want to talk. He wanted to see her. But he had no doubt things would heat up. She liked it just as much as he did. And he'd be gone by Sunday. They both needed to get their fill before he left.

Alex pulled up to his mom's place five minutes later and knocked hard, hoping to get this over with quickly. He heard her talking on the phone as she approached, her voice high and excited.

"Oh, Alex!" she exclaimed as she opened the door. The tiny gray kitten shot out the door and down the stairs. Apparently it belonged to his mother, as if she could take care of an animal in this clutter. "I was just talking to your brother! He was telling me about all the places you've been. I am so proud of you."

"Thanks," he said gruffly as he followed her into the kitchen. "I'm just dropping these off."

"Oh, you're so good to me. Do you want some coffee?" He looked around at her mess of a kitchen.

It wasn't filthy. Nothing smelled bad, but there were piles of papers and canned goods everywhere. He shook his head, then accidentally kicked something when he moved to put the manila folder full of paper samples down. The bowl he'd kicked spilled cat food everywhere.

When he bent to pick it up, he saw that tiny ants were crawling in the bowl. "Mom, there are ants all over this cat food."

"Oh, I keep putting out traps, but they come in from the garden. But the cats don't mind ants. Extra protein." Cats? Multiple? That wasn't good. Not when the place was already so cluttered.

"Jesus." He grabbed a paper towel to clean it up, then marched the whole mess out to the garbage can. When he came back in, she was tearing open the envelope.

"Oh, these are lovely! You're going to stay and help me choose, right?"

"No." He washed his hands. Twice.

"Well. All right." She only lapsed into silence for a few minutes. "So how in the world did you ever become an engineer?"

"I went to college."

"I'm sure, but… Well, sweetheart, you weren't exactly a good student."

He froze to shoot her a hard look, then threw the paper towel into the trash can. "Are you kidding me?"

"You almost failed ninth grade, remember?"

"Yes," he ground out. "I definitely remember. That was the year you pulled me out of school four times to go on cross-country wild-goose chases. *Remember?*"

"Well, we had to. Your father—"

"My father was right here in Teton County, good and dead."

"I didn't know that!" she cried. "So many people were telling me so many things!"

"You mean you were harvesting rumors to keep you going. Regardless, after I had to go to summer school in ninth grade, I refused to go on any more trips with you and Shane. Amazingly, I managed to get my grades up by my junior year. Who would have thought that taking a kid to school every day would result in better grades?"

"Alex," she sighed. "You've always been so rigid."

He laughed. "Sure, Mom. I'll see you later. Enjoy your paper samples."

"Wait a minute! I wanted to talk to you about this awful lawsuit! What am I going to do? If that evil little man—"

"Mom. I'm leaving."

Amazingly, she didn't follow him out the door, weeping and wailing. He stepped outside and almost tripped over the tiny cat that wound between his feet. "Hey," he murmured. She purred against his ankle.

Alex picked her up and nearly winced at how cute she was. Her tiny meow made him shake his head.

"You're not trying to survive with that woman, are you?"

She meowed again, and her purr vibrated through his palm.

"Take it from me. You need to get out of there."

He glanced back at the house, thinking of the dangerous piles of papers and the ants in the cat food. "Shit," he muttered. He couldn't leave this baby here to get hit by a car or eaten by coyotes. He tucked the kitten inside his coat and headed for his bike.

Even without the warm bundle against his chest, he felt silly riding his bike a hundred feet, but he couldn't leave it there for his mom to see, so he drove to Sophie's and eased his bike into the narrow space between her garage and the next house.... Just in case he was still here when the sun rose. When he knocked, she answered the door wearing a modest blue dress and a frilled pink apron.

"Are you baking cookies?" he asked.

"Cupcakes, actually. Do you want one?"

"Hell, yeah."

She led him to the kitchen and popped a little cake in his hand. The white frosting was covered with sparkly pink sugar crystals. "Pretty."

"Thank you."

"The cupcake, too."

When she smiled he realized how tired she looked. Her makeup was smudged. Her eyes slightly red. "Are you okay, Sophie?"

"I'm okay. I'm really sorry about what my brother's done. I had no idea. Nobody did."

"It's got nothing to do with me." He ate half the delicate little cake in one bite.

"But it's your family's money."

"My family doesn't really have any money. There's the trust. And my brother's land, I suppose."

"That's awful!" she gasped.

"Hopefully it'll be settled by the insurance company if it comes to it. Though if it does put his land at risk, then I'll get pissed and come looking for your brother." He held up the cake. "This is really good," he said before he popped the rest into his mouth.

"Thanks," she murmured. "But…your father's memory. It shouldn't be hurt like this. It's not fair."

He dusted his hands off over the sink with a chuckle. "I'm not the least bit worried about my dad's memory. Many years of effort have gone into making that man into a saint. He could use some tarnishing. Especially considering that we're about to have a ceremony honoring his sleazy death."

When she winced, he muttered a curse.

"I'm sorry," he said quickly. "I'm not used to talking to someone who was involved."

"No, it's okay. It was sleazy, unfortunately. But there's nothing wrong with honoring his memory."

He wasn't sure about that, but it was too complicated to figure out tonight. "What about your mom? Did you have a ceremony?"

She swallowed hard before she turned and busied

herself with piling bowls and pans in the sink. "Not really." Clearly, she wanted to discuss it as much as he did. Good.

"You look awfully cute in that apron," he said, eyeing the ribbons that curled over her ass.

She flashed him a bright smile and dried her hands on a dainty towel embroidered with berries. "Thank you."

"You look awfully cute in everything. And nothing."

"Stop." She giggled, her cheeks flushing with a much healthier color than she'd had a few seconds ago. A tiny meow broke the silence.

Her eyes went wide.

"Oh. Um… Listen. Can you do me a big favor?" He unzipped his jacket and pulled out the kitten.

"Oh, my God," she gasped, immediately taking it from his hands to cuddle against her chest.

"I found her wandering outside. I can't take her to the motel, but I didn't want to leave her outside. I'll check out shelters tomorrow, but if it's not too much trouble for tonight…?"

Sophie didn't answer. She was too busy burying her nose in the kitten's fur. The kitten purred like an engine. "Oh, my God," Sophie breathed. "Yes, she can stay with me. How do you know she's a girl?"

He shrugged. "She's pretty?"

"I don't think that's how it works. But we'll settle on 'her' for now."

She got a can of tuna from the cupboard and set it

on the ground. The kitten quickly abandoned purring and began eating like a pro. Sophie set down a bowl of water, too. Within minutes, the kitten was curled up in a chair, asleep, her fat tummy rising and falling with each breath.

"I'll try to take her off your hands before the weekend."

"Sure. I'll make up a litter box. She'll be fine." She wiped down the kitchen counter.

"You said you wanted to talk."

"I did."

"What do you want to talk about? The lawsuit?"

"God no." She took off the apron and turned to leave the kitchen, but he snatched the apron off the counter.

"Hey, no need to leave that behind. You might need it later."

"Oh, my God!" She laughed. "You're naughty."

"Oh, I'm the naughty one?" he teased, loving the way she laughed until she collapsed into the couch.

"Shut up. You're not supposed to bring any of that up!"

"So, just do it and never mention it after?"

"Exactly. I'm shy."

That ridiculous lie was like a stroke of fingers down his belly. She wasn't shy, she was a coy little vixen, and he had a sudden urge to make her admit it in the most breathless way possible. "That lie is even naughtier than what we did yesterday."

"Not even close to true. And I am shy. A little."

He shook his head and shot her a look that let her know he wasn't fooled. "So no talk of last night? Or the lawsuit?"

"Nope. Tell me more about Alaska. Or tell me where else you've been."

"Where else? Canada, California, Texas, Colorado, South Dakota, the Netherlands—"

"The Netherlands!" she yelped. "That's crazy! I don't know anything about it. Tell me everything."

It was his turn to laugh. "I don't know all that much. Some of the food was good. Some was really...fishy."

"Were you on the sea?"

"No, strangely, their production is mostly on land. I only work on groundwater. Ocean hydrology is a whole different thing."

"Did you see a lot of windmills?"

"Yep. It's a beautiful country. Flat but really green. The people are fairly reserved, but friendly as hell when you get to know them."

"Did they speak English?"

"Most of them."

"Wow," she breathed.

He suddenly remembered the pictures on his phone. "Here. This was my favorite place. The biggest town where I was working was a university town. Every single building is older than anything you could see here." He called up the picture of the ancient row homes on the main canal and handed the phone over.

"Oh." Eyes wide, lips parted in wonder, she stared at the picture. "Oh, Alex, I can't believe you were there. Can I...?" She gestured at the screen, and he nodded, giving her permission to scroll through.

She slid through the photos slowly, pausing over each one to study it. Her eyes sparkled. Alex glanced at each picture, but his eyes always rose to her face again. Jesus, she was cute, with her little nose and black glasses and wide-eyed fake innocence.

"Oh," she said suddenly, and pushed the phone back at his hand. "Sorry."

She'd gotten past his pictures of the Netherlands and stumbled over a picture of a woman perched on his bike, her tank top dipping low over tan cleavage and her sunglasses hiding her almond-shaped eyes.

"I probably should've asked before now," Sophie said. "Do you have a girlfriend?"

"No. She's my ex."

"Ex-wife?"

"No," he answered. But then heard himself add, "We lived together for a while." He wasn't sure why he said it. It hardly mattered.

"I'm sorry," she said simply.

"It just didn't work out. It's been six months now. It's fine."

"That doesn't seem very long."

"Well," he added with a sardonic smile, "I hadn't been home for three months before that. I'm not so good at settling down."

Sophie curled her legs under her and watched him for a moment. "I understand that."

"Really? I wouldn't think you'd be sympathetic. Seems like you were born to settle down."

She winced as if he'd struck her, and Alex immediately regretted whatever he'd done to offend her. "Hey—" he started, but she spoke over him.

"I'd like to travel. I'd like to move on. But I help with my dad's ranch, and he needs me. He's getting older. I wouldn't walk away from that."

Now he was the one wincing. "Like I did, you mean."

Sophie shrugged. "I wouldn't judge that. I grew up with the same scandal you did. You saw your chance to escape and you took it."

"And you didn't."

"I haven't seen my chance yet."

"You went to college, obviously."

Her smile wasn't natural and wide this time. It was tight. "I took most of my degree work at the University of Wyoming online. I only spent a year in Laramie. Then I commuted to Salt Lake City for two years to get my master's, but I only had to be there six or seven days a month. My brother..." She paused for a long moment, but then just shook her head. "I don't know. He's always been a little lost. He was so young when she disappeared."

Alex's mind cruelly flashed back to those first few weeks after his dad had left. Alex had been nine, his brain more than solid enough to record every moment. "I'd think maybe that would be a blessing," he finally said.

"I've thought the same thing. But I guess not."

"How old were you?" he asked.

She smoothed a hand over her skirt, her gaze gone distant. "I was almost five. My birthday was three days later."

"Jesus," he said, the hair on his nape rising in horror.

"I wasn't even that scared at first. I knew she'd be back for my birthday. She had to make a cake. She had to—" The words ended in a strange little hiccup. Sophie took a few breaths and then cleared her throat. "It feels like it was a hundred years ago, doesn't it?"

"Yeah," he said quietly.

"And then sometimes it's right there all of a sudden, with no warning. It must be easier when you're not here."

"It is easier. No one knows about it, so after a while it's almost like you don't know about it anymore either. It's almost like it didn't happen. You should try it sometime. Get away."

"Run away," she corrected, but he couldn't tell if it was an admonition or a yearning.

"Maybe. I don't know."

Her gaze stayed distant for a long time, but then she shook her head and smiled. "I can't. Maybe someday."

Alex wasn't sure why he felt a stab of disappointment. He'd be moving along in a few days, what she did or didn't do with her life was none of his business. Maybe it was only that it felt like a judgment of his own life.

Other people stayed. To take care of a mother. A father. Or the woman they loved. They stayed because normal people didn't drift the way Alex did.

He and Andrea had tried it that way for a while. She'd traveled with him on and off for a year. She'd thought it would be fun. He'd loved it for a while. But then it had been a disappointment for them both. She'd been homesick and lonely while he worked; he'd hated coming back to the hotel to an argument.

So they'd tried it her way instead. They'd rented an apartment outside Seattle. Picked out furniture. He'd moved his few belongings in with hers. That had been happy for a while, but only a while. Then Alex had gotten a little too relieved when it was time to hit the road again, and Andrea had gotten a little too pissed about each successive trip.

He wasn't made to settle down, and nobody wanted a relationship with a man who couldn't stay in one place for more than a few months.

Or had his childhood made him so afraid of holding on tight that he just let everything go?

"Tell me more about your travels," she finally said.

He shook his head. "Tell me about your dad's ranch."

"Ha. Your family is in ranching. You know all about it. There's nothing to tell."

"Cattle?" he pressed.

She nodded.

"South of here, right?"

"Yes," she said. "About forty minutes out. That's all there is to tell. It's beautiful, but I only stay to help my dad. He's always been good to me."

"He sounds like a good guy."

"Yeah. He is. He's my stepdad, you know. I mean, I assume you know everything."

He nodded. Of course he knew. Everybody knew. Greg Heyer had met a woman on a trip to Casper and brought her and her young daughter home to live with him just a month later. *What had he expected from such a quick and dirty start? Nobody even knew her people.*

Yeah. He'd heard all about that. Many times.

"Tell me where you'd go," he said.

She frowned in puzzlement.

"If you left here, where's the first place you'd go?"

"Oh." She kept frowning, but now he could see the thoughts turning in her eyes. "There are so many places. Alaska, for sure. But first?" She looked at him like he might have the answer, but he couldn't help.

Finally, she smiled. "I've never seen the ocean. I'd go to California. But not L.A. or San Francisco. Not to a city. I'd go to the coast and see the ocean and redwoods and… God," she sighed. "Can you imagine?"

Yes. He could. He'd seen that coast a dozen times. But he didn't say that. "It'd be beautiful."

"Yes. Everybody always says you can smell the ocean. Is that true?"

"Sure."

"What does it smell like?"

Alex opened his mouth to answer, then realized he wasn't sure how to put it. "It smells…humid, I guess. But cool."

"Like rain?"

"No. More complicated. Sometimes a little fishy or a little green. And salty."

Her head tilted and a frown showed between her eyebrows. "Salt doesn't have a smell."

Alex laughed in exasperation. "You're right. I don't know. It's like trying to explain that aspen smells crisp."

"Okay, you got me there." She watched him, her mouth soft with amusement, her eyes still bright.

"What?" he finally asked.

"You have a nice laugh."

He raised an eyebrow at that.

"I like it. You look so dangerous and dark with your tattoos and your scruff." Her hand rose to stroke his jaw, her fingers scraping softly over his stubble. His skin tingled. "And then you laugh."

"I'm glad you like it," he said, his voice already rough with need for her. He curved his hand around her knee and felt the soft warmth of her stocking.

God. "I like your laugh, too," he said. "It sounds so sweet and innocent. Just the way you look."

Her eyes crinkled with mischief.

"Tell me again how you're shy," he challenged, sliding his hand up her thigh.

"I am," she said, just as his hand touched bare skin. He pushed higher, bunching her skirt up until her stocking was revealed, half a shade darker than her skin, clipped to a pale pink ribbon that was decorated with swirls of tan. His skin looked impossibly dark against all that pale, and far too rough to touch such sweetness. They both watched his blunt fingers spread over her thigh. "I'm shy," she repeated, her breath coming faster now. Something dangerous uncurled in Alex's gut.

"Right. You're shy. You're a nice girl."

"I am," she insisted, but her words ended on a gasp when he tugged her leg closer, pulling her thighs apart. He pushed her skirt up into a crumpled pile, exposing pink panties. Lust spread through him like a drug as he slid his hands along the line of that delicate fabric until his fingertips slipped between her legs. Her plump lips were a sweet cushion under his touch. He stroked her through the fabric, tracing the seam of her body until she was panting.

"I guess nice girls like this," he growled.

"Yes," she whispered.

"What else do they like?"

"I don't—" He brushed her clit and she drew in a quick breath. "I don't know."

"Oh, I bet you know. You just can't say it. Because you're shy."

"Yes." He barely heard her this time. The delicate, innocent pink of the panties was getting darker under his touch as her wetness soaked through the fabric. That was getting to be one of his favorite sights.

Alex reached for the row of tiny buttons that started at the collar of her dress. She didn't stop him. She didn't touch his arm. She just ducked her head and watched as he unbuttoned them one by one. Feigning patience, he made it all the way to the last button, just at her waist. Then, instead of shoving the dress off and fucking her right there against the arm of the couch, he very slowly spread one side of her dress open and down her arm. The bra was pink, too. He wanted to see all of it together.

"Stand up," he ordered.

She uncurled her legs and stood, the skirt of her dress falling to cover her thighs. Not for long. He opened the other side of her dress and tugged it farther down her arms. It caught for a moment, and he liked that, Sophie half undressed, arms restrained, and her nipples pushing against the scraps of fabric that covered them. But he only paused for a moment before tugging the dress all the way down. He let it fall to a heap on the floor, and he took her in. The bra, the panties, the garter belt, the stockings, and all of it still sweet and innocent. All of it cut modestly in muted colors of pink and tan. Like she was just a nice girl on her way home from school in the 1940s.

He was so hard it hurt.

"Do nice girls like to show off?" he asked.

Her chest rose and fell with every nervous breath. She nodded.

"Yes, they do," he murmured, raising one hand to cup her breast. He flicked a thumb over her nipple and watched the muscles of her stomach jump.

He dragged the fabric aside just enough to expose the hard nub of her nipple, then circled it slowly with his calloused thumb. It grew harder against his touch. "Take down your hair."

While she reached up, he leaned forward and caught her nipple between his teeth.

"Uh," she gasped, but her hands were occupied with the knot at her nape. He heard one pin fall to the floor as he scraped his teeth over her and made her jerk. Then her hair fell and brushed against his head. He leaned back and took her in.

Now she looked violated and vulnerable. Hair wavy and tumbling, the bra shoved aside, her nipple wet and reddened. Alex hooked his fingers into the sides of her panties and slipped them down. They were quite conveniently put on over the ribbons of the garter belt, so once he let the panties fall, her sex was framed by pink ribbons and the tiny strip of tan lace that decorated the edge of the belt. Pale, plump flesh and the slightest hint of pink lips peeking from her slit. He could see how slick and wet she was already.

"Yes." He didn't try to keep the violence from

his voice. "You like showing off, don't you, Sophie? You like walking around like this all day, knowing what a hot little piece you are if someone would just fucking look."

"Yes," she gasped.

"You are hot. Look at you."

Her chin rose and she stared defiantly at him. He stood, needing to show her that he was bigger and stronger and she couldn't defy him. But her gaze didn't change. She wasn't scared. That knowledge jacked his lust into overdrive. She liked it like this.

He curved his hand around the back of her neck and gripped her skull to hold her still as he slipped his fingers over her mound. His fingertips slid along her folds and she jerked against his hold, but he didn't let her move.

"You're a nice girl who likes to have dirty sex, aren't you, Sophie?"

She didn't answer this time. She only closed her eyes and nodded, so Alex kept stroking her. Lightly, so lightly, until she was whimpering with need. She wanted more, but he didn't give more than that, just the lightest stroke of his fingertips over her clit. God, she was slick and soft. He could touch her like this forever.

But that wouldn't go over well with her, apparently.

He resisted the way her hips pushed toward him. "Please," she finally begged, her hand reaching to cover his.

"You didn't answer me," he murmured, ducking his mouth close to her ear.

"Yes! Yes, I like it."

"Mmm. Good." But he didn't give her what she wanted. Instead he kissed her cheek, her ear, her jaw. When he got to her mouth, her lips parted eagerly for him.

He took her mouth but pulled his hand free from her grip. Sophie growled in frustration, but she opened wider for his tongue. He kissed her deep and long, reaching back to unclip her bra and slide it off her arms. She let it drop.

Alex raised his head to look down at her. God, she was a treat. A beautiful, precious treat. She made his hands shake and his heart pound. Heart pounding even harder, he kept one hand at the nape of her neck and, with the other, reached down to unbuckle his belt. He opened the button of his jeans and unzipped them.

"Show me what else you like," he said quietly, remembering how eagerly she'd sucked at his thumb that first night.

Her heavy eyes slid down his chest and focused on his open jeans. Her breath tore past her parted lips as she panted. Finally, she whispered, "Yes," and she went to her knees.

Despite that he'd told her to, Alex had a brief moment of thankful disbelief, but he recovered quickly and dragged off his T-shirt.

"Oh," she breathed, looking up at him as she put

her hands to his bare stomach. Her hands smoothed up to his chest, brushing over the hair, shaping the muscles. Then her touch moved down again, down his belly, past his navel, and then to the band of his briefs. The heel of her hand brushed his cock, and Alex held his breath to keep from moaning. But it was in vain. She tugged his briefs lower and her fingers closed around his cock and Alex moaned in near pain. He loved her hands on him. Loved her touch. Loved the sight of her on her knees and staring at him like her mouth was watering.

"Show me," he murmured as she drew him free.

Sophie nodded and glanced up at him with a little lick of her lips that made his nerves jump. *Yes,* he thought, *just like that.* That little pink tongue and those wet lips. On him. Around him.

She stroked him first, her fist working slowly up and down his shaft as she watched. His vision narrowed to nothing but that. Her hand on him, her face eagerly watching.

She squeezed harder, and a little drop of pre-come formed. Sophie hummed, and then she licked it. Slowly. Sweetly. She cleaned the head of his cock and then flashed him a small, wicked smile.

Dark pleasure washed over him, soaking into his muscles like heat. When her tongue swirled around him, that heat turned to fire that traveled up his nerves.

Her mouth closed over him then, enveloping him in warmth that shocked him even though he'd been waiting. Fuck, he felt like he'd been waiting his whole life for that sweet draw of her mouth on his cock.

She took him in slowly, her mouth sliding up and down. Her fist kept the same rhythm, so that by the time she'd taken half of him into her throat, it felt like she was swallowing all of him. Alex groaned and watched the beautiful sight past a haze of lust.

But he wanted more, more, even as he went nearly dizzy from the pleasure. More.

"Touch yourself," he rasped.

Her gaze flew up to meet his. She drew back in surprise until only her lips touched him.

Alex eased her fingers free and fisted himself. He slipped his other hand into her hair. "Touch yourself," he repeated.

She did as he asked, her hand disappearing between her thighs even as her mouth opened. She let him ease her back onto his cock, and took him as deep as she had before. Her moan hummed through his shaft.

"Fuck," he groaned as she pulled at him with her mouth. It was all pressure and wetness and heat and the sight of her mouth stretching wide around his cock.

She moaned again, shifting on her knees, and he knew this was getting her off. "Show me," he said. "Show me how much you like it." He palmed her head and eased deeper into her throat. She didn't resist at all.

The pleasure was weight inside him. Weight and tension that drew his whole world down to where her tongue slid up and down around his wet shaft. Alex watched. He watched himself disappear into her mouth over and over. Watched the way his rough fingers clutched at her smooth red hair. And beyond all that, the pretty pink tips of her breasts and her hand disappearing between her legs.

She jerked back and Alex let her. His cock slid free of her mouth, the air a sudden cold grip around him. Sophie threw her head back and cried out, the muscles of her neck tight as she came, her hips spasming against her own hand. Her cry went hoarse, and then faded to a whimper. Alex squeezed his cock hard, determined to hold back his own orgasm for a few more moments.

Her eyes opened, dazed and heavy when she looked up at him. Her mouth was red and wet. Her cheeks pink with a blush that had nothing to do with shame.

"Good," he whispered.

She nodded. Yes, she was very good and she knew it. A nice girl who liked it hard and wet and filthy.

"Now open your mouth." She did as he asked, just as he'd known she would. Alex slid his cock between her lips and cupped her head with both hands. He pushed in as deep as he could. She didn't pull away. She braced her hands on his hips and she let him fuck her that way. Slowly, carefully, her mouth the most perfect thing he'd ever felt. And when he finally came, the world collapsing into that drawn-out moment of climax, she swallowed every drop.

His head dropped, too heavy for his neck to support anymore, and he watched in shock as she drew back just enough to lick his cock clean. He shuddered at the swipe of her tongue against oversensitive flesh, but he didn't stop her. He'd never do that.

When she finally sat back on her haunches, Alex let his legs give way and he collapsed onto the couch. "Holy shit," he breathed, dropping his head back for a moment to catch his breath. Once the room stopped spinning, he tugged his jeans up, then reached down to pull Sophie onto the couch.

When he drew her close, she curled onto his lap, her body fitting into his like she'd always been there. He couldn't move. He never wanted to move. Her fingers spread over his bare chest and her cheek was warm against his shoulder. He wrapped his arms around her and stroked her back, marveling at the softness.

"Are my hands too rough?" he asked, worried that the slide of his fingers over such perfect skin might annoy her. But she shook her head and sank a little more deeply into him.

He didn't feel much like a loner right then. It felt nice here with her. Comfortable and warm. He wondered how late it was and didn't particularly care. He just tucked her head under his chin and closed his eyes. "Sophie?"

"Hmm?"

"You open to me crashing here tonight?"

She nodded and Alex sighed. He didn't want to move, much less get on his bike and ride through the cold night to his dreary hotel room.

But apparently Sophie wasn't as ruined as he was, because a few minutes later, she stretched and sat up. "I'm going to take a shower. There's beer in the fridge, I think."

"Thanks."

She stood as if her legs weren't weak at all, but Alex didn't take offense. Instead, he took the opportunity to watch her move nearly naked around the couch, picking up clothing as she went. Her little round ass made his mouth water.

She caught him watching as she walked out the room and flashed a smile over her naked shoulder.

"I should've taken a fucking picture," he muttered to himself. He'd like to remember that sly look forever.

He must've dozed for a moment, because he snapped awake when he heard the pipes whoosh to life on the other side of the wall. After sex like that, he could've just tipped right over and slept on the couch for eight hours, but he didn't want her thinking she'd ruined him, even if she had. A man had his pride, after all. Plus, a cold beer sounded damn good.

Alex forced his exhausted muscles to work and got to his feet. He fastened his jeans and grabbed a beer from the fridge and downed half of it within seconds. He hadn't thought the night could get better, but the ice-cold beer was a perfect cap to the hot-test blow job he'd ever had.

Smiling, Alex wandered the room to try to get a feel for Sophie, but everything here clearly be-longed to her great-uncle…unless Sophie was an outdoorsy vampire who'd won the Snake River Fly Fishing Championship of 1963. He'd have to ask her about it later.

Still, he took in the old photographs and Western fiction and moved around the room, if only because he knew he'd fall asleep if he sat down again. The kitten jumped up and followed him.

He recognized a lot of the places in the photo-graphs. They came from the same place, he and So-phie. The same place, the same circumstances, the same defining event. Funny that they'd turned out so differently. She took care of people. He cut them loose. She was a dreamer. He kept moving and didn't dream about anything.

He was almost done with his circle of the room when he saw the open boxes near the small dining table. One box was filled with large photo albums of some kind. The other was overflowing with paper and scissors and tape and various sparkly things. On the table, one of the albums was open. He could see pictures.

Alex glanced toward the bedroom, feeling guilty, but it wasn't exactly snooping if the thing was open, so he stepped forward and looked.

The picture wasn't a photo; it was a postcard of a

beach. Glittery script spelled out FLORIDA in green letters and ended in a colorful beach umbrella. The other side of the album featured a postcard of an alligator sunning itself in a swamp. Facts about the Everglades were printed out on paper shaped liked an orange.

Alex blinked and turned the page, only to find more postcards. These were from New York. The next page was different, though. This was a brochure for camping in national parks. Not at a campground, though. This was the chance to spend the night in an old fire tower, two hundred feet above the forest. Nothing decorated this page except pale green shading that disappeared halfway up the paper.

Another page was a postcard from a cave in West Virginia. Colored lights lit up the stalactites, making them glow. A trail of sparkly jewels swept across the page above it.

Alex glanced at the box full of albums and counted at least six. Were they all the same? Places she wanted to go, things she wanted to do? Why was she making these scrapbooks instead of just getting in her car and going to Florida or West Virginia or any other place she could drive to?

Just as he was reaching to draw another book from the box, the water shut off and he jerked his hand back. Looking at an album on the table was one thing, but digging through boxes was a whole other. She'd said he could spend the night, not investigate her life.

Alex finished his beer and went to set it by the sink and grab another. By the time she came out, wearing a little pink nightgown that ended just beneath her ass, Alex was dead tired.

"Want to watch TV in bed?" she asked, her voice sounding almost hesitant in a way that made him grin.

"Hell, yes," he answered. He toed off his boots while she turned off lights, then stripped down to his briefs and joined her in bed. It wasn't very big, so they had to stay close. He wrapped his arm around her and she snuggled close.

"Thanks for letting me crash," he said.

She smiled up at him. "No problem. I wanted more later anyway."

More. All right. Then he didn't need to ask if he'd been too rough or demanding. She wanted more. He'd do his best to give it.

They settled in as if they'd always fit together. Alex fell asleep to the sound of her laughter and the faint flicker of the TV playing against his eyelids. Despite the old bed and the television playing, it felt nothing like falling asleep in a hotel room. Nothing at all.

CHAPTER TEN

"HEY, GIRL!" LAUREN called through the front window. "I brought cinnamon rolls!"

Sophie froze and stared bug-eyed at the front door. The blinds were drawn over the window next to it, thank God, but Lauren knew Sophie was home. Her car was under the carport. *Shit.*

Alex was still in the shower. She could probably get rid of Lauren in a few minutes. And at least she'd showered and dressed after she'd climbed off Alex that morning.

Sophie tiptoed toward the door, even as she wondered why the hell she was tiptoeing.

"Hi!" She meant to keep Lauren in the doorway, but Sophie had never kept her out before and Lauren just walked on in without an invitation. Sophie had never had to keep her out before. She didn't bring men home. She didn't let them hang out and raise suspicions. She went to their hotel rooms instead.

"Here," Lauren said, holding out the tray.

"Your mom is still here?" Sophie asked, taking the tray of cinnamon rolls. They were still warm and she moaned as the scent finally hit her.

"You don't think I made cinnamon rolls from scratch, do you? Mom is baking and I figured you could use some cheering up."

"Buying my emotions with sugar. You know me well."

"Yeah, it was a really brutal quest for the truth. Anyway, it's in the paper."

This time her moan had nothing to do with deliciousness. "The lawsuit?"

"Yes. Your copy was in the drive. I left it on the porch in case you wanted to ignore it for a while."

"God, I wish I could. Maybe there was a freak windstorm that blew most of the newspapers away before people could read them."

Lauren nodded. "Maybe. But I added an extra couple of cinnamon rolls just in case that doesn't work out."

"Okay. I'll just stay home and stuff myself. It'll help. Thank you."

"Hang in there," she said, pulling Sophie into a quick hug. "Jake and I are taking my mom up to Yellowstone before she has to leave, so text me if anything else comes up. But it'll be over soon."

That's what Sophie had thought, too. She'd been wrong. It would never be over. But she smiled and said, "See you tomorrow," as she led Lauren back to the door.

Lauren opened the door and Sophie was finally starting to relax when an awful silence fell over the house. She hadn't thought an absence of sound could ring in your ears, but ring it did. Alex had turned off the shower.

Lauren froze. Her eyes flew toward the far wall. The shower door squeaked.

"Anyway!" Sophie sang, as if that would distract her friend. Strangely, her ploy didn't work.

Lauren's gaze began to stutter over different parts of the room. The man's T-shirt crumpled on the couch? Check. The empty beer bottles next to the sink? Check. The bedroom door opening to reveal a big, naked, tattooed beast of a man wearing nothing but a white towel around his waist? Oh, fuck yes, that was probably a big check mark, too.

"Oh, shit," Lauren murmured. "I guess that's better than a cinnamon roll."

Alex just raised his eyebrows.

Sophie thought she might die right there, but her heart kept rebelliously beating on. "All right," she squeaked. "See you tomorrow."

"Okay," Lauren whispered, then tore her gaze off Alex to look at Sophie. "Sure." She widened her eyes as if she could convey a hundred questions with that one gesture.

Sophie jerked her head toward the door, but before she left, Lauren took the opportunity to ogle Alex one more time. Once she'd looked her fill, she backed outside. "Bye!"

Alex raised one hand in farewell. Sophie slammed the door. The silence rang in her ears again. It must have been ringing for Lauren, too, because Sophie didn't hear her footsteps head down the stairs for quite a while.

"Coworker?" Alex finally asked in the quiet.

Sophie turned and leaned weakly against the door. "Yes."

"Damn. Sorry."

"It's okay," she whispered, then cleared her throat. "She's a friend, so…"

"So she won't tell everyone in town?"

"Exactly."

"Good. I don't want to fuck things up for you."

She managed a smile at that. "That's sweet."

"You have a strange idea of sweet."

She relaxed a little and laughed. It would be fine. Lauren might give Sophie shit for years, but she wouldn't tell anyone else. And there was an upside. Now Sophie had someone to talk to. Because she had *so* much to tell.

Just looking at him standing there was enough to inspire hours of conversation, and Lauren had seen it, too. Yeah, this might get her through a few long, cold winters.

She pushed off the door and walked toward him. "Need something?" she asked.

Alex groaned. "I had to crawl to the shower. Are you trying to prove your superiority? I give. Uncle."

Sophie laughed. "It was a genuine question! Coffee? Pants?" She wrapped her hands around his neck and leaned back to look up at him. "What'd you come out here for?"

"I don't remember," he said. She felt him growing hard against her. "Jesus, you're a witch. The kind that can raise the dead."

"Maybe you're more of a man than you thought."

He groaned again. "I'll punish you for that later."

"Promise?"

"No. I probably won't have the strength."

She laughed and kissed him as he closed his arms around her and lifted her a few inches off the ground. Yeah. He had plenty of strength.

"Mmm," he hummed into the kiss before setting her down. "I remembered. I came out to tell you that I parked the bike on the side of your house, but I'd better get going now that it's light. I guess I really screwed up that quest for discretion."

"Well, you put on a nice show, at least." She traced her fingers over the wide tattoo that covered most of his chest. This one was an ominous wave that covered nearly his whole torso. It looked like a Japanese woodblock print. Her own little ocean right here in Wyoming.

"Will I see you later?" he asked.

She bit her lip to keep from smiling triumphantly. This man was sex on a cycle, and he couldn't wait to see her again. The feeling was nice and so very mutual. "The dedication is tomorrow. Won't it be a busy day for you?"

"Shit. I guess it might be."

"I'm working until seven tonight. I'll get in touch later and see what's going on."

"Deal." He kissed her nose and retreated back into the bedroom. She touched the spot he'd kissed and tried not to feel warm inside. It was just sex, and it would be over within days. And if that made her stomach knot up, that was only the kind of affection you felt for a man who was that spectacular in bed.

He was everything she'd always wanted. Things she'd touched on with other men, but the connection had never quite been there. She'd had intense, kinky sex before, but she'd never felt hollowed out by it afterward. And she'd never wanted to beg the guy to crawl back into bed and spend the day there, just talking.

Okay, not just talking. But mostly.

God. This wasn't good.

But it didn't matter what she wanted. He needed to go before someone spotted his bike. Sophie was alarmed to realize she hadn't even considered where he'd parked it. She was losing her discretion over this guy. That was probably worse than the prospect of losing her heart. At least that would still be private. No one would see it. Any heartache would belong to her.

She watched him stop to look around the dim bedroom in confusion. "Your shirt is out here," she said.

He flashed a smile and picked up his boots. "Thanks. That part was a bit of a blur. I mean *my* clothes coming off. I remember every moment of taking yours off."

"Not many of yours came off," she said drily.

"Ah. Right. Not very gentlemanly of me." His lazy smile let her know he wasn't apologizing.

"You made up for it later."

"Yeah." His smile faltered a little as he sat down and pulled on his shirt. "That was really nice last night."

It had been nice. Having his whole big, naked body pressed against her, taking over all of her bed. It had been damn nice.

She watched as he pulled on a boot and tugged the laces tight. The muscles of his back flexed and bunched beneath his T-shirt as he worked. She liked the way he moved. He was so self-assured. So easy with his body.

She was confident enough about her body, but she was also conscious of it. Aware. Alex just *existed*. His body was his, to do what he wanted with. To use and mark.

She smirked. Maybe that described her body, too.

"All right," he said as he scratched the kitten under the chin. "I'll see you girls later."

She absolutely, unequivocally did not melt a little at those words. She melted a lot. But she somehow managed to stay where she was standing and say goodbye from there. She didn't need a kiss. She didn't need a scratch on the chin.

But once he'd gone, she collapsed onto the couch and pulled the kitten close. "Why does he have to be so cute?" she whispered into the warm fur. The kitten purred in response. "I know. It's terrible. We should stop seeing him."

His motorcycle roared to life from a comfortable distance. He must have rolled it down to the street before starting it. His caution reminded her that she had bigger problems than this little crush.

She set down the kitten—who promptly curled up in the space where Alex had sat—and went out to grab the paper. Her brother had made the front page. Tweny-Five-Year-Old Mystery Revived by Brand-New Lawsuit.

Well, they'd damn well summed it up perfectly, hadn't they?

Not much more was revealed about the lawsuit. It seemed that it was pretty straightforward. David Heyer was suing for a million dollars in actual and punitive damages for the untimely death of his mother due to the negligent or reckless driving of Wyatt Bishop. The lawsuit also mentioned that the accident had occurred on a private road on land owned by the Bishop family.

But the worst part of the article was that the reporter had used the lawsuit as an excuse to rehash the entire scandal. Now even the youngest generations of Jackson could experience the deliciousness of the story.

How Dorothy Heyer and Wyatt Bishop had disappeared on the same summer day twenty-five years ago after purchasing a camping trailer. How their months-long affair had come to light. The writer even listed some of the discarded rumors that had circulated over the ensuing years, though she failed to mention that every one of them had been perpetuated by Rose Bishop.

Eventually Greg Heyer had petitioned for his wife to be declared dead. Thankfully the article didn't mention that the petition had started the very worst rumor of all: that Greg Heyer had discovered the lovers together and killed them both. Sophie had been surprised by that one. It had been sprung on her during gym class. She could still remember standing in the locker room clutching her sweatshirt to her chest and pretending the awful words had meant nothing.

The article then detailed the evening last summer when Shane Harcourt had found his father's truck and the skeletal remains inside. There was even a picture of the crash site.

Sophie had managed to avoid the picture last time around, but this time she found herself staring at the grainy black-and-white photo of the crumpled truck nearly hidden by tall grasses and trees.

Had her mom died on impact? The truck had tumbled seventy-five feet before coming to rest nearly upright. Had she been unconscious, at least? Or had she lain there awake and dying for days?

Goose bumps rose on Sophie's arms and spread over her whole body, then deep inside until she shuddered.

Sophie would never know. No one ever would. And no one would ever know what had caused it.

Her brother had brought all this back to the surface for no goddamn reason at all, except money. *Money.* He didn't even work for a living. He thought because of one tragedy in his life, he deserved to get everything easy.

She scowled at the page. She'd pay a million dollars for it all to go away. How could he have done this?

The article wrapped up with a paragraph about the dedication on Saturday at the Providence historical site. Sophie was skimming the ending when the bomb dropped, setting off an explosion in her chest. A quote from Rose Bishop. "After everything my sons and I have gone through, I finally thought we'd get some closure. This lawsuit is a violation of my family's suffering. Clearly, no one in the Heyer family has any shame. They never have."

God, the reporter must have salivated over that. It wasn't often that feuds were laid out so gleefully for public consumption. And this one had everything. Sex, death, one of the founding families of Jackson, and now, money.

Sophie looked at the photo one more time. Her mom had lain in that truck for over two decades. She'd been lost. Forgotten. She still was, her ashes sitting on a shelf in a closet of the funeral home. Sophie didn't want to bring her home.

She refolded the paper, carefully moving the front section to the back and stacking the lifestyle section on top. Then she went to the kitchen, plated two cinnamon rolls, and curled back up on the couch to eat them both. They stopped the burning in her stomach, but she still had to swipe tears off her cheeks while she ate. The kitten slept on, too wrapped up in the scent of Alex to care what Sophie was up to, but Sophie didn't mind. She'd do the same if she could. In fact, she hoped to do exactly that tonight.

She just didn't want to think about this anymore. She didn't want to go to work and be asked about it, and she didn't want to be around people who were pretending not to know. She didn't want people looking at her, recognizing her, watching to see what happened. She didn't want to run into Rose again. She didn't want to pick up her mom's ashes. She didn't want to grab her little brother and shake him until his ears rang. She just wanted it to *stop*.

All of it.

Alex was right. She should leave. Walk away from everything like he had. Let these damaged people fight it out amongst themselves for eternity while she flew free.

But just the thought made her cry so hard she had to set the plate down and curl up into a pillow. She couldn't walk away from her family like that. She was the only one her dad could depend on. If he were fifty, maybe that would be okay, but he was slowing down. He needed help, and her brother showed no signs of growing up and carrying part of the load. She couldn't just leave.

The only solution she could come up with in that

moment was to lie there and feel sorry for herself, so that was what she did. She sniffled. She clenched her eyes shut. She cried a little more. When that got boring, she reached out and swiped some frosting off the plate and licked her fingers.

It turned out that wallowing in self-pity was kind of boring. And there were so many people who had bigger problems than she did. Real problems. Sick kids. Foreclosed mortgages. Terrible injuries from wars. Really, she was just being a big baby.

She sat up and stared blindly at the paper sitting in front of her. As her energy returned, she slipped the next section free of the paper to read the local advice column. *Dear Veronica* was her favorite part of the paper. It was selfish, maybe, but Sophie liked knowing that other people in town had secrets and problems, too.

Still, she stared blindly for a moment at the advice section, too tired to even focus. Then her swollen eyes cleared, and unfortunately she wasn't staring blindly anymore. Her eyes had focused right on the bolded headline: Vixen Has Her Claws in My Son.

"Nope," Sophie said aloud. It wasn't about her. It was some other vixen with her claws in some woman's poor, unsuspecting son. Sophie wasn't the only slut in town, surely.

Dear Veronica,
My son just came back to town after many

years away. As you can imagine, I'm overjoyed
to be reconciled with him.

Jackson has a fairly fluid population, Sophie told
herself. People come and go.

The problem is that as soon as he set foot in
town, the neighborhood floozy set her sights
on him.

There were several neighborhoods in the Jackson
area. And probably several floozies. It absolutely
wasn't her.

He's a man, so I can't expect him to see past
her harmless facade when she's offering free
sex.

Harmless facade. She glanced down at her cardigan.

How do I get rid of her? I just got him back
and I don't want to cause another rift, but this
little tramp will ruin his life!
Signed,
There's a Strumpet on My Street

Yeah. Shit. It was definitely about Sophie.
This crazy old woman was never going to leave
Sophie alone.

Maybe she should move back in with her dad. And maybe dye her hair. Sophie's resemblance to her mom was just too much for Rose Bishop to deal with. It probably didn't help that she actually was sleeping with the woman's son.

At least she hadn't been named. Sure, people might be able to figure out that Alex was the prodigal son described in the letter, but no one knew he was hooking up with anyone, much less that it was Sophie. So this was more of a private jab than a public taunt. All right, it was both.

Out of curiosity, Sophie read the answer, and it made her want to whoop with triumph.

Dear Strumpet on My Street,
First of all, men are fully capable of resisting free sex, no matter how it's disguised, so please don't excuse your son for his actions. Now, as far as I can tell, the transgression here is sex between two willing participants, so my advice to you is to get over it. People like sex. In fact, our bodies are designed to like it very much indeed, so if this so-called floozy has a merry sex life, then more power to her. Your slut shaming is far more embarrassing than anything she could ever do in the privacy of her home.

If your son is actually in danger of throwing his life away for the sake of free sex with a stranger, then maybe you should've raised

him to be a better man. Yet I somehow suspect you're overreacting and he will emerge
from this trap with nothing more than a few
scratches for his trouble.

If you want any chance of making this reconciliation with your son work, keep your
mouth shut, look the other way and stop shaming women and coddling men.

Well. That wrapped Rose up in a nutshell. But
somehow Sophie didn't think the woman would take
the advice to heart.

The outrage Rose was going to feel as she read
that actually cheered Sophie up. She wasn't the ma-
licious one here. She didn't have anything to be
ashamed of.

Okay, she had some things to be ashamed of, but
not nearly as much as the woman wanted to pin on
her. Sophie couldn't spend her days hiding from
every little rumor. If she were that much of a cow-
ard, she'd never have seen sunlight.

She'd go to work and volunteer to deal with all
of the kids' programs today. She'd interact with the
parents and sign people up for future programs and
she'd look everyone straight in the eyes as she did
it. This scandal wasn't going to defeat her. Not that
she'd let anyone know, at least.

But first, she'd have one more cinnamon roll.

CHAPTER ELEVEN

THE SIGN SAID Providence—2 miles, but Alex wasn't exactly hopeful that he'd find good fortune there. They were meeting to walk through the final plans for tomorrow's dedication, and Alex couldn't help but think it was an appropriate site for the ceremony. Dead buildings, dead town, all to commemorate their dead family.

His dad's disappearance had been the original injury, but it hadn't been definitively fatal. They could have recovered. They could have survived.

His mom had always been difficult. She'd always been dramatic. She'd been fond of declaring people her enemies and making sure they knew it. She'd collected friends easily and just as easily turned on them. Life had been chaotic, but it had been life.

Their dad had been the calmer one. The steady one. But the less stable their mom had gotten, the more likely he'd been to walk away. To calm things down, maybe, but he hadn't taken his sons with him. He'd just say, "I'll be back," and he'd leave them behind with a crying, raging mother. But he had always come back. An hour later. A day. He'd always come back until he hadn't.

But dads walked out all the time. In small towns and big towns, in Wyoming or anywhere else in the world. People lost parents to death or divorce or abandonment. Alex could've dealt with that as well as anyone else did. A little damage, a few dings, but he could've gotten up and ridden on.

But he hadn't lost his dad, he'd lost his entire family. First his father, and then, within days, his mother had lost whatever balance she'd had. There was no way her husband would've left, and anyone who said otherwise was the enemy. They were evil, cruel, idiotic. Maybe they were even in on his disappearance. At first, she'd said he must have been hurt or killed, but that idea had quickly become too awful to tolerate. If he was dead, he was gone forever, and Rose Bishop *knew* he was coming back.

He had to come back.

For Alex, the worst loss of all had been his older brother. After all, his mother had always been unstable, and his dad had always been working. But Shane… He'd always been *there*. The smart, strong brother who was only one year older but had seemed so much bigger.

Shane had been his friend, his brother, his protector, his hero. And then he'd been lost, too, sucked into their mother's delusions. *He's coming back, Alex. Mom thinks she found him in New Mexico. He's been living on an Indian reservation. We're all driving down tomorrow.*

I don't want him back, Alex had started thinking. Who wanted a dad who didn't want you?

It hadn't taken him long to start saying exactly that out loud. And then worse things. That he hated his mom. That he hated Shane. That he hoped Dad was dead because that was what he deserved.

His anger had only grown as he'd gotten older. As their mom had lost job after job. As they'd moved from house to duplex to cabin to apartment.

Shane had been perpetually sympathetic, echoing things he'd heard from their mom. *We have to help her. She can't do it on her own. We have to be the men of the house.*

By fifteen, Alex had been determined not to be anything to anyone. At eighteen, he'd made sure of it by disappearing just like his dad had. It had felt cruel and empowering. It had felt right.

He didn't know if it had been right anymore. On one hand, their mom hadn't gotten any better. He'd avoided years of dealing with whatever was wrong with her, be it mental illness or self-absorption.

On the other hand, maybe he and Shane could've had a relationship if Alex had stayed in touch. Maybe they'd have been brothers again.

Shit. Who could say? There was no changing anything now, and no point wasting more time thinking about it.

He pulled into the parking lot of the ghost town

and parked the bike next to his brother's truck. The place wasn't quite as dead as it had been, but Alex refused to see that as any sort of metaphor.

This was where the Bishop money had gone. The place had been forced alive with cash.

He'd been here long ago with his brother and dad, but there'd been no parking area and no big glossy sign to mark the place. The road that ran through Providence had been nothing more than a wide expanse of tamped ground broken liberally by sagebrush and grass and an occasional scrub oak. All the vegetation had been cleared away now and the road smoothed until it looked like a wagon full of hay could come rolling down it at any moment. The buildings looked better, too, from what he could see.

Alex walked down the road.

Yes, the buildings definitely looked better. The Bishop money had been put to good use. Nothing had been painted or buffed to a shine, but the fallen boards and collapsed roofs had been repaired. Signs that had long ago been buried in the dirt had been resurrected and rehung. The saloon and mercantile had their identities again. A couple of the small houses even looked almost livable. And almost all the buildings had a placard set in front of them with text and sometimes pictures identifying the buildings and who had used them.

Alex heard voices ahead just before Merry Kade stepped into the road at the farthest end of the town and waved at him. He raised a hand and took a deep breath to try to gather some patience before seeing his mom.

"Hi," he said to Merry when she met him halfway through town. "It's quiet out here."

"Yeah, weekdays during the slow season aren't exactly our busy time. But this summer was pretty exciting! And we've set up a few field trips for the elementary school later this month. I can't wait. They're going to love it."

"Absolutely," he said, wondering how many kids she knew who got that excited about history, but he kept that thought to himself. If anyone could inspire school-age kids to love history, it would be Merry.

"Come on," she urged. "I have something so great to show you. The signs were installed yesterday. Your family is the first to see them!"

Apparently he was moving too slowly, because Merry grabbed his hand and pulled him forward, her feet sending up tiny puffs of dust as she dug in.

Alex shook his head at her enthusiasm, but he picked up the pace, raising a hand to his brother as Shane turned around to watch.

"You weren't trying to resist her, I hope?" Shane drawled as they drew closer.

"I could see it was futile."

"Alex!" their mother gushed, and rushed over—an awkward, limping kind of rush—to give him a hug.

"You okay?" he asked.

"Oh, you know. I'm old. The cold doesn't help."

He frowned at her weary sigh, but gave up. If there was something seriously wrong, she'd make a big deal out of it.

"Well?" Merry finally asked. "What do you think?" She gestured toward a tall sign, which stood next to a foot trail angling through the grass ahead. A narrow creek flowed next to it, though it was nearly dry at this time of the year.

Their mom moved back toward the sign with a satisfied nod. "'The Wyatt Bishop Memorial Trail,'" she read in a booming voice. "Look at that. Shane, Alex, your father is finally getting the recognition he deserves."

Below the name of the trail was a picture of the town of Providence taken just after the flood had destroyed most of it. *The Fox Creek, which this trail follows, was the lifeblood of the Providence community, providing clean drinking water and irrigation for crops. However, a series of environmental catastrophes led to the destruction of most of the town when the creek flooded in 1899.*

There was a description of a landslide and then the eventual burst of that natural dam along with some other historical details, but Merry was waving them forward along the trail. "There's more," she said excitedly.

They all followed her down the trail another fifty feet or so and there it was, a metal plaque set on a

stake overlooking the creek bed. A picture of his father was etched into the silvery metal.

Wyatt E. Bishop
1948–1989
Beloved husband and father, and cherished
member of the Bishop family,
one of the founding families of
Providence, Wyoming.
This trail is dedicated to his life and memory.

"Oh, boys," their mother whispered. "Oh, it's so
beautiful. Look at that."

Alex looked, but all he saw was hypocrisy. They'd
left off the part about him being the beloved lover
of a married woman, not to mention that the Bishop
family had turned its back on his young sons. But
Shane seemed to like it just fine. He put his arm
around their mom and they both stared at the plaque.

Alex just cleared his throat. "It's nice. Thank you,
Merry."

She was grinning but had to wipe away a tear.
"Your mom helped me come up with the inscrip-
tion. We couldn't fit everything she wanted, but I
hope it's all right."

His mom had likely written three paragraphs.

Shane turned to pull Merry into a hug. "It's beautiful," he said. "And I'm so glad there's something
here to remember him after he spent so many years
in that canyon."

Alex looked up the trail to where it disappeared into a slash of broken rock and climbing trees.

"So awful," their mom murmured. "Here all this time. Right here with us. I knew he'd never leave."

Shane glanced over Merry's head and met Alex's eyes. "Have you been up there yet?"

"No," Alex said. His skin prickled. He wanted to turn and leave.

"Come on. We'll walk a little ways up."

"We'd better not," Alex said. "Mom doesn't look up for it."

"I'll stay with her," Merry volunteered. "The office has a space heater. We'll sit and have a coffee and work out the last-minute details for tomorrow. You two go on."

Well, shit.

He glanced toward the trail. "We should really help," he insisted.

"Oh, sure," Merry answered. "Because you boys will contribute a lot to how the chairs should be set out."

Shane nudged his shoulder. "Come on. Let's get out while the getting is good."

Alex didn't have any better arguments at that point. He supposed he could have just offered the truth, but he wasn't sure what that was. Why didn't he want to walk up the trail with his brother? His father's body was long gone and Alex didn't believe in ghosts.

So he shook off his hesitation and stepped onto the

Wyatt Bishop Memorial Trail. It felt like any other trail, so he walked on.

After a few moments, he glanced back to see his mom and Merry walking through the town. "I wouldn't think Mom would support any of this. Shouldn't she be raging about how the money should belong to us? About how Gideon Bishop left this money to a ghost town just to spite her and shut her up and cover up the truth?"

Shane chuckled. "Yeah, there was plenty of that for a while. When I filed my lawsuit against the estate, she was over the moon. She wanted me to teach them a lesson. Shit, I guess that's what I wanted, too, but I got over it. And she did, too."

"Really?" he asked, shocked.

Shane flashed a smile. "Okay, she had a little trouble getting over it."

"A little?" Alex asked.

This time Shane burst into full-out laughter. "Yeah. A little. The same amount of 'little' trouble she has getting over everything."

"Yeah. She's stubborn. I'll give her that."

"When her psychiatrist suggested that we have a funeral or a memorial or something, Merry offered this trail, the plaque, and Mom jumped on it. I don't know. It was like she wanted to let it go if someone would just acknowledge *something*."

Alex watched the canyon coming closer as they walked. "Doesn't seem like she wants to let it go too much."

"I'm hoping that it's just coming to a head. It's almost over. She's panicking a little at the thought, but once it's done… I don't know. If it's not over after tomorrow? Shit. If she won't help herself, there's nothing I can do anymore."

Alex rolled his eyes, but Shane watched him without a hint of anger.

"Let's just get through this and see. You're already here. What's the harm?"

"Fuck, man. When did you become the personification of patience? You got kicked out of school for fistfights a half dozen times."

"The truth?" Shane asked.

"That'd be a first in this family."

Shane shrugged. "All right. The truth is that I was just as angry as you for a long time. After you left, I was pissed as hell. I wanted to make people pay. That's why I tried to take my pound of flesh after Granddad died. And then I met Merry."

"Really? Love of a good woman?"

"No. It's not that. She's had a rough life, she's had challenges and pain, but she sees the good. And that shamed me."

Alex felt his whole body tighten at that. With shame or something like it. For mocking his brother. For thinking he knew anything about it. After all, Alex had been in love, too, and he hadn't been able to do a damn thing with it. He'd fumbled it and dropped it and walked away from the mess he'd made. What the fuck did he know?

He swallowed the thickness in his throat and nodded. "All right."

He noticed then how far they'd walked. How narrow the trail had gotten. Grass bent over the dirt. Their legs brushed it aside. The smell of aspen touched him, and then it was inside him. Every time he smelled that scent, he was home again. He never wanted to be. It just hit him. Home. Hiding from his brother during a game of tag. Running from the house after an argument. Sitting at a campfire with a girl, hoping to lose himself in her body for a few minutes.

His leg brushed sagebrush and that bright menthol scent broke over him, too. That was an earlier memory. Of being here. With his dad, with Shane.

"You found him," he said as they reached the mouth of the canyon.

"Yes."

The shade swallowed them and the air was suddenly cold. "Here?"

"About thirty minutes up the trail. I was on horseback."

"Happenstance?"

Shane barked a dry laugh. "No. Merry again. I'd taken her up a higher trail to show her something, and I spotted a flash of white. I didn't think it had anything to do with Dad. I only rode up out of curiosity."

Alex stopped and looked up the narrow canyon. The tumbled rocks looked like they were frozen, just waiting for a signal to start rolling down again, straight toward Alex.

"Do you want to walk up a ways? Get an idea of where he was?" Shane asked.

"No," Alex snapped before he could temper the word.

"The truck's gone. It's just a clearing."

"No." He crossed his arms to hold back a shiver. This was the place. The mysterious spot their mother had searched for. The place that had kept her husband from her for reasons she couldn't understand or sympathize with. This canyon had swallowed Wyatt Bishop whole and kept him from his family for so many years.

"She was right, after all," he murmured.

"What?" Shane asked.

"He really didn't mean to leave."

"No. He didn't. They were taking the trailer up to that clearing by the old settler's cabin. It's the only place that road led."

Alex couldn't figure out why it didn't make it better. It should. He could recognize that. But it didn't change anything, somehow. All the things he'd felt as a kid, they were still there. And he still hadn't had a father for a dozen years. Not until he'd met Oz.

Alex shifted a rock and saw the moisture underneath, waiting just beneath the surface. There was no creek here that anyone else could see, but it was there, flowing slowly just beneath the rocks, making its way down the mountain.

The real flow of the world was always beneath the surface. Oz had taught him that.

"We'd better get back," he said.

He turned before Shane could answer and headed back down alone.

CHAPTER TWELVE

ALEX WATCHED THE sun creep past the trees next to the motel parking lot and wiped a hand over his eyes before crouching back over his bike. That little trip down memory lane had exhausted him. Alex made a point of not looking back in his life, but he didn't have much choice these days. There wasn't a present in Jackson. Or a future. It was all his past and he couldn't get away from it.

The two hours they'd spent in the office with Merry going over the details hadn't helped either. His mother had wept bitter tears when he'd insisted—eventually, in a very loud voice—that he wasn't giving a goddamn speech about his dad. She accused him of rejecting his father and everything the man had ever done for his children. Alex had just barely managed not to counter that at least he hadn't changed his name like some people in the family. He'd avoided reverting to childhood levels of immaturity, but just barely.

He'd tried to lose his mind in work after, studying the reports for the site he'd be visiting in Alaska, but he hadn't been able to shake the tension, so he'd washed his bike instead. He'd lost himself in that, finally, then found himself tinkering with the throttle for an hour.

That was something he loved about his bike. He could ride it, fix it, maintain it. He didn't have to depend on anyone else. If it broke down, he ordered a part and fixed it himself. He knew his bike inside and out. It never changed. It was the one constant in his life, waiting for him whenever he got back from his travels. It centered him, somehow.

By the time the trees completely blocked the sun, Alex was totally relaxed. He stood up and stretched, feeling the breeze against his neck. A warm front was shaking off the cool that had settled in that morning.

Perfect.

Sophie had said she got off work at seven. Alex got out his phone.

Interested in a sunset drive? he texted her.

YES!!!! she wrote back immediately.

Alex could picture her delight perfectly. She took such joy in pleasure. Of course, everyone liked pleasure. But she was *fed* by it. Wine, pretty dresses, wicked underthings, travel, motorcycles, sex. It was all beautiful to her.

He wished he could see more than Jackson Hole with her. He wanted to watch her face the first time she saw Alaska, the ocean, the world. If she ever left this place, she'd come alive.

Considering how alive she already was, it'd be a fucking wonder to behold.

But all he'd get was Jackson, so he'd take it.

When should I pick you up? he texted back.

7:15 at my place. Or maybe around the corner?

He smiled. I'll sneak up.

Perfect.

Yeah. One more perfect night with her before he had to go.

SOPHIE ENJOYED THE look on his face when she stepped outside.

"You look different," he said simply, but his eyes took their time sliding down her body.

She didn't often wear jeans and boots, but this time she wanted a long ride on the bike, and heels and a skirt wouldn't cut it. "Have I lost all my feminine mystique?" she asked.

"You're made of feminine mystique," he said as she slid on her favorite bright pink coat, "and you know it."

She laughed because she did know it, but then she pressed a hand to her mouth and glanced down the street. "Where's your bike?"

"Around the corner."

"Let's go out the back." She led him through the

house and out the back door. "This feels like high school. Except I was never bad in high school. Were you?"

He grinned and said nothing. Sophie took in the rough stubble on his head and the wide shoulders and leather jacket and big hands and shook her head. "Yeah, you were really bad."

"Come on. I wouldn't say bad. I'd just say that I took smart advantage of the benefits of living in a ski town."

"Spring break?" she asked wryly.

"Man. I had a great affection for college girls at that age."

"Player," she tossed out, feeling a little jealous. Not that he'd had his fill but that she hadn't.

"I'm not surprised you were a good girl in high school," he said as they sneaked through her neighbor's bushes to the sidewalk beyond. "So when did you get so naughty?"

Now she flashed her own grin. "A girl doesn't kiss and tell."

"No? Does she fuck and tell?"

"No." She stopped next to the bike and waited while he got out the helmets. Glancing around to be sure they were alone, she leaned close to his ear to purr, "And she doesn't say things like 'fuck' either."

She loved the way his eyes immediately went dark. "God, I love the way you say that word. Your mouth makes it sound like a whip."

"A whip, huh?"

One big shoulder rose in a shrug. "If that's what you want, bring it on."

"I'll try anything once," she said, her heart speeding a little at the idea of hurting him. Not because she wanted to, but because it would piss him off. She wanted to see him pissed off. He'd be fucking magnificent.

"All right, my little dominatrix. On the bike."

She mounted up behind him and slid her arms around his waist. He smelled good. And felt even better.

"Do you want me to teach you how to ride?" he asked over his shoulder.

Yes! her brain shouted. Yes, she wanted to learn how to ride. But… She shook her head. "There won't be time. You can't teach me in just a few days."

He was still for a moment before he nodded. "You're right." He flashed a smile. "Next time?"

"Next time," she said, both of them in on the joke. There'd be no next time.

As he urged the engine into a roar, she closed her eyes and felt the rumble of power around her. Under her ass, between her thighs, shivering up into her whole body through his back. He pulled onto the street and sped toward the highway.

It was strangely soothing to her, the danger of this man she barely knew flying her through the world. It felt like she was real.

That was what sex was like for her, too. The good kind anyway. The brutal, messy, dirty kind. It felt *real*. No pretenses or pretending. Just taking and giving pleasure. Just losing your thoughts and fears and *feeling*.

That was where Alex took her every time. They wanted the same things. They needed those feelings. They were animals together. In bed, yes. Or against a wall, or on the couch. But here, too. Running, flying, feeling the wind tearing at your body, trying to slow you down. But they didn't slow down. They reached the highway and Alex hit the throttle and they were gone.

Sophie opened her eyes to a sky on fire. The sun burned behind high clouds above the Tetons. The mountains were dark, jagged spears stabbing into that orange sky, sending out flames of red and pink and silver.

Tears pricked her eyes. She pretended they were from the wind and held tighter to Alex's body.

"Where do you want to go?" he shouted over his shoulder.

She pressed her cheek tighter to his back. "Anywhere," she answered, and meant it to her very soul. Anywhere. Just away.

The sun dropped as they drove, sliding down until it touched the peaks of the mountains before it began to disappear behind them. The oranges and pinks blazed even brighter for a moment, then deepened to fiery red. Alex slowed just as the fire darkened to purple.

He set his foot down and Sophie stretched behind

him. "Where are we?" she asked over the rumble of the idling engine. Desert grasslands stretched out toward the foothills that surrounded them.

"You've never been here?"

She looked around in confusion until she finally saw the sign that pointed toward the east. Providence, it said. She set her mouth and nodded. "Only once."

"When they found them?"

"Yes." His back was a straight, hard line against her.

"I was here today. For the first time since..."

She nodded, but didn't say anything. He'd have to spend the whole day here tomorrow, but she hadn't planned on ever coming back. Still, it was something being out here at dusk, the quiet broken only by the occasional car that passed.

"Would you mind?" he asked, and she knew what he meant, but didn't know how to answer it. She didn't want to go, but she was ashamed of that. She was too strong to cower away from something so harmless, and yet she wasn't strong at all, was she?

Sophie swallowed her reluctance and nodded. "Not at all."

He turned the bike down a lonely ranch road and off they went, driving toward the darkness this time. The first stars were just rising above the hills. The sky was all purple and blue here, just edging toward black. By the time he slowed the bike and pulled into a gravel lot, the sunset was nothing more than a lightness at their backs.

It was twilight, her favorite time. Not dark enough to be night, but nothing close to day. But when she took off her helmet, the twilight didn't feel peaceful. It felt eerie. Too quiet now that they were far away from the highway and close to that *place*.

"How many people will be here tomorrow?" she asked just to chase off the silence.

"I have no idea. Hell, I'd thought it would be no more than however many people are on that damn board, but now… Who knows."

"The lawsuit," she murmured.

"Yeah. Not great timing on your brother's part. Though it'll make my mom happy if we're mobbed. She's been under the impression that the whole town will turn out to honor him."

"Why?" she asked in surprise. He'd been dead for twenty-five years and even though his grandfather had been an important man around town, Wyatt Bishop had just been an average citizen.

"Why?" he repeated with a humorless laugh. He tipped his head up to look toward the stars. "Because she's just as delusional as she's always been."

"I know she's always been, um…staunchly defensive of him."

"Jesus, it's more than that. Do you know that after he disappeared, she had my brother and I convinced that our father had been kidnapped and held hostage and that's why he wasn't home?"

"Kidnapped?" she asked in shock. "What do you mean?"

"I mean after he'd been gone a week and there was no sign of him, she decided something had happened to him. That he'd seen some sort of corruption or crime and he'd been taken to keep him quiet."

"But…why would she think that?"

"Because she needed him not to have abandoned her. More than that, she needed him to be a hero. She always did. So she made him into a hero however she could."

"But he was with my mom. What did that have to do with anything?"

He shrugged. "For a while, my mom just left her out of the story. She was convinced your mom's disappearance had nothing to do with Dad. It was coincidence. And she had us convinced, too. But I finally wised up."

Sophie heard the bitter note in his voice and recognized it. "School?"

"Yeah. There were a lot of stories. I guess you know that."

"I do." She'd always assumed they'd been crueler to her because it was so easy to call a woman a slut, a whore, a jezebel, a man-stealer. Not to mention all the things they'd called her dad, too. But she realized then that Alex and Shane had been older, so they'd probably heard more. There were only so many names that a first-grader knew, and by the time she'd gotten older, the story had had less shine on it.

"I'd say kids are cruel, but you know that," she said softly.

"Kids are cruel, but it was way crueler for my mom to give us that kind of hope."

"I'm sorry," she whispered. She wasn't sure if she should touch him, wasn't sure they had that kind of relationship. But he was telling her something secret, wasn't he? He was sharing a pain that maybe only she could understand. Sophie wrapped her arms around his waist and laid her cheek on his chest. "It was scary, wasn't it?"

His arms folded her in tighter. "Hmm?"

"It was scary," she whispered again. It had terrified her. She'd been scared for years. Not because Sophie had thought someone had kidnapped her mom or killed her or taken her away, but because she thought they hadn't.

His arms were so warm around her. He surrounded her. He filled up all the terrifying doubts inside her for that one brief moment. She held on and listened to his heartbeat and she didn't think about how cold it was up there on the trail. How dark and terrible.

When she pulled back again it was fully dark and a million stars shone above them. The moon hit the pale gray wood of the closest buildings, and the walls caught just enough light that they looked like ghosts lurking in the distance.

"I shouldn't have brought you here," Alex said.

He shouldn't have. She'd wanted to go *away,* not come back to this place.

"Let's just ride," she said. "Just a little farther. Okay?"

"Yeah. That sounds good." She'd started to move to the bike, but Alex said her name. She turned back to face him.

"I'm sorry. I didn't plan to come here. I just looked up and there it was, and… Shit. I don't know. There's this ridiculous dedication tomorrow, and I fucking hate it and I realized that at least you'd understand. That I could tell you."

"You don't have to apologize. I do understand. Tomorrow's going to be hard."

The outline of his shoulders slumped a little. He was facing away from the moonlight. She couldn't see his face, just the glint off his scalp and the delicate scallop of one ear.

"I know you can't talk to anyone else about it," she said. "I can't either. You have your brother, at least."

His head tilted. "You have your brother, too," he said wryly.

"Ha! Okay. I see your point." She turned and faced the town, thinking this was the time to talk if she ever wanted to. Alex would be gone soon. Tomorrow or the next day. He'd be gone and she'd go back to her life. Librarian and daughter and sister by day. Her real self once or twice a year with men who'd never know anything else about her.

Alex was the only one who really knew there were two Sophies. Lauren knew a little bit, but only a little.

So she looked at the ghostly wisps of the town and the black edge of the hills rising above it.

She took a deep breath. "This is where they died," she whispered. She'd never said it. Not out loud. She'd always said missing or disappeared or gone or vanished. But that wasn't it anymore. Her mother was dead.

Alex took her hand and they watched the darkness together. "Strange that they were always so close to us," he said.

She nodded, wondering how many times she'd passed these hills. "Do you want to stay the night again?" she asked.

His hand squeezed hers. "I'd like that."

"Me, too."

But neither of them moved for a long time. She'd finally gotten comfortable with this place somehow. Alex's big hand wrapped around hers made it seem almost peaceful. Almost.

"I don't know what to do with my mother's ashes," she admitted to the town.

She felt Alex turn toward her. "What?"

Sophie laughed nervously, self-conscious even in the dark. "I don't know what to do with them."

"Well, you don't have to do anything with them. Keep them on the mantle or in a closet, even."

"I mean I haven't even picked them up yet. I can't. I don't know why."

"Oh, Sophie," he breathed, and then he surrounded her again, pulling her close to him, making it all go away. "I don't know why either, but I get it. I do. You're okay."

She breathed through her mouth to try to keep the tears at bay. It mostly worked. She didn't sob. She didn't break down, but a few tears escaped. She had no idea why. It was so stupid. She'd go pick them up on Monday. What to do with them after wasn't even her decision to make. Her father could keep them or bury them or spread them over his land. It wasn't her responsibility.

Somehow she still didn't feel better.

A coyote howled somewhere in the north. Another answered. Sophie wished she and Alex were already back at her place, warm under the covers and falling asleep. But when Alex asked if she was ready to ride, her heart leaped again. Yes.

She didn't want to sleep yet. She wanted to fly.

CHAPTER THIRTEEN

"Has anyone seen my kitten?" his mom asked.

Alex slanted an impatient look across the table. Yes, he'd seen her kitten exactly one hour before. It had been curled up against Sophie's naked back before Alex had chased it off with a friendly nudge. He'd needed that back to himself.

"There's one right there," he said, pointing to a tabby slinking across the floor.

"No, the kitten is gray—" his mom started, but he cut her off.

"Maybe she's lost here in the dining room."

"It's not that," she snapped. "She goes outside."

"Kittens aren't safe outside," he snapped back.

Shane rolled his eyes. "Let's worry about the cat another day."

Alex glared at both of them. He was too tired and irritated to be sitting at this so-called dining room table that was piled a foot high with papers and pictures and mail.

"All right, is everyone ready?" Shane asked.

Alex glanced down at his black jeans. Not exactly funeral wear, but this wasn't exactly a funeral.

Black jeans were the most formal thing he owned at the moment, but he figured he looked okay with the white shirt and gray tie that Shane had loaned him. He'd shaved his scalp and face, at least, so he wouldn't scare any of the other guests.

"I'm ready," their mom said. She was dressed in a black dress and sweater and even wore a little hat with a black veil. Yeah, she was ready, and pretty excited about the whole thing. "Alex, I just wish you'd reconsider. It's not right."

"I'm not making a speech, Mom, and that's the end of it."

"After everything he did for you, it's the least you can do for him."

"He's dead, Mom. He doesn't really care at this point."

She gasped as if he'd slapped her. "He laid there for twenty-four years and you—"

"That's right. He was there for twenty-four years. He wasn't in Mexico. He wasn't on the beach. He wasn't kidnapped or injured or wandering the country with amnesia. All those days and weeks and years you made us look for him were wasted. Every single one. I don't remember much about him except that wasted time and those made-up stories, thanks to you. I don't remember the real man anymore. So no, I won't be making a speech about him."

He expected Shane to jump in and shut him up, but Shane didn't say a word.

Their mom pressed her knuckles to her mouth. "That's outrageous!" she cried.

Shane finally spoke. "Leave him alone, Mom. It's time to go."

"Leave him alone? He's the one saying crazy things! Not me! I'm not crazy!"

"Nobody said you were crazy."

Alex opened his mouth but Shane shot him a quelling look. Alex shrugged. Fine. Not today.

"Come on, Mom. Let's get going."

She wiped tears from her face and sniffed. "Fine. I just need to find my papers."

Alex stood, knowing he'd lose his temper if he watched her search through this mess for the speech she'd printed out. "I'll wait outside."

He stepped out onto the stoop and suddenly wished he still smoked. He hadn't had a cigarette in ten years, but Jesus, he needed one now. That place made him feel almost panicked, surrounded by all the lies she'd lived with for decades. Any reasonable person would've tossed that stuff as soon as the body was found. Why would she want to remind herself that she'd wasted so much time?

At least the front yard was free of that clutter. The grass was neatly cut, and the fall leaves raked away. He wondered if Shane took care of it for her. She certainly didn't do it herself.

And suddenly there was a memory. Of his father. A real memory, not something filtered through his mother's twisted mind.

They'd had a decent house back then on a couple of acres with a big barn. During the summer his dad had mowed the lawn on a riding mower. Shane and Alex had each begged to be taken for a ride. He'd always made them play rock-paper-scissors to see who went first.

But that last year, just a few weeks before he'd disappeared, his dad had started teaching Alex how to use the mower. Alex could still remember the pride and nervousness that had filled his chest as he'd sat between his dad's knees and steered the mower. "You have to remember it's not a toy," his dad had said every single time. "You could hurt yourself or someone else. You have to take care."

He'd taken care.

Unlike Shane, Alex hadn't had a lot in common with their dad. Alex hadn't liked training horses or camping or ranching. But riding on that stupid lawn mower, they'd bonded.

He could still remember the hot sun and the sharp scent of grass that cut through the duller cloud of diesel, and his dad's big hands over his, showing him how to shift and steer and lift the blades during turns on the driveway.

And over the nearly deafening roar of the motor, his dad's voice in his ear. "Good job, Alex. I think you're better at this than I am. Next year it's all yours."

The next year it had been. But only until the bank had taken the house.

But for those few weeks, it had been the two of them, doing that chore together, sharing that time.

That was a real memory.

God, he wished he had a cigarette.

A bright flash of color drew his eye, and Alex caught sight of Sophie walking from her front door toward the street. Her head turned and she hesitated, but even from this distance, Alex could see her tentative smile when he raised a hand. She waved back, then turned away, heading the opposite way down the street, probably to avoid his mother's house. But Alex still watched as she got farther away, his gaze glued to the vivid pink of her skirt as she walked.

The way she moved was already familiar to him. Something in her walk and the sway of her hips and the way she tipped her head. He'd recognize her just by her shadow, and even that shadow would make his heart trip just like it did now.

He didn't want to leave her behind.

Alex looked away from her just before she disappeared around the corner.

It didn't matter what he wanted. He was leaving. There was no question of that. But the feeling shook him. Even when he'd loved Andrea, he'd always felt a secret relief when it had been time to get back to work. A feeling that he was moving on, even when he knew he'd be returning.

He didn't feel any relief about this goodbye, but that was probably an illusion. He could let himself feel attached because he knew he wasn't. He'd known from the start that it would be nothing.

Then again, he'd had plenty of nothing in the past, and it hadn't ever crept into him like this. He was actually taking a step down to follow her when a hand fell on his shoulder.

"Are you going to ride with us?" Shane asked.

"No, thanks. I'll take the bike."

"But if…" Shane paused for a moment, then cleared his throat. "Sure. Looks like a nice day for it."

Alex started down the steps, but paused halfway down. He turned to face his brother, noticing then how much Shane looked like their dad. His eyes, of course, and the hard edge of his jaw, but he had his calmness, too. That steady strength. He definitely hadn't had it at nineteen. Alex would never know when he'd grown into it, because he hadn't been around to see.

"Thanks," Alex finally said. "I'll meet you there."

His mother called out, but Alex walked away and left Shane to deal with it. For the first time, he could feel that it wasn't right, but he kept going. He wouldn't know how to go back if he wanted to.

CHAPTER FOURTEEN

THREE MEN WERE looking at the Providence ghost town display when Sophie walked in. There was a flyer for the dedication ceremony taped to the glass. When the men turned at the sound of the door closing behind her, she saw that they were all firemen from next door.

"Oh, hi, Sophie," Will said.

"Hi," she said with a falsely bright smile as she sailed past them.

"You doing okay?"

"I'm great! Running a little late. Gotta go!"

She hurried past the circulation desk, feeling eyes on her the whole time, but when she glanced over, no one was looking. She was imagining things. Still, she rushed for the door to her office and was just about to breathe a loud sigh of relief when she realized Lauren was waiting for her. Before Sophie could make an excuse and back out, Lauren grabbed her arm, pulled her in and shut the door.

"Your shift doesn't start for eight minutes. I need details. *Now.*"

"What details?"

"Oh, my God, you know what details. I tried to be respectful and not call yesterday. Okay, Jake told me to be respectful, but—"

"You told Jake?"

"I had to tell someone! I walked in on you with a naked man. A really naked man. With tattoos. And *biceps*."

"Lauren! It's a secret."

"I'm sorry! Jake was waiting in the truck and I was in shock! I just blurted it out without thinking, but he won't tell anyone. You know he won't. He thinks you're so sweet he actually told me I was probably misinterpreting something. God, men are idiots." She grabbed Sophie's hand. "I'm really, really sorry. Please don't punish me by not telling me about your bad boy. He looks like he'd do terrible things to you. Did he?"

She looked so hopeful that Sophie's irritation fell away. She smiled and shook her head.

"He didn't?"

"Of course he did. I'm under a lot of stress. Do you think I'd want to hang out and play Scrabble or something?"

"Well, you do love Scrabble."

That was true, and she'd actually love to play Scrabble with Alex, preferably half-naked and stretched out on the bed.

"Sophie!" Lauren poked her arm. "Focus! Who is he?"

She shrugged. "Just a man. He's passing through."

"You mean you just found him walking down the highway and took him in for a few days?"

"No, he has his own place to stay! And he was on a motorcycle."

Lauren's jaw dropped. "Oh, my God. If I didn't have a hot firefighter waiting at home, I'd knock you out and assume your identity."

"Oh, please. I'm the one who's had to watch you fall madly in love with the hottie next door. Give me my few days of dirty sex."

Lauren leaned forward, eyes going even wider. "Is it dirty?"

Sophie answered with a proud grin. "Yes. It's been pretty shameful, I have to be honest."

"God, what are you even doing here? Why didn't you call in sick?"

"Is that your solution to everything? You're supposed to be the older, more responsible friend."

"I'm the *wiser* friend, and I'm telling you that you need to be on bed rest, sister."

Sophie rolled her eyes and tossed her purse in a desk drawer. "It doesn't matter. I think he's leaving tomorrow anyway."

"Fine. Enjoy him while you can. But you're being careful?" Lauren pressed.

"Of course, Mom. Sheesh. This isn't my first rodeo."

"Tell that to Jake. I swear he thinks you're untouched."

"Aw, that's sweet." Jake really was one of the nicest guys around, even if Lauren had spent years spying on his shirtless jogs. "Tell Jake he was right and it was actually my plumber you saw."

"Naked with a towel?"

"Plumbing accident. He had to strip down. Jake will totally buy it and my reputation will be safe."

Lauren snorted. "Not with me, you lucky little hussy. And I'll expect more details at girls' night tomorrow. I want to hear everything."

No way was Sophie going to spill everything, but she supposed it wouldn't hurt to tell Lauren a little bit after Alex was safely gone. And Isabelle wouldn't tell a soul. In fact, she was so scatterbrained she'd probably forget everything once she was out of sight.

Sophie swallowed hard and straightened a few papers on the desk. "I'd better get to work."

"Okay, I'm on my way out anyway."

"Where are you going?"

Lauren cringed. "The dedication. Jean-Marie wants us to have a presence there and she has a meeting with the city council. So I volunteered."

Sophie's eyebrows flew up in shock, but Lauren reached out to touch her arm.

"I knew you couldn't go, and I didn't want anyone else going and…talking about it afterward."

She had to blink hard when she realized that Lauren was trying to protect her. "Thank you. Seriously. I really appreciate that." It was only after she reached to give Lauren a hug that the disaster of it all hit her square in the gut. Her hug turned into a clutch. "Wait. No. You can't go."

"Why not?"

She turned a hundred possibilities over in her mind, frantically searching for library projects to keep Lauren here. Or she could claim that she wanted to go herself, to pay her respects or—

"Hey," Lauren said. "What's wrong? I know it's a stupid idea and nobody needs to go, but you know how Jean-Marie is when she gets an idea."

Sophie tried not to let panic take her over. It wasn't like she'd done something illegal. She'd just slept with the wrong guy at the wrong time.

"Lauren… Crap." A look at the clock confirmed that Sophie was on the clock and didn't have time for a lengthy explanation.

Shit. It was confession time. "Lauren, please don't tell anyone this. I'm begging you."

"What?" Lauren asked, her voice a little frantic now. "What's wrong?"

"That man at my house… His name is Alex Bishop."

Lauren started to shake her head, her face blank, but then her mouth formed a little O of shock. Sophie let her head drop in shame.

"Bishop?" her friend whispered.

"Yes."

"Oh, my God."

"His mom suspects, but no one knows. You can't tell anyone. *Please*."

"Of course I won't. Just…don't worry. I won't tell anyone. I won't even acknowledge him at the dedication. Okay? Calm down."

Sophie realized she was feeling more than a little panicked and breathing too fast.

"Okay," she whispered. "Okay, this is almost over. One more day. Right?"

"Right. And then you're going to tell me how you ended up in bed with that woman's son."

Sophie shook her head, suddenly feeling the horror fall over her. *That woman's son.* She'd stopped thinking of him that way, somehow. He'd just become Alex to her. But Lauren was right. He was Rose's son. The child of a woman who'd made her life hell. A woman who had every reason to hate Sophie's family, because Dorothy Heyer had *damaged* her. Hurt her. Broken her heart.

"I've got to get going," Lauren said. "If I'm late, Jean-Marie will kill me." She pulled Sophie into a hug. "Are you going to be all right?"

Sophie nodded.

"Everything will be fine. I swear."

She nodded again and pulled back before she started crying. "I know. I'm good."

"Hey, just be glad she didn't volunteer the whole staff to serve drinks or something."

Sophie laughed. Lauren was always good at making her laugh. "God, Rose might've loved that."

"See? Things could always be worse."

"All right. Enough with the sayings from cat posters. We've got enough of those around here."

Lauren winked. "Some day Jean-Marie will retire and I'll take over. We'll put up posters of shirtless men in glasses reading books."

"I love you," Sophie said.

"Don't be maudlin. You're a librarian, for God's sake. Toughen up."

Right. Toughen up. If she could deal with all the bored children whose parents treated the library as a drop-off day care in the summer, she could deal with one day of mild emotional discomfort. And the avid interest of everyone in town. She could do that.

And it turned out not to be that difficult. The library was quiet today. Maybe because everyone in town was at the dedication. Or maybe because it was a sunny day in fall, and the locals all sensed winter coming. They didn't want to be indoors with books. They wanted to be out under the clear sky.

Normally Sophie would want that, too, but today she took comfort in the quietness of the library. The scent of books and copy paper and the old documents that held the history of the whole region.

She had sun here, after all. It streamed in through the side windows and warmed the bean-bag chairs in the corner of the children's section. She stuck close to that area, putting out new displays of kids' books for fall. She always enjoyed September. The kids were back in school and the section was quiet and not yet filled with books about Thanksgiving and

Hanukkah and Christmas. Sophie could choose her very favorite kids' books on any subject.

After she finished the kids' display she felt calm enough to work on reorganizing the Spanish language section of magazines and popular novels. It took a little more concentration as she didn't read a word of Spanish. In fact, she was focusing so completely that she didn't register that her phone was buzzing in the pocket of her cardigan until it had stopped.

"Oops." She looked guiltily around to be sure no one was watching. No cell phones in the library, after all. Just as she was pulling it out, it buzzed again. When she saw that it was Lauren, Sophie rushed toward the office and closed the door.

"Hey, is it over already?"

"No! Oh, my God, Sophie, I don't know if I should tell you this."

A dozen possibilities raced through her mind in a split second. Rose had ranted about Sophie, or Alex had shown up with a wife, or Wyatt Bishop wasn't really dead, or—

"Your brother is here."

"What?" she yelped.

"Your brother is right here in the audience! It's really crowded, and I'm not sure if the Bishops have noticed, but—"

"Oh, my God. Why would he go?"

"I don't know. I tried to talk to him, but he just brushed me off. Right now, everybody is just hanging out and looking at the displays. No one has started speaking yet. You don't think he's going to get up and say something, do you?"

Horror slammed through her. "No," she breathed. He wouldn't do that. Why would he? It would be hurtful and wrong and—

"Sophie?" Lauren said.

Oh, God. "They haven't started talking yet?"

"No, I think it'll be a few minutes."

Sophie grabbed her purse and keys. "I need to stop him. I'll be right there."

She stopped at the circulation desk to pull their weekend clerk aside. "I'm so sorry. I have a family emergency. I'll be back in an hour. Maybe two. Do you think you could call Betty and see if she can come in?"

The woman seemed alarmed by Sophie's demeanor and nodded. "Absolutely. You go on. It's slow. There shouldn't be a problem."

Sophie was already moving as she called out "Thank you!" then ran to her car. She fumbled her phone out as she turned the key in the ignition. She was in no state for driving and talking on the phone at the same time, but she had to get to her brother. She tried his phone, then tried again, then left a frantic voice mail.

"Please leave, David. Please. I don't know what point you're trying to make, but those people have a right to grieve any way they want to. *Please*." She hung up and tried again, but he didn't answer. Why would he? He knew what she'd say, and he obviously didn't care to listen.

She couldn't let this happen. Whatever his motivation was for going, she had to get him out. For selfish reasons and for unselfish reasons, as well. Yes, it would create a scandal for her family, but more than that, it would ruin what Wyatt Bishop's family wanted to do for him. A small moment that meant something to them. She'd never resented that they were doing it, just that it revived stories she'd rather keep buried.

Sophie tried her brother's phone one more time. When it went to voice mail, she hung up and tossed the phone onto the passenger seat with a shouted curse.

She was going to kill him for this. She was going to cut him out of her life, as effectively as you could cut off someone who you lived with most of the time.

Where the hell had he gone wrong? She'd done her best to do all the things for him that Mom would have. She'd done laundry and dishes and cooked and cleaned. She'd bandaged his scrapes and read to him. And they'd both still had their father, who was hardworking and loving and *good*. How the hell had David turned out to be so completely opposite?

"I babied him," she muttered to herself. "I did all the hard work so he never had to."

Now he just wanted a payout. Some excuse to never have to work hard in his life. He thought he was owed it because he'd lost something. Well, she'd lost something, too, damn it, and now he was going to destroy the peace she'd managed to dig out of the ashes.

For a brief moment as she sped down that long highway into the valley, Sophie considered texting Alex. She could warn him, at least. He wasn't emotional about the dedication. He'd remain calm and take control of the situation.

But what if her brother didn't remain calm? What if he was stupid enough to cause trouble with Alex? David would lose that brawl, without question, but Alex would be the one standing there as the man who'd gotten into a scuffle at his father's memorial.

Her phone buzzed briefly, and Sophie dived for it.

Everyone is taking their seats.

Lauren.

Merry Kade is going to give an historical talk.

Another text popped up. David hasn't said or done anything. It's fine.

Maybe it really was fine.

Sophie didn't have time to text back, and she couldn't risk it at seventy miles per hour anyway. Praying that she didn't pass a cop, she pushed the car up to seventy-five, the adrenaline coursing through her veins making it seem like a logical decision.

It paid off, thank God. She was at the turnoff to

Providence within a few minutes of the last text. She couldn't go seventy-five on the dirt road, but she pushed it to forty-five, gritting her teeth as her car flew over ruts and furrows. Dust exploded behind her, like she was leaving ruin in her wake. She hoped that wasn't true.

When she fishtailed around a curve and almost slid right into the irrigation canal that ran next to the road, Sophie had to hit the brakes. She skidded to a stop, her hands clutching the steering wheel so hard that she could no longer feel her fingers, just ten big heartbeats pulsing down her hands.

"It's okay," she panted aloud. She could only make this worse by being found unconscious, her car half-buried in a drainage ditch, after her brother interfered with the ceremony for Wyatt Bishop. "It's okay."

She blew out a deep breath and inhaled another. When she could hear past her own pulse, she started down the road again, this time a bit more slowly.

When she started seeing cars parked along the road, Sophie thought she was almost there. She'd only been here at night, after all, the last time safely snug against Alex's back, unaware of exactly where they were going.

So she slowed down, hoping not to miss the turn, but as the road curved, she saw that the cars went on and on.

"Oh, no," she muttered. Half the town really had turned out. No, not half. Not really. She could see the sign not a quarter mile ahead. It wasn't so bad. But she still heard herself murmuring "Oh, no," over and over again.

Telling herself she'd only be there for a moment, Sophie pulled into the packed lot and parked behind a row of cars. It wouldn't be a problem. She'd sneak in, grab her brother, and sneak right back out the way she'd come.

She stepped out of her car and, for a moment, there was silence. For those brief few seconds, Sophie felt a terrible relief. She was just losing her mind. That was all. None of this was even happening. It was an awful dream and she'd wake up and laugh in horror.

But then a voice said something over a speaker far away and applause drifted to Sophie on the wind. "The Providence Historical Trust…" she heard. As she took a step forward, there was more applause. She ignored it and walked forward down the long street.

There were the buildings that had loomed like ghosts that night, but beyond them were pure blue skies, not a cloud in sight. It seemed so wrong.

A few stragglers lingered near the saloon, reading the placard that was planted in the dirt. Sophie ducked her head and hurried past them.

The town of Providence lay on either side of a wide dirt lane. At the end of it, a line of backs greeted her. Hundreds of people. She didn't know whether to feel relieved that she'd easily keep hidden or worried that she'd never spot her brother.

She could hear the speaker now, an older woman speaking about the legacy of the Bishop family. She didn't seem to know much about Wyatt Bishop, though she went on and on about the man's father.

As the woman's voice rang out across the crowd, people began to shift restlessly. After all, none of them were here to see a member of the Historical Society speak. There was nothing juicy about that.

Sophie stood on her tiptoes and scanned the crowd. Most people were seated on white fold-out chairs. The rest of them stood around the seating area in a semicircle. At the front, next to a microphone, stood a big picture of Wyatt Bishop. She'd seen that in the paper, but never in color, and never draped with white carnations. But her eyes didn't stay on the photo, because stretching out in a row next to it were chairs for the Bishop family. Rose sat next to Shane and his girlfriend, Merry, and Alex sat on the end.

The sun caught the side of his face and emphasized the hard angles of his cheek and jaw and nose. He'd shaved his head so there wasn't one hint of softness about his profile now. Even his mouth looked hard.

Sophie ducked back down and said a prayer that he hadn't seen her. That no one had seen her.

The speaker droned on, her voice rising on important words like *Bishop* and *Jackson* and *"the mission of this trust."* Sophie sneaked to the left, keeping behind the backs of as many people as she could. There was no sign of her brother. Once she got toward the front row, she stood on tiptoe again and peeked past the shoulders of the people in front of her.

She had a clear view of the seated audience from here, and her brother wasn't among them. She spotted Lauren right in the middle, but didn't manage to catch her eye. Maybe Lauren had been wrong. Or maybe her brother had found a lick of common sense on the ground and taken his stupid butt home.

When the crowd began to applaud, Sophie shot a startled glance toward the front. The woman from the trust was stepping back and Shane Harcourt was taking her place at the microphone.

This was almost over. Shane would speak, and then his mother, and then they'd unveil the plaque or whatever it was and her brother wouldn't cause any trouble and they'd leave.

Then she spotted him. David was standing almost exactly opposite from her, but he wasn't looking over the crowd. His eyes were locked on Shane as he began to speak.

"My father loved this place," Shane said, his voice so much like Alex's that it made Sophie's stomach hurt. "He used to bring me here on horseback, up the very trail he was on the day he died."

Pressing a hand to her twisting stomach, she looked back and caught her brother scowling at the solemn words.

Oh, God. Sophie moved as fast as she could toward the back of the crowd. She couldn't run. That would draw attention, but she ducked her head and walked determinedly back the way she'd come, and then around to the far side.

The crowd laughed at something Shane had said, but her ears were buzzing with panic now.

Don't let him ruin this. Don't let him cause a scene.

Sophie slowed as she got closer to the front. Alex was seated on this side. If she got too close to the edge of people, he might spot her.

When she'd walked as far as she dared and still couldn't see her brother, panic grabbed her heart in a fist and squeezed. She closed her eyes, took a deep breath, and tried again.

There. She'd gone too far. He was a few feet to her left and two or three people deep in the crowd. Sophie edged closer and reached out to grab his sleeve. When she tugged, he glanced down at her hand, then back to Shane.

"This land meant a lot to him. It means a lot to my whole family," Shane's microphoned voice continued.

David snorted. She tugged harder.

He glanced her way and did a double take. She glared at him, and he glared back for a moment before crossing his arms and setting his shoulders. So she pinched him. Hard.

When he jerked away, the two people between

them edged away with irritated glances. Sophie mouthed *sorry* and sidled closer to her brother.

"We need to leave," she whispered.

He gave his head one shake and refused to look at her.

"Right now."

His jaw ticked in response. His arms folded more tightly against his body. Great. He was pretending to be a three-year-old now.

She leaned closer and hissed in his ear, "Let's. Go."

"I'm not leaving," he murmured just before the crowd broke into wide applause.

Shane raised a hand. "Thank you so much. And thank you all for coming. My mother would like to say a few words...."

He paused, and Sophie looked up, afraid they'd been spotted. But no. Shane wasn't looking at her. He was looking at Alex as he stood up from his chair. "I'd like to say something," Alex said quietly.

Sophie blinked in shock and dug her nails into her brother's arm. Alex hadn't planned to speak. If he got up there and saw Sophie and David...

She jerked so hard on her brother's elbow that he stumbled a step toward her.

"We have no right to be here," she whispered furiously. "I don't know what the hell you think you're doing, but I'm not going to let you do it."

The audience clapped as Alex approached the microphone.

David tried to jerk his arm from her grip. People were beginning to back away. "I have as much right to be here as anyone. *More* of a right."

Sophie looked frantically around at the crowd surrounding them. People were staring now, frowning, putting two and two together. So much adrenaline rushed through her that her limbs began to ache.

"Please, David," she said. "I'm begging you. Please."

He finally looked at her. Really looked. "You don't understand," he said.

And then she heard Alex's voice and tears of desperation sprang to her eyes as she prayed he didn't look in her direction.

"I don't remember as much about my dad as Shane does. I tried to forget a lot. But I do remember a few things." He paused as if he were taking a deep breath, and then a gasp rang out across the crowd.

Sophie knew what it was. She knew, even as she turned to watch Rose Bishop stand and point right at Sophie, her whole hand trembling, her face turning red. "What is *she* doing here?"

There was a strange shuffling sound, the noise of hundreds of people all turning in one direction. Every single face turned to look at Sophie. Every face, including Alex's. Her vision narrowed to just him, just Alex, his brow furrowing with confusion, mouth parting in shock.

"You trespassing whore!" his mother yelled. A

rush of shocked gasps passed through the crowd like a wave. "You're just as bad as she was!"

"Oh, no," Sophie whispered. "No."

"And you!" Rose pointed at David.

The people around Sophie and David backed away as if their awfulness might spread. Sophie was left standing with her hand around her brother's arm, frozen. She couldn't move.

"Haven't you ruined enough?" Rose screamed.

"Mom," Shane said. "Calm down."

"I won't calm down. Those people destroyed our family and now that this is all we have, they're trying to destroy this, too."

Sophie shook her head, but her brother laughed. "You've always wanted to erase us. You don't even want us here, but we lost someone on that trail, too."

Horror helped her break through the ice holding her still. Sophie jerked David's arm hard and pulled him a few steps away. "Stop it," she said, then, "I'm sorry," to everyone else.

Alex finally seemed to break through his own shock and took a few steps toward her, but his mother started forward, too. Sophie pulled harder on David's arm.

"No," David growled. "We don't have to hide in shame. God knows they never hid. What did we do that was so wrong?"

"*This* is wrong," Sophie snapped. "Stop it."

But Rose had her own answer. "I'll tell you what's wrong. She's exactly like her mother. Look at her."

She stabbed a finger at Sophie, still stalking forward, closing the space between them. The crowd parted, giving her room to do her worst. "Same hair. Same face. Spreading her legs for a man who doesn't belong to her."

This time the crowd's gasp was a roar that rumbled through Sophie's head.

"Mom!" Alex and Shane snapped the word at the same time, but Alex got to her first. He grabbed his mother's arms in a steady grip and pulled her to a stop.

"You cut this out right now," he growled at his mother, but his eyes were locked with Sophie's.

"I'm sorry," Sophie said again, but his mom was decidedly less conciliatory.

"I know what you're doing with her! How could you touch her? She's no better than a dog. A red-headed slut pretending to be a decent woman!"

"Mom." Alex started pulling his mother back. "Go!" he yelled at Sophie. "Just get the hell out of here, for God's sake."

Sophie tugged her brother in the other direction. This time, he actually moved with her.

Rose snarled like a wild animal. "You're monsters!" she yelled. "No one wants you here!"

They were monsters. Her brother should never have come here, but she'd made it worse by following. Before Sophie turned away, she saw Rose Bishop collapse into her chair, sobbing. Shane and Merry both spoke frantically to her, but Alex stayed quiet, his hands still locked on her shoulders as if to hold her down, but his eyes were on Sophie. And they were blazing with blue fury.

Sophie's stomach turned. She felt like throwing up, especially when she tore her gaze from Alex and saw the pale, shocked faces of the audience. Some of them watched her, some watched the Bishops, but they all looked stunned. And excited. She'd created the exact thing she'd been desperate to avoid.

Tears welled in her eyes and spilled down her cheeks. She clawed at David's arm and dragged him backward until he finally turned and followed. Then he was in front of her, leaving her behind, storming out as if she was the one who'd dragged him here.

"Wait," she gasped, jogging now, past the press of people, and then the stragglers, then the empty houses and shops of the dead town. "David! Wait!"

"You wanted me to leave, I'm leaving." He shook off her hand when she reached for him.

The fury she'd seen in Alex's eyes burrowed inside her and became fury in her gut. She hated David. She wanted to hit him. Wanted to make him hurt the way she was hurting. But she could never hurt him that badly, because he didn't give a damn about anything.

He never had. Not her, not their father, not the ranch.

She chased after him as they reached the parking lot. "Why did you come here? *Why?*"

He didn't answer. He didn't stop. She followed

him through the lot and out to the road, wishing she could kick off her heels, and knowing there was no way she could run barefoot across gravel. "You have to talk to me. You owe me that."

"I don't have to talk about shit," he said over his shoulder.

Before she could get to him, he was in his truck. She banged on the window, but when he started the engine, she changed course and raced back toward her car. Sophie reached it just as the first early deserters were walking out of Providence.

She lowered her eyes to avoid their stares and slipped into her car. She tried to control herself, tried not to throw any gravel up as she left, but she had to catch him. And she had to get away.

It took a few minutes. She was almost to the highway by the time she saw him. His truck was better equipped for the washboard road and she was blinded by the dust his tires threw into the air, but once they were on the highway, she caught up.

He was driving south, which could mean he was going into Jackson, or could mean he was heading home. It didn't matter to her. She was following him wherever he was going. He wasn't just going to walk away and sulk like some sullen teenager this time. He could damn well answer for himself like an adult.

This was really bad. It wasn't some decades-old scandal dusted off. It wasn't even something as dry as the black-and-white text of a new lawsuit. This had happened in living color in front of at least two hundred locals, most of whom had only been there in the hopes that something just like that would happen. This would be talked about for years, passed on in whispers anytime a Bishop or Heyer left a room.

She glared at the back of her brother's head, hoping if she put enough anger into it, his hair would start to smoke. But it didn't work. In fact, her head was the one aching within a few minutes. She caught her brother's gaze in the rearview mirror and made a phone sign next to her head. He ignored her and sped up.

But his efforts were in vain. They reached the town limits and he had to slow down. The highway patrol were spread a lot thinner than the town police, and the town made a bundle off of tourists speeding their way home from Yellowstone.

Her head ached worse as they inched their way through town. Sophie unclenched her hands from the steering wheel and rolled her shoulders. Her brother headed south. He wasn't stopping here. He glanced into the mirror to see if she was still following.

"You're not getting away," she muttered. "And you're not going to hide behind Dad this time."

Shit. Dad. She had to call him before someone else did. Her phone rang just as she was reaching for it, and Sophie gasped and jerked her hand away. It could be Alex or her dad, or it could even be someone from the newspaper. It hit her then that this was going to take over her life, for days or even weeks.

Hell, this might be the rest of her life. The old spinster whore librarian.

Or maybe just the old spinster whore. Jean-Marie was going to be really, really pissed, after all.

Fear stabbed her through the heart, but Sophie shook it off. It would be okay. If she got fired, she'd move back home and do what she'd always done: take care of the house and her dad and— No. Not her brother. That little shit could starve to death in dirty clothes, for all she cared.

When her phone stopped buzzing, she reached gingerly for it and turned it over. *Lauren,* it read, *Missed call.*

Thank God. It had only been someone checking on her. One of the few someones who would. She ignored it and called her father.

When it went to voice mail she felt a deep, cowardly relief. "Dad, it's me," she said, her voice cracking over those simple words. She took a few deep breaths and tried again. "David went to the Bishop dedication. I don't know why. I tried to stop him, and…Rose Bishop saw me and went crazy. I'm so sorry. It was really bad. I'll…I'll see you when you get home."

Saying it out loud made it real, and Sophie began to sob. She tried to shake it off so she could drive, but the tears wouldn't stop. She reached into her back seat to grab a spare sweater and mopped her face, then kept it in her lap to use again.

She deserved this. She'd slept with Alex, knowing it was wrong. Knowing it was some sick, sad repeat of what had happened twenty-five years before. Maybe that had been the entirety of the attraction. To try to understand her mother and what had driven her to do something so wrong. Or maybe she'd just wanted something that reckless and bad.

Well, she'd gotten it. And she was paying the price. She should probably just be thankful she hadn't ended up paying as high a price as her mother had.

But she didn't feel thankful as she turned onto the long ranch road and watched her brother pull away as his truck flew over the rough road. He could go as quickly as he wanted to. If he tried to hide in his room, she'd kick the damn door down. She took the turn onto her dad's drive so quickly that gravel flew into the fence.

Finally, she broke through the dust cloud her brother had laid and saw him disappearing inside the house. Sophie slammed on the brakes, wrenched the keys from the ignition and sprinted up the steps.

"You idiot!" she yelled when she spotted him. Still taking off his jacket, he looked surprised that she'd made it in so quickly. "I thought you were going to come to your senses. I thought you'd drop the lawsuit after you got a little attention. But now you do *this?*"

"I had a point to make," he muttered.

"What point, huh? That our mom is dead, too? Everyone knows that, David. They're pretty fucking clear on the details."

"No. The point is that we don't need to hide our

faces. We deserve as much respect as those Bishops do."

"Well, great job, David. You really drove that home by crashing a dead man's memorial."

"You don't know what it's been like for me."

"What?" She screamed it so loudly that she startled even herself and had to swallow hard and try again. "You are a stupid, selfish ass. I've lived through everything you have, and I'm old enough to remember every single moment. You have no idea how scary those first few days were. How terrifying."

"I know enough."

"You don't know *anything!*" she yelled, the words nearly lost on a sob. "If you knew anything, you wouldn't be bringing it all back like this. How could you do this to me?"

He sneered at her, as if her tears disgusted him. "It's not all about you, Sophie. You're not the center of the universe, even though you always try to be."

"I am the center of *this,*" she insisted. "You're her son, it's not the same. I'm her daughter. I look just like her. Everyone looks at me and sees *her.* They always have and they always will."

"Yeah, well, everyone looks at me and sees *him.*" The words rang through the room before dying into silence. They made so little sense that Sophie's rage tripped over itself and stilled.

She frowned. "What do you mean?" she asked in confusion. "They see who?"

"Him." When she only stared blankly, he rolled his eyes. "Wyatt Bishop."

"Why would they see him?"

"Jesus, Sophie." He blew air through his teeth and looked at her like she was a fool. "They see him because he's probably my dad."

"What?" she whispered. Then she yelled it. *"What?"*

He nodded as if he'd just dropped a deep truth on her.

She crossed her arms. "Are you completely insane?"

"That's what I've had to live with, Sophie. Never knowing. People reminding me that I'll never know. And the Bishops never once acknowledging that I might be their brother."

This was what had been bothering him his whole life? This was what it was all about? Sophie moved slowly toward him. She uncrossed her arms. And then she pushed him. Hard.

David stumbled back and almost caught himself, but then his calves hit the ottoman and he went down. "Goddamn it, Sophie!"

"You're an idiot, David. Do you hear me? An idiot. You have a father. You have his eyes and his long legs and weird thumbs and his ears. He's your dad."

He clambered up, his cheeks mottled with red. "I'm not sure and neither is anyone else."

She wanted to feel bad for his doubts, she wanted to comfort him, but so much anger boiled up inside her that she felt faint from it. He had no idea. None at all.

"You have a father, David. You have a dad right here! Do you know who doesn't have a father? Alex Bishop. And Shane Harcourt. And *me*."

He rolled his eyes again, and despite the fact that she knew violence was wrong and knew she shouldn't have pushed him, she wanted to shove him back down again and slap him. Slap him over and over.

"He's your dad," she repeated. "He's not my dad. Do you get that? I'd do anything for him to be my real dad, and you're listening to idiot gossip when anyone can look at you two together and see the truth."

He shrugged. "You've always been closer to him than I was."

They glared at each other, but before she could explain what an idiot he was being again, someone cleared his throat from the kitchen. Sophie turned and gasped at the sight of their dad standing there. Her stomach dropped.

He ran a handkerchief over the back of his neck and looked at David. "If you want a DNA test, we'll get one."

"Dad!" Sophie gasped. "No. You don't have to do that."

"That's up to David," her dad said. "Not you. If it'll make him feel better, then we'll do it." He sounded so matter-of-fact. As if he hadn't just heard his two children disclaim him as their father.

"Oh, God, Daddy. He doesn't really think that. He's just letting gossip get under his skin, that's all. David, tell him you don't mean that."

David didn't say anything. He just raised his chin like a stubborn child.

Their dad nodded. "If we take this test, are you going to stop all this nonsense?"

"It's not nonsense," David insisted.

Sophie had rarely seen her dad angry. He was more given to silence when something upset him, but this time his eyes narrowed and his jaw went hard as steel. "It is nonsense," he barked. "It's disrespectful and sneaky and nasty, and I didn't raise you to act this way. You don't disrespect the dead. Not with lawsuits or nasty lies or childish tantrums."

"They have no right to—"

"You've humiliated your sister and embarrassed yourself. And if you think I enjoy listening to people talk about what my wife was doing with another man twenty-five years ago, then you apparently don't know me too well, either."

Sophie pressed a hand to her mouth and even David seemed to suddenly realize how much he was hurting his father. His chin dipped down, dropping the arrogant outrage.

"Now…" Her dad took a breath and let it slowly out. "We'll take the test, and then I never want to hear another word about Wyatt Bishop."

"Fine."

"And you'll drop the lawsuit."

They stared at each other for a long moment. Her father's gaze was cool and hard, and David had no moral ground to stand on. He finally shrugged one shoulder and looked away. "I'll consider dropping the lawsuit."

"You'll do it or you'll get the hell out of my house."

"Dad!" he yelped, like a little dog who'd been kicked. "Where would I go?"

"No idea. But the lawsuit is wrong and I won't be any part of it. If you want to be your own man, then I suggest you get to it." He turned and left before David could argue further.

Sophie heard the back door close and then the sound of his truck starting. She should stop him. Say *something*. But she didn't know what to say.

The door to David's room closed, too, quietly for once. She was alone and she couldn't do anything to make this better for either of them. So she took off her heels, tied on an apron, and grabbed the vacuum. After she'd cleaned the living room, she headed for the kitchen. When her phone rang again, she saw Lauren's name but didn't answer.

In all the chaos, Sophie had forgotten to go back to work. Sick and ashamed, she called the front desk and left a message that she wouldn't be back. She didn't give a reason. They probably all knew why by now. She was in danger of being fired, but probably not because she'd left work. She'd embarrassed the library in front of the trust, one of their biggest new supporters in the community. It was bad.

She couldn't face anyone today, not even Lauren. But the guilt of ignoring her would eat her alive, so Sophie quickly texted that she was okay and would be in touch later. Then she turned off her phone, washed her hands and opened a jar of stewed tomatoes to start spaghetti. She'd make dinner and show her family that everything was okay. Everything would be fine.

But she'd been pulling this same trick since she was five years old, and she was beginning to suspect it had never worked at all.

CHAPTER FIFTEEN

"THAT WAS THE most singularly fucked-up thing I've ever seen," Alex growled, trying his best to keep from shouting. He paced through his mother's living room, or tried to, but her stacks of insanity blocked his way at every turn. This house was a goddamn diorama of his ruined childhood.

His mother wept in the corner, but she wasn't grieving or ashamed, she was outraged.

"That redheaded little *bitch!*" she yelled.

Alex closed his eyes and breathed.

"Mom," Shane said calmly, though Alex could hear the frustration that edged the word. "When was the last time you saw your doctor? I just talked to Manny and he says you haven't called for a cab ride in at least three weeks."

"I don't need therapy!" she wailed. "I need that woman out of my life!"

"You know how important therapy is right now. You were finally starting to get past this. You—" A loud ring cut him off. Shane pulled his cell phone from his pocket and stepped outside.

Alex wished Merry hadn't needed to stay behind

to help clean up that mess. He didn't want to be alone with his mom. He was afraid of what he'd say to her.

"Alex," she said, her voice suddenly a whisper. "Alex, you were going to say something about your father. I'm so proud of you, baby. So proud. And then that woman had to go and ruin it."

"You ruined it," he countered. "She was just standing there."

"Well, why do you think she was there? To *help?*"

He didn't know why she'd been there, actually. Or why she'd been with her brother, who had just filed a lawsuit against Alex's family, after all.

All he knew was that he'd been up there, trying not to see the crowd, trying to stop his hands from shaking, and he'd meant to tell that story. Of his dad and the lawn mower. Alex had no idea why he'd decided to share it, but he had. And then he'd looked up and seen her.

The worst part was that she'd looked so beautiful and frail and he'd wanted to go to her, even as the horror she'd brought had swelled around him.

"You men are all the same," his mom muttered. "Blind to everything if there's an easy piece of tail around."

He shook his head in disgust.

"Did you think she was in love with you? Because she looked at you with those pretty eyes and fluttered her lashes? You hardly knew her! She was trying to hurt *me*."

His mom had always loved to paint herself as

the victim. The ultimate victim of everything. A cheating husband, callous in-laws, vicious neighbors, money-hungry banks and power companies and landlords. Rose Bishop had always been a victim of the whole cruel world. It came as no surprise that Sophie Heyer was out to get her, as well.

Alex followed his brother out the back door, not to listen in, but just to get out.

Sophie hadn't slept with him to hurt his mom. That was completely absurd. He knew why she'd slept with him: because there was an insane chemistry between them. It'd been there since the moment he'd laid eyes on her. Hell, maybe it ran in the family. Thank God his dad and her mom had never decided to get married and set up house. That would've made for some damn awkward teenage years.

No, there was no way in hell Sophie had slept with him to enact some scheme of revenge. But why had she come to the dedication?

She hadn't said she was coming. In fact, she'd made it pretty clear that she wasn't. Why would she?

"Yeah," he muttered. "Why would she?"

He checked his phone to see if there were messages. In the rush to calm his mother down and get her out of there, Alex hadn't had time to check his phone, and when he saw there'd been no calls, he realized he was shocked. He'd been expecting her to call, to apologize, to explain. She hadn't.

What the fuck did that mean? He didn't blame her for his mom's outburst, but she must have known that she'd cause problems if she showed up. Even without his mom's difficult behavior, her brother's lawsuit was the kind of thing that would cause bad blood between any two families.

Had it been a publicity stunt? Some sort of perverted effort to keep the Heyer family in the public eye leading up to a court fight?

But she'd said *I'm sorry.* He'd watched her say it.

He was trying to decide whether to call Sophie when his brother got off the phone and shook his head. "I don't know how long it's been since Mom's gone in, but her doctor has been concerned. She's out of town this weekend, but she wants us to bring Mom in first thing Monday morning."

"You," Alex corrected.

"What?"

"You bring her in. I'm leaving tomorrow."

"Alex, come on."

"If you think I'm sticking around for more of this shit show, you're as crazy as she is. I'm done."

Shane blew out a long breath and looked up at the sky. It was still clear blue and cloudless. The perfect day to mock their ridiculous drama. "Maybe you're right. Maybe I should've just left you alone. Let you disappear forever. Is that what you want?"

"Yes," Alex said automatically, ignoring the pain that twinged like a phantom stitch in his side.

Shane shoved his hands into his pockets. He rocked back on his heels.

Alex felt his brother turn to stare at him, but he

kept his gaze straight ahead. He didn't want to look at him as they said goodbye. This time, he knew what it meant, to leave behind everyone you've ever loved. Every place you've ever known.

He'd done it before. It should be easier this time. It *would* be easier. And if it felt like a death looming just beyond the horizon, that was just his old age showing. He needed to get off his ass and move on.

Shane finally spoke. "I'm pissed that you left me with this, you know. I need help."

"With her?"

"Yes, with her. And hell, if you wanted to hang out and help me build my fucking house, I wouldn't say no."

Alex rolled his shoulders. "Put her in a home. She's not right in the head."

"She's only sixty-five. She can't—"

"And I don't know shit about building houses. There's nothing I can do to help you." He stared at the trees behind his mother's house. He didn't look at Shane.

"Alex," Shane said, as if he meant to say something more, but the silence dragged on and he just cursed under his breath.

"Yeah. I know how you feel," Alex said.

"Please. Just a few more days. I don't know what the hell I'm doing either."

"You seem to have it under control."

Shane's laugh sounded more like a bark. "Was that a joke?"

"Kind of." Alex ran a hand over his head, half startled to feel how smooth it was. "There's nothing I can do for the woman."

"She's your mother."

"Ha." It was Alex's turn to sound unamused. "Was that a joke?"

"No, it wasn't a fucking joke."

But it was. That was what his brother could never see. It was all a joke. "She was supposed to take care of us after Dad disappeared. She wasn't supposed to disappear, too."

"So you're just going to go ahead and be like both of them?"

Alex sneered. "I never said it was the higher ground. It's just ground that's nowhere near this fucking place."

Shane grunted. "Well, if that's the way you want to live, there's nothing I can do about it. And nothing I can do to make you stay. But I still love you. You're my brother. That won't ever change."

Jesus. Alex rolled his shoulders, trying to shake off the tightness in his chest. "It doesn't have to be the way it was. We can talk. I'll check in. I just can't be here."

"All right."

Alex finally looked at his brother, but now Shane wasn't looking at him. "I'm staying the night. You wanna grab a drink later?"

"I'll see how Mom's doing. Right now I need

to help Merry. She put a lot of work into this, and now…"

Yeah. Now.

He suspected that Shane hoped Alex would volunteer to stay with their mom for an hour or two, but if the woman couldn't be left alone, she was too far gone for him to help. Anyway, she'd been out of control for decades. This was nothing new.

"Maybe I'll see you later, then. Tell Merry I'm sorry about all this shit. Pretty amazing she's willing to put up with it just for you."

"I know. She's the best."

Maybe. Or maybe Shane was a lot easier to put up with than someone like Alex. Women liked security. Stability. A man who knew how to stay put. Alex wasn't ever going to have that. He didn't know how to stop moving.

He headed through the house toward the front door. "Bye, Mom."

"Alex, where are you going? I thought you'd stay for dinner."

She always did this, acted like nothing had happened. She'd once dragged Alex and Shane all the way to Arizona to chase down a lead. She'd banged on a stranger's front door, accused the man of hiding her husband, then proceeded to take her kids out for ice cream before getting back in the car for the return trip to Wyoming. No big deal. Just a normal day in Rose Bishop's world.

She'd cast herself as the hero in her story, and there was no changing that narrative.

"Goodbye," he said as he pushed out the door. He wasn't going to make a speech or a grand gesture and give her an opportunity to bleed her hurt all over him. She'd indulge her loud mourning whether he said a real goodbye or not. He didn't have to stay and participate.

He breathed a sigh of relief once he was on his bike. He was doing the right thing. He'd get an early start tomorrow and get back to his real life. He still had a few weeks before he needed to be in Alaska, so he'd work his way northwest and spend some time in the Cascades before it got too cold. Then he'd store his bike in Seattle and head up to Alaska. After that, it was down to Texas for his next contract.

"Fuck yeah," he muttered. Freedom.

Yet he was still sitting there on his bike, kickstand up, thumb hovering above the start. His hesitation wasn't exactly a mystery. After all, his eyes were locked on Sophie's front walk.

He checked his phone again. Nothing.

Shit.

He should at least tell her he was leaving. See if she had an explanation. He supposed whatever she said wouldn't matter, since he was saying goodbye regardless. But damn…he couldn't deny that it felt strange that he'd never see her again. Never taste her or touch her.

If he said goodbye, if she explained…maybe they

could hook up when she finally came to California. He could show her around, take her for a ride. It didn't have to be serious. It could just be a day.

He tossed a glance at his mom's house to be sure she wasn't standing in the window, then he eased the kickstand back down and headed up the sidewalk. But he needn't have bothered. Her car wasn't in the carport and there was no answer when he knocked. Shit.

He was just stepping off the porch when a car pulled up and the woman he'd seen in Sophie's doorway the day before stepped out.

"Is she home?" she asked as she approached.

He shook his head and they stood in awkward silence for a moment.

"I'm Lauren," the brunette said, sticking out her hand.

"Alex," he said as he shook.

"Um. Sorry about today. I was just coming to check on her."

He nodded. "Yeah."

Lauren cleared her throat. "Have you talked to her? She's not answering when I call."

"I haven't tried."

"Mmm." Her eyes slid toward her car. "She's probably at her dad's."

He swallowed back the questions he wanted to ask. It was none of his business. "Right. Well. Good luck."

He felt her eyes on his back as he walked away.

Maybe he should just go. If someone forced him to tell the truth, he'd have to admit that the reason he'd planned to hang around tonight was because he'd hoped to spend one more night with Sophie. But that wasn't going to happen, and his brother didn't even want to grab a drink, so Alex should just hit the road.

He headed for the motel to pack. The sky was clear and he could put Wyoming behind him by sundown. What more could he ask for?

When he hit the throttle, the roar of the engine drowned out any answers his mind had to that question.

It was only 4:00 p.m. when Sophie pulled up to her house, but it felt like she'd been gone for days.

Her father had returned at two and they'd shared a big midday meal in silence before he'd headed back out to work. Her brother had disappeared into his room again, and Sophie had put the leftovers in the fridge and washed the dishes. Then she'd found herself sitting at the kitchen table, trying to figure out how to apologize to her dad for what he'd heard.

She hadn't said anything wrong, per se, but he must have been hurt. She'd never said that to him, not even during her darkest teenage years. *You're not my real dad.* Even thinking it felt wrong. He was as real as any dad had ever been to any child.

In the end, she couldn't think of what to say, so she'd just left. Now she felt like her limbs were made of lead as she climbed out of her car and walked to her door. She glanced toward a passing car and saw both the driver and passenger staring at her as they slid past. Shit. She'd been so worried about the hurt she and her brother had managed to cause that she'd blocked out the bigger picture.

Her secret was out. Everyone knew she was just like her mother. There was no hiding it now.

The weight of her body multiplied again. She made it up the stairs and through the door and gave up any idea she'd had of stopping in at the library before it closed. She'd call Jean-Marie tomorrow. She'd call everyone she needed to call tomorrow. Not tonight. Tonight she'd draw the curtains and crawl into bed and sleep for as many hours as she possibly could.

She locked the door behind her and dropped her purse.

"Where is my husband?"

Sophie squeaked in shock at the voice drifting from the dim of her living room. She slapped her hand to the wall and slid it in a wide arc until she found the switch, but she realized who the voice belonged to just before the lights revealed Rose Bishop.

"Mrs. Bishop," she gasped, "you can't be here."

"Where's my husband?" She wore the same black dress she'd worn at the dedication, but her feet were bare and red, her face blotchy and eyes swollen. Her short gray hair stood up in strange swoops as if she'd clutched it over and over.

"Mrs.—"

"Why can't you just leave him alone? He's mine. You have your own husband, your own kids. Leave my family alone or I'll tell everyone what you are!"

Sophie's startled fear turned to a different kind of alarm. Something was very wrong here, beyond the fact that this woman had somehow broken into Sophie's house. She hadn't gotten off the couch, at least. She wasn't charging at Sophie or trying to attack.

"Mrs. Bishop, where are Shane and Alex?"

"They're at home where they should be. Where Wyatt should be. Why won't you just give him back to me?" She began to cry, her face crumpling before she hid it in her hands.

Keeping a careful eye on the woman curled onto her couch, Sophie dug her phone from her purse and called Alex. There was no answer, but she waited for voice mail. "Alex," she whispered. "Your mom is at my house and I think there's something really wrong. Can you come by? Please?"

A tiny meow pierced the room just as she ended the call.

Rose's head popped up. Her puffy eyes narrowed, then they focused on the furry gray ball that curled up at her feet. "Pastel?" she whispered. She picked up the cat and cuddled it close. Then she looked around as if she were trying to get her bearings.

"Mrs. Bishop?"

Her head came around and her eyes cleared. "You stole my cat."

"What?"

"You little bitch, you stole my cat, as if everything else weren't enough."

Her heart dropped. Was that where Alex had *found* the kitten? At his mother's? "Ma'am, I'm Sophie, not—"

"I know who you are!" she screeched. She pushed herself to her feet, the cat clutched tight to her bosom. "It wasn't enough to co-opt my son, you took my cat, too? You're a monster! You'll be hearing from the police about this. I won't put up with your vicious attacks anymore."

"Mrs. Bishop," she started, trying to gather her flying thoughts. "You broke into my *house*."

"You're a liar and a slut." With that simple defense, Rose Bishop limped forward on her bare feet.

More than a little freaked out, Sophie moved sideways toward the kitchen, circling the path from the couch to the door. Rose watched her just as warily until she got to the door. She fumbled with it for a moment, and Sophie was faced with the bizarre decision of whether or not to unlock the door for her trespasser. But Rose finally realized the problem. She unlocked the door, then threw it open as if she were the one under threat.

A few seconds after she disappeared, Sophie tiptoed forward and carefully peeked her head out, half expecting the woman to be lurking in the corner of the porch. But the porch was clear and Alex's mother was limping down the sidewalk toward her house.

Sophie was frozen, half crouched and clutching

the doorjamb as she craned her neck to keep track of the woman's progress. Was she delusional? Had she suffered some sort of spell?

"Shit," Sophie breathed. "Holy shit." What the hell had just happened?

She leaned farther out, but Mrs. Bishop was out of sight now, and Sophie felt suddenly guilty. What if she just kept walking and wandered out of town or into the street and got hurt?

When she stood and stepped outside, Sophie realized her hands were shaking. She laced her fingers together and held tight. "This is crazy," she whispered to herself as she moved down to the walk and crept forward.

She caught sight of Mrs. Bishop just as the woman stepped into her house. The door closed behind her with a solid thunk that Sophie could hear from her house.

Now what?

She couldn't just stay out here staring at the woman's house. Someone would see her and add stalking to the epic tale of the Hcyers versus the Bishops.

Sophie sprinted back into her house. She had no idea why she was the one feeling guilty. Rose was the criminal here.

Before she even got to her door, she heard her cell phone ringing and gave up any pretense of calm to sprint up the steps. "Hello?" she asked on a gasp. "Alex?"

The wind stole his voice for a moment, blowing into his phone and crackling into her ear.

"Alex?" she asked again.

"Are you okay?"

"I'm fine. I just… I didn't know who to call."

"What happened?"

"I came home and your mom was in my living room."

"Are you fucking kidding me? I hope you called the police."

"What? No. She wasn't okay, Alex. She was confused."

"She's been confused for a long time."

"I mean it! She thought I was my mom. She kept asking where her husband was."

Alex sighed. "Listen, Sophie, I'm already on my way out of town. You'll have to call Shane about it."

The shock of the whole day must have finally caught up with her. Sophie nearly dropped the phone. Her knees went so weak that she had to sit down. He was gone? Just like that?

But of course he was. After today he wouldn't have felt any obligation to even say goodbye to her. "Okay," she finally managed to croak. "She's home alone and I don't think she should be. I'll call Shane if you'll give me his number."

The wind caught his phone again. She wondered where he was. If he'd left right after that nightmare today, he could already be in Utah or Colorado or Idaho.

He said her name.

"Yes?"

"I said I'll text you his number."

"Thanks." She hung up before she could say more. If she told him she was sorry, all the emotion inside her would come bubbling up. She was so damn tired, anything could've pushed her to tears, and hearing that he was already gone was more than just *anything*.

But she had to hold it together. She couldn't crawl into her bed just yet. Or could she?

If Rose had been such an awful mother that her own son didn't give a damn about her, did Sophie have an obligation to take care of her? Rose had been calling Sophie's mom a slut and a whore and home wrecker for a quarter of a century. She'd transferred all that spite to Sophie. After all the awful ways Rose had tried to hurt the Heyer family, why help her at all?

But the devil on Sophie's shoulder had nothing on the very loud angel sitting on the other. She checked her texts for Shane's number, then closed them and checked again. Nothing. Just as she was checking a third time, her phone rang. Alex's name popped up.

"I called Shane," he said gruffly. "He'll be at Mom's within the hour. It'll take me about that long to get back to town."

"Okay."

"I got a late start," he said as if she'd challenged him.

"Sure. All right. I hope she's okay. I'd offer to go over, but…"

"Yeah. You'd better not. I'll see you in a while."

He hung up before she could apologize, but she was thankful. She didn't know what to say. The next forty-five minutes ticked by. She paced from the porch to the living room to the bedroom. She changed into yoga pants and brushed out her hair. She poured herself a glass of wine, then changed her mind. What if she had to file a police report or something? But she managed to screw that up, too, by spilling half the wine on herself when she tried to get it back into the bottle. *Reeks of alcohol,* any police report would start with.

Finally, just as dark was setting in, she heard the roar of Alex's bike approaching. She opened the door before he even knocked.

"My brother says she seems normal. Whatever that is."

"She's not. Or she wasn't. She was talking to me like I was my mother."

"Sophie." He ran a hand over his head, drawing her eye to the smooth skin. She shook her head and looked away, but he kept talking. "Her whole thing has been treating you like you're your mother, right?"

"It wasn't like that. She was confused. She was looking for your dad."

"Again, pretty standard." His words were hard. Removed. Far cooler than they'd ever been with her before. He was pissed. At her and his mother and the whole world.

"I'm sorry," she said.

He shook his head like he didn't understand.

She felt a brief moment of irritation, but she knew it was ungracious. "About today. I'm sorry that I showed up and set her off."

"Yeah." He shoved his hands in his pockets. "What the hell was that, Sophie? Why were you there?"

She'd thought she was ready to talk about it, but his questions made her insides quake. "I'm so sorry. My brother was…" She waved a helpless hand.

Alex stared hard at her. "He was what?"

"I don't know. I was just trying to help."

"Right. He's your brother. You want to support him."

"No!"

His eyebrows rose in question, but his mouth was still a flat, cold line of doubt.

"Alex, I wasn't supporting him! I heard that he was there. I only wanted him to leave. That's all. I didn't… I'd never have gone. Never."

His stiff shoulders relaxed a little. "What was he doing there?"

"I don't know. He wanted to make a point."

"What point?"

"A stupid point! How should I know? It was cruel of him and terrible and I only wanted to stop it. I'm so sorry, Alex."

"Jesus. Don't cry."

She shook her head and swiped at her cheeks. "He thinks you're his brother."

Alex's head drew back. "His *what?*"

"I guess there were rumors that he was your dad's son. Like an idiot, he listened to them." A little hiccup escaped her throat and she swallowed it back. "He looks like my dad, but I don't think he got anything else from him. No dignity or work ethic or common sense… God, what am I going to do?"

"It's not your fault."

"No, but I have to live with it." She blinked her tears away and caught his eye. "I'm sorry. This isn't about me. Your mom. She needs help."

"She's always needed help."

"I've been on the sharp end of her obsession for a long time, but this is different, Alex. This isn't martyrdom or stubbornness. There's something wrong."

"Maybe. Or maybe she was just trying to freak you out. Do you think that's beyond her? She broke into your house just a few hours after she called you a whore in front of the whole town. She's nobody's victim."

"And after everything she's done to me, I'm still worried about her. Why aren't you?"

He didn't answer her question. Instead, he dug his phone from his pocket and scrolled, looking angry that she'd even asked the question.

"And you didn't tell me you stole her cat! I thought she was going to kill me!"

He grunted, but didn't glance up from the phone. "She's seeing her psychiatrist next week."

"Good. Okay."

"My brother's texting me. I'd better get back." He hesitated for a moment, but he didn't say anything else. He only studied her face and then walked toward the door. "Thanks for calling."

That was it. He was gone again. As far away as if he was still on his bike, heading anywhere but here.

Sophie locked the door, turned off the lights and crawled into bed. She couldn't help anyone else today, not even herself. Tomorrow she'd try to clean up the mess. Again.

CHAPTER SIXTEEN

ALEX PRETENDED THERE wasn't a kitten curled up and purring under his chin as he scowled at his brother. "We'll see how she's doing in the morning. I'm obviously not going to get out of town tonight."

"You weren't supposed to leave tonight anyway," Shane countered. "What the fuck was that?"

"You were busy. There wasn't any reason to stay." The kitten nuzzled his throat. He gave up ignoring it and scratched the back of its head. The purring rumbled more loudly. "She's sleeping?" he asked, tipping his head toward the back room.

"Yes."

"I'm sure she's fine."

"What did Sophie say exactly?"

"That she kept asking where her husband was, as if Sophie was actually her mother. Has Mom ever done anything like that before?"

Shane shook his head.

"Yeah. Maybe it was an act. I wouldn't put it past her. I mean, Jesus, she sneaked into Sophie's house and waited for her to come home."

Shane scrubbed both hands over his head. "I don't

know, man. We'll see what her doctor says. Can't you just stay? Maybe there's something wrong. I know you think I'm as delusional as she is, but this summer it was almost like I was getting to know her again. I mean, before Dad disappeared, she was a real person with interests and hobbies—"

"And grudges and feuds," Alex interrupted.

Shane smiled. "Okay, I'll concede that she's always been dramatic, but she was a whole person once, and it felt like she was inching back toward that. And this—" He swept a hand out to take in the whole room. "It wasn't like this."

"She's obviously been saving this crap for years, Shane."

"Yeah, but it was all in that little study."

"You mean the room where she sleeps? On a couch instead of a bed?"

"She has a bedroom upstairs and she stopped using it. That's my point. Things have gone south really quickly."

Alex sighed, then winced when the kitten dug her claws into his collarbone. "Fine. I believe you. But I still don't know what that has to do with me. Frankly, she's practically a stranger to me."

"We're the only family you have."

"Well, Jesus. Way to make me feel better."

Shane laughed and reached for one of the beers he'd brought over. "I'll sleep down here in the living room. There's a spare bedroom upstairs, or you can stay at my place."

Shit. Alex knew exactly where he wanted to stay, and even though he knew there wasn't a chance in the world, making another commitment felt like sacrilege.

"So it's true?" Shane asked softly after a moment.

"What?"

"You and Sophie?"

Alex cursed and tensed up so much that the kitten uncurled and went to sit on Shane's lap. Alex's neck was ice cold without her. "It's not true that she's a whore who has her claws in me, if that's what you mean."

"No. I mean there's something between you."

Alex shrugged.

"So...hell, yes?" Shane drawled.

"It's temporary."

"Clearly."

Alex bristled, but he couldn't say why. "She doesn't want anyone to know."

"Shit, it's a little late for that, brother."

Shit, indeed. The full damage of the day finally penetrated his thick skull. He'd been so wrapped up in his own anger that he hadn't realized how screwed up everything had gotten. Of course Sophie hadn't gone there willingly. She had to live in this town. She had to live with the fallout.

"Nobody will believe it," he growled.

"You're either joking or you're an idiot. They'll believe anything if it's scandalous enough. Especially when it comes to our families."

"Damn it." He shifted and crossed his arms. "Do you think she'll be okay?"

"It's the twenty-first century. Women have sex."

Right. But that wasn't the point for Sophie. She wasn't just a woman. She'd grown up in scandal. In a fishbowl. She needed to get the hell out of here, so she could be whoever she wanted to be.

"You want another beer?" Shane asked.

"No, I'd better hit the road."

"Okay. I need to get over to Merry's. She's pretty torn up about today. She hates for people to be unhappy."

Alex cracked a smile. He could see that. She always seemed cheerful. Carefree. Nothing that he could understand, but she definitely made him smile. "I'll meet you here tomorrow, then."

Alex made sure the kitten wasn't following him before he slipped out the door, eager to escape and equally worried that he had nowhere to escape to.

It was late. She had no reason to see him. He'd stood there and watched her cry and done nothing. Jesus. Why hadn't he seen what had happened to *her* today? He'd spent too damn much of his life on the defensive, worried about himself, guarding against others.

He'd been watching out for himself so long that he didn't know how to take care of anyone else. Not even a damn kitten.

But he still wanted to be with Sophie tonight. He wanted to climb into her bed and draw her close and sleep like that. Just for one more night. That'd be enough. He'd make it enough.

Alex wasn't often given to indecision, but he stood in the cold moonlight and stared down the street for a long while before he started toward her place.

She had no reason to let him in. All he could do was ask. And hope.

He breathed in the night air, crisp and clean and scented only with aspen. He'd been so familiar with that in his youth that it seemed too common to have forgotten. But he'd gotten used to the ocean smells of California and Alaska and most of the places he went. There were no aspen on the plains of Canada.

Alex inhaled and turned toward her house.

The windows were dark. Dark as the night around them. "Damn," he breathed. He took out his phone.

Sophie? Are you awake? I'm outside...

Christ, that sounded pitiful. But he was pitiful, wasn't he? Wandering around the dark streets of Jackson like a homeless dog. This place was bad for him. Diminishing or regressive or just sad.

She didn't write back. He was almost relieved. He could go back to that hotel and feel sorry for himself, tell himself he was a damn victim. Carry on the legacy.

He texted one last time. I'm sorry. And started back toward his bike.

The porch light snapped on.

He spun on his heel.

"You were already gone," she said, standing there in a T-shirt that came down to her thighs and hair that stood out in a wild mess.

"What?" Alex murmured, too distracted by the sight of her.

"You left. So what are you doing here now?"

"I was at my mom's…"

"No. I mean you were headed out of town when I called. So why are you *here?*"

He didn't know what to say. He wasn't good at this sort of thing. He'd left without a word, and he'd known it was wrong when he did it. "I came by," he finally said. "More than once." In fact, that had been the reason for his late start, though he couldn't make himself admit that.

She watched him for a few long seconds, her face golden in the porch light but still impossible to read. Then she turned and walked away, but she left the door open. Alex refused to let his shoulders slump with relief. He kept his head up and stepped inside.

When he closed the door, it was dark again. He heard the creak of floorboards as she moved around. A light came on toward the back of the house and her shadow stretched out as she moved down the hallway.

Alex took one step forward, unsure if he should follow or not. A couple of days ago, he would've taken it as an invitation, but whatever her kinks were, he didn't think ice-cold sex was one of them.

He was right. Her shadow reappeared, and then Sophie, her hair smoothed down a little and the T-shirt covered by a little pink robe edged in white lace. This was the Sophie he was more familiar with, but when she turned on the kitchen light, he saw the circles under her eyes and the tightness around her mouth. She looked so vulnerable without her makeup and hair twist and prim little heels.

"How is your mom?" she asked.

"She's fine."

"Is she really fine, or do you just want to get back on the road?"

Alex bristled, but he tried not to snap at her. He'd obviously woken her up and she was obviously pissed. She poured herself a glass of water and leaned against the kitchen counter. He noticed that she didn't offer him a drink.

"I just wanted to apologize," he said. "When I came by earlier, I was pissed about the dedication, and I didn't think about what that scene meant for you."

"You mean that everyone in town now thinks I'm a whore and a home wrecker just like my mom? No big deal."

"Sophie—"

"No, it's fine. You were upset. It makes sense that you were focused on yourself and your family. I get that. Except that I was worried about you and your family, too, so I guess I'm just a fool."

"What am I supposed to say?" he asked. "I'm

sorry it happened, but I didn't do anything wrong. There was nothing I could've done to protect you today."

"I didn't do anything wrong either!" she bit out.

"Your brother—"

"My brother didn't *do* anything. He was just there. That's the way it's always been. We can't even *exist* because that's offensive to her. Do you know what it's been like, living with that?"

"I think I do."

"I don't know if that's true. She's on your side, Alex, and even that was unbearable to you. Imagine what it was like for me as a little girl, to hear all those rumors *she* started. And now she's doing it to me! How am I supposed to live with that? My entire job, if I still have one, is dealing with the people of this town. Not cattle or horses or even tourists, but the people who live here and know everyone and everything. About *me*."

"Then *leave*," he bit out impatiently.

"What?" she snapped.

"Leave. You're a grown woman now, Sophie. There's no reason for you to stay."

"No reason?" Her laughter was sharp as a whip. "I have reasons, but I wouldn't expect you to understand. You don't think there's ever any reason to stay."

"That's not fair."

"I'm pretty sure it is."

"I had to leave," he snapped. "This place was killing me just like it's killing you."

"My family needs me. You wouldn't get that."

It was his turn to laugh. "*I* don't get it? You've given up your whole life to take care of two grown men who'd be fine without you. Jesus, Sophie. Live a little. For once!"

Her cheeks turned bright red. "I'm living just fine. Not everyone wants what you want."

"Shit." Alex glanced toward the dining room, then rubbed a hand hard over the back of his neck. "I saw the scrapbooks. Don't tell me you don't want more."

She'd opened her mouth to snap back at him, but she stayed silent as her eyes went wide. Her head snapped toward the dining room, then her gaze shot back to him. "What?"

"You left one out. I saw the picture, the places. And the way you talk about traveling. Jesus, Sophie. You've got to leave this place behind. No one would know anything about you if you ever bothered to get more than an hour from home."

"I know that!" she snapped. "You don't have to tell me that. You think I'm so stupid that it hasn't occurred to me?"

"Of course not. But I can't figure out why someone as smart as you can't see what she needs to do."

"I'm not you, Alex. I don't *need* to flee every serious relationship and live like a nomad."

"No, you need to stay here to prove to yourself

and everyone else that you're a better woman than your mother was."

As soon as the words left his mouth, he wanted to take them back. He was pissed, she'd hit a nerve, and he'd decided to fight back. But he knew he'd gone too far even before she slammed her water glass down on the counter and stood up straight.

"Fuck you," she growled. "It doesn't have to be anything screwed up or pathological just because I love my family. My dad is a good man who needs my help. God knows my brother isn't going to do anything for his family. He's kind of like you that way."

"Maybe he doesn't feel like he owes his family anything more."

"Well, I do."

"Why?"

Her sigh was a quick, sharp breath of impatience. "Because I love my dad, Alex."

"You say that like it's an obvious explanation, but people who love their families still grow up and leave. They get married, they move away, they travel. They don't just cut out pictures of places and glue them into books for their whole lives, Sophie."

She stepped forward like she wanted to push him or hit him or slap him, but instead she pointed at the door. "Go. You already left once. That's what you do, right? You leave when anything gets the slightest bit difficult. So leave. We're not going to fuck, and that's clearly what you came here for. 'I didn't really want to see you again, but I'm here now, so…'"

"I did want to see you again. I came by three times!"

"Why?"

He shrugged. "I just—"

"Why would you want to spend time with some pitiful, dried-up loser who's never been more than a few hours from home? My God, time must have really dragged when I wasn't on my knees for you."

"Damn it, that's not what I meant at all. I meant that you're amazing and interesting and you're wasting your fucking life here."

"You don't know anything about it!"

"I know what's out there, Sophie. I know what you could see and do if you'd stop being so damn terrified to leave. What do you think is going to happen? Do you think your dad won't survive? Do you think he won't love you anymore?"

She jerked back as if he'd slapped her, all the color draining from her face. "Shut up."

"Hey." He reached out to take her arm, but she pulled it away. "Sophie."

"Just go."

"You don't really think that, do you?"

She shook her head, her jaw clenched tight.

"I'm sorry. It frustrates me that you're so wild and bright and you're stuck here like a bird with clipped wings."

"I'm not *stuck* here. That's how you see it because you can't stay in one place for more than a month. I love people, Alex. I take care of them."

"And what happens if you don't?" he asked.

"I...I don't know. I don't have to know. I won't find out."

"So this is it, huh, Sophie? You're going to stay in Jackson, move back home, keep your head down and your real self secret?"

"Yes."

"Is that what you dream about? Living at home, taking care of your dad, working at the library? Over and over, every day, every year, broken up by the occasional roll in the hay with a man who won't ask questions? Is that all you're ever going to be?"

"Shut up. I'm not going to be a person who walks away. I won't ever do that."

"Like me?" he asked.

"Like *her*," she growled. "I can't leave, Alex. I won't do that. I may look like her and sound like her and fuck around like her, but I won't walk out on the people who depend on me. My dad needs me and if he doesn't..." The raw, hoarse words stopped and her ragged breathing filled the room.

"If he doesn't need you, then what?" Alex pressed.

She shook her head.

"He's your dad, Sophie. He'll always be your dad."

"No." She blinked and two fat tears trailed down her pale cheeks. "He's not my dad. And when my mom left..." She swallowed hard and drew in a breath that was so broken Alex had to fight not to wrap his arms around her and force her closer. "I knew he wouldn't want me anymore. Why would he?"

"Oh, Sophie." He did reach out then. He couldn't stop himself. She didn't pull away. She let him slowly put his arms around her and draw her to his chest. She was stiff, but her head bent and rested against his heart.

"I was so scared," she whispered. "For years. But that first year or two, I was just waiting for the day when some nice woman would show up at the door and tell me I was going with her. That's how I thought it would happen. That I'd be taken to an orphanage and never see my family again. Because I was *just* like her, Alex, and why would a man who wasn't even my real dad want to keep me after that?"

He pressed a kiss to the top of her head and held her tighter. "I'm sorry," he whispered. Sorry for her, and sorry he'd never thought that deeply about how it must have been for her.

"I made myself essential. I took care of all the things she should've been there to do, so even if he didn't want me anymore, he'd let me s-s-stay."

She broke down then, finally. Her body gave up its stiffness and she wilted into him, shaking and crying quietly. Quietly, as if she'd learned that when she was little. Not to be a bother. Not to cause trouble.

Alex didn't say anything. His throat was too tight. He swallowed several times, but that didn't help, so he just pressed his cheek to her head and breathed her in. It was so clear now why she kept everything hidden, why she couldn't make herself leave.

After a few minutes, she relaxed. Her back softened under his hands.

"It's okay," he whispered.

She nodded.

"You know he loves you, Sophie. You know he's your dad."

Another nod.

"So don't tie yourself down. You can walk away from this place."

She lifted her head and looked at him, her eyes soft and vulnerable.

Alex leaned in, slowly lowering his mouth toward hers. He wanted to comfort her. Wanted to make her forget.

He was abruptly shoved away.

"I tell you how much it means to me to belong to my family and you tell me to just walk away?"

He backed up. "You need to get out of here. You *want* to get out."

"How am I supposed to trust you telling me to leave when you won't even stay and take care of a woman who needs you? Your mother is sick."

"She's always been sick."

"That's your excuse? That she's always needed you? You're no better than my brother, you know that? Shane takes care of everything, so *you* don't have to."

For the first time, Alex felt true anger take him

over. He spun away from her and paced into the living room. Then back. He scrubbed his hands over his scalp and squeezed his eyes shut. "That is not my fault," he growled. "I can't be responsible for what Shane does with his life. I can't be responsible for what *you* do with your life."

She stared him down.

"We were kids, Sophie. They were adults. All of them. We don't have to carry them or pay for their sins or clean up the mess they made."

"They're family," she said.

"And saying that over and over again isn't a fucking life! Do you get that? Do either of you get that? Saying that someone is family isn't a magic spell. It doesn't make anything better. It doesn't make things right, damn it!"

"Well, what else do we have, then?"

"A goddamn life, Sophie. Anything you want. You can have everything."

She stared at him with that infuriating cool. "As long as I'm like you and don't care about a home."

Did she think he didn't care? That he didn't *want?* "Sophie—"

"You need to leave, Alex."

He shook his head.

"I'm never going to be like you. I'll never walk away from everything just so I can hope for something else."

Right. Sure. Alex nodded. He knew what she was saying. He saw it in Shane's eyes every time. "I'm glad you feel like you have something here, then. Because I never had even that."

Every nerve in his body pulled back as he walked away. He wanted another shot. Wanted Sophie to stop him. But as he reached her front door, he told himself he was relieved. After all, what would he do with another shot? Hang around for a day or two before he moved on to the next job? He'd tried that already. It hadn't worked with Andrea. It wouldn't work with Sophie. She was right about that, at least. She wasn't like him.

So he walked out. "Call me when you get to California," he said from the doorway. "I'll show you a cove that no one else knows."

When his foot hit the first step, she closed the door. Alex walked on.

CHAPTER SEVENTEEN

ALEX CRACKED HIS eyes open, then squeezed them tightly shut at the piercing light that greeted him. His mouth felt dry as dirt and his head ached. He was hungover. Great. This town continued to bring out the best in him.

He tried again, easing his husk-dry eyes open and focusing on an unfamiliar wall. Where the hell was he? He remembered going back to that dive bar. He remembered ordering Scotch. Several times. That same blond bartender had been there, giving him the same friendly once-over.

Shit. He hadn't ended up at her place, had he? Surely he'd remember something of the sex, if not the ugly reasoning for it.

He rolled over and lifted his head from the pillow. No. Not her place. Just a different room in the same motel. He remembered now. He'd checked out that afternoon and when he'd come back last night, his old room had been rented out already.

"Fuck," he breathed, letting his head drop. Even if he'd never see Sophie again, he was glad he hadn't ruined their affair by ending it with someone else.

It wouldn't have been a high note after what he'd had with Sophie. With her, it was something… different. Intense and brutal, yet still sweet. He hadn't thought those things went together. Thank God he hadn't fucked it up.

Well. He'd screwed it up in all kinds of ways, but at least he hadn't gotten drunk and fallen into bed with someone else. That would've tainted everything. And if Sophie had ever heard about it, it would've hurt her. Alex dared a glance at the clock and cursed. He was supposed to meet Shane at their mom's house in fifteen minutes. He needed a long, scalding shower and several cups of good coffee before he'd be fit company. Neither of those were going to happen, but he forced himself out of bed anyway and fired up the pitiful one-cup coffeemaker.

The shower was scalding, at least, but it only lasted two minutes. The almost-hot, high-acid coffee was waiting for him when he got out. Alex downed it in three gulps. He was out the door five minutes later.

Clouds greeted him and he felt the occasional drop of rain hit his neck as he drove. It was a shitty day to leave town, but that seemed like the appropriate way to go at this point.

He gave the door a perfunctory knock before letting himself in, moving quickly to avoid staring toward Sophie's house like a kicked puppy.

"Hello?"

Shane walked out from the kitchen. "Thank God you're here. I'm starving and the only thing around is stale bread and a bunch of leftovers that do not look recent. Mom seems good. She's in the bathroom. We'll leave as soon as she's ready."

Alex glanced toward the kitchen. "I don't smell coffee and I could damn sure use another cup."

"Yeah, you look like shit. Not the relaxing night you were hoping for?"

He shot his brother a narrow look.

"That bad, huh?"

"It was pretty damn bad."

"Well, at least you're on your way out of town."

"Yeah, at least," Alex muttered. "How's Merry?"

"Better. She bounces back pretty quickly. We'll pick her up on the way to the restaurant."

"I can't believe that place is still open."

"And still the best breakfast in the state."

Alex shot a look toward the hallway. "I'm going to head over and start in on some corned-beef hash by myself if she doesn't hurry up."

"Give her another minute. She's moving slow lately."

"Good thing, or yesterday she might have jumped right over those chairs and pounced on Sophie's back."

Shane smiled. "She was pretty riled up. Hey, at least she taught us to follow our passions in life."

Alex snorted and shook his head, then started down the hall. "Let's get this circus going. Mom?" He tapped lightly, not wanting to intrude. "Are you ready?"

She didn't answer, so he knocked harder. "How long has she been in there?"

"Ten minutes. Maybe fifteen."

Alex frowned, suddenly picturing an open window and curtains flapping in the breeze. What if she'd decided to bother Sophie again?

The door was locked, so he pulled a pocketknife from his jacket and turned the locking switch. "Mom, I'm coming in. Stop me now if you're not decent."

She didn't stop him. She didn't say a word, and Alex felt real worry as he slowly opened the door. The worry exploded into alarm when he saw her slumped on the floor between the toilet and the bathtub, her head tipped back and mouth open.

"Shane!" he yelled, rushing in to touch a hand to her neck. Her pulse was steady, but seemed slow to him. He heard his brother curse from the doorway. "Call an ambulance!"

"What's wrong?"

"She's passed out. I've got a pulse." He looked around for a pill bottle or some other hint of trouble, but saw nothing but hair spray and deodorant and other normal bathroom items. "She's cool. No fever."

He stroked a hand over his mother's hair as Shane began talking to 911. "Mom." She lay limp against the wall. "Mom," he said again, patting her cheek this time. Her eyes fluttered a little, but when she mumbled something, the words were incoherent.

Shane came back, the phone still near his ear. "They're on their way."

"She's coming around a little. Mom, are you hurt anywhere?"

She breathed something about a car, then shook her head. Shane handed Alex a blanket. He draped it over her, then scrunched it up on the edge of the tub and eased her head down toward it.

"Has anything like this happened before?" Alex asked. Shane shook his head. "Could she be doing drugs?"

His brother raised a doubtful eyebrow. "Aside from what her doctor has prescribed, I can't imagine."

"Maybe you should find her prescription. The hospital will probably want to know."

Shane disappeared for what felt like an eternity, before returning with empty hands. "There aren't any down here. Did you check the drawers?"

Alex pulled open the bathroom drawers but found nothing. Finally, the ambulance squawked to a stop in front of the house and the bathroom became controlled chaos as the paramedics checked and poked and prodded before loading her onto a stretcher. She shook her head in vague protest.

"I'll meet you there," Alex said as Shane climbed into the ambulance with her.

For the first time in his life, Alex had been stopped from leaving, and he was thankful. If he'd left, the guilt would've kept him from ever coming back.

"GIRLS' NIGHT OUT!" Lauren shouted as she pushed her way into Sophie's house.

"That's not funny," Sophie said.

"It's not supposed to be funny. It's Sunday. We have a date, remember?" Lauren waved her hand and Isabelle popped inside, too.

Sophie groaned, but Lauren was unsympathetic. "She already knows what happened, so you don't have to worry about telling her."

Was that supposed to be a relief? "I am not going out with you two."

"Why not?"

"Because, one, I don't feel like it, for obvious reasons. And two, you can't be seen with the town slut."

Isabelle smiled. "Are you kidding? That's exactly who I need to be seen with. If a rumor spreads that I'm a slut, maybe I'll get a date this decade."

"Yes," Lauren agreed. "And it'll really cement my identity as the bitch who entranced the gullible widower of a truly nice woman."

"God," Sophie groaned. "Don't make me laugh. I'm too miserable. I'll probably break something if I try."

Lauren pointed toward the hall. "Go get dressed. We'll wait. And put on some makeup. You look like you've been crying all day."

"Shit." Sophie felt her composure begin to crumble. She pressed a hand to her eyes.

"Oh, sweetie," Lauren sighed. She tugged Sophie down to the couch and wrapped her arms around her. "You didn't do anything wrong. You don't have to hide."

"I know," she said, even though she didn't know. She'd done lots of things wrong for lots of years. Alex had helpfully pointed that out.

"Listen, you're going to have to get this over with. People are going to whisper. Better to meet it head-on with your best friends right next to you. The longer you hide in here, the harder it will be."

"I should go see my dad," she mumbled.

Isabelle offered a disapproving snort. "It's almost seven. You're not going out to your dad's tonight."

She was right. Sophie had been putting it off in half-hour increments, and now the whole day was gone, wasted hiding under blankets on her couch. She'd wanted to go see her dad, but she hadn't known what she would say. There were a hundred things. A thousand. And none of them were right.

"It was so awful. You guys have no idea."

"I was there, remember? It was awful, but do you know who people were talking about when it was over? Not you. *Her.* I'm not going to patronize you and tell you no one was excited about your involvement, but most people felt bad for you, Sophie."

Was that true? She'd felt like Hester Prynne in *The Scarlet Letter,* standing there while the whole town judged her a whore.

Lauren nudged her. "Go wash your face and brush your hair and get dressed."

Isabelle nudged her other side. "We're not taking

no for answer. You need to get out. Isn't that what you always tell me, even when I really, really don't want to go?"

Sophie groaned. "I'm not up for flirting with men tonight."

"Oh, please," Lauren said. "This has nothing to do with men. We won't even look at them. We'll growl if they come near. This is just about us."

She wanted to curl up under the blankets and cry some more, but that was probably a pretty good reason to listen to her friends. "Okay," she sighed, then smiled when the whole couch bounced with their celebration. "But I won't look pretty," she warned.

"We don't care," Isabelle said. "We'd still do you."

"You're so sweet." She stood up and trudged toward the bathroom, then winced when she saw her eyes. She really did look like she'd been crying all day. And night.

Fifteen minutes of intensive reconstruction made enough of a difference that she could go out without looking like a hospital patient, but she wasn't quite up for heels and stockings. Instead, she pulled on the jeans she'd worn the other night and a loose cashmere sweater. Maybe the ivory color would make her look innocent. She grabbed her brown leather boots and rejoined the girls.

"Oh, my God," Lauren exclaimed. "You look almost presentable! Good job."

"Thanks."

"Let's go. I'll drive. Your only job is to get drunk."

"And ruin Isabelle's reputation."

Isabelle gave her a thumbs-up.

Despite Sophie's bravado, her stomach hurt the whole way to the bar. She clenched her hands tight and tried not to change her mind. She could quit her job, move back home, order everything she ever needed online. She'd never have to see another person again. After all, she'd never been brave about anything. Why start now?

She opened her mouth to say she didn't want to do this, but Lauren slapped her leg. "We're here!"

"No," Sophie groaned. "The saloon?" This time of year, it would be packed with locals. "Why don't we go to that wine bar on—"

"Oh, did I forget to tell you to wear your big-girl panties? I must have, because you're obviously wearing some sort of inferior underwear."

"I hate you."

"No, you don't. Have you eaten anything?"

"Yes. I made a pot of mac and cheese for breakfast and then I ate it all day."

Lauren got out and rounded the car to open Sophie's door. "Good. I don't think pretzels will be able to absorb this much alcohol."

Isabelle gave another thumbs-up.

Sophie really did love these women, even if they were pains in her ass right now. No one else had bothered to check on her today. Her dad was dealing with his own sorrow. And her brother was a shit. And Alex...Alex had moved on. Good riddance.

So why did she have to blink back tears as she got out and followed her friends into the Crooked R Saloon?

It had just been a fling. And he didn't understand her. He didn't know what it was to have other people depend on you. He was selfish and placeless and—

"Stop frowning," Lauren ordered. "Look like you don't give a damn."

"I need a drink," she snapped.

Lauren poked Isabelle. "Go talk to that hot bartender. Sophie needs a martini, stat. We'll find a table."

Sophie glanced behind the bar and almost spun around. Benton was there. A really cute, really sweet guy that she'd accidentally slept with when she'd thought he was only here for one ski season. She didn't want to see him tonight. She didn't want him to see her.

But when he glanced up and caught her eye, he just offered a wide grin and a wave. He didn't look pitying or scandalized. She waved back.

His hair was done up in wild twists tonight. They should have made him look a bit mad. Instead they made him look like an even-more-beautiful sibling of Lenny Kravitz. He had to be the most popular bartender in town, but he still had a friendly, open smile for Isabelle as she leaned close to order.

He was nothing like Alex, who scowled way more often than he smiled, and who would definitely move on like she expected him to. He didn't know how to listen or comfort. He didn't seem to know what she wanted to hear. But he also made her shiver with something close to fear when he touched her and told her what he wanted.

Shit.

"You're frowning again," Lauren said as she tugged Sophie to a table and sat down. "But that's okay. No one is even looking at you. See?"

She was right. Sophie looked around and saw that nobody seemed very interested. Only one face turned toward her, a woman Sophie recognized as a library patron. But that woman just gave a chagrined smile and looked back to her drink.

But Sophie was unconvinced. "They're probably waiting for a few more people to get here to be sure the mob is effective."

"Or it's really not as big a deal as you think it is."

Sophie felt almost resentful of that. It was a big deal. It was a goddamn community disaster.

Or just a personal embarrassment, she chided herself. She slumped in her chair as Isabelle returned with drinks. "A martini for Sophie, and beers for us. Well, one beer for you, Lauren. You're driving."

"Hey, you have to drive home from my place."

Isabelle shrugged. "I'll crash on your couch if I need to."

"Only because Jake is working overnight. Otherwise, I'd kick your ass right out. Speaking of overnight friends…" Her gaze slid to Sophie. "Did Alex ever find you yesterday?"

Sophie shot Isabelle a panicked look, but she seemed unsurprised. Right. Everyone knew now. She only raised interested eyebrows.

Sophie tried to look just as casual. "Was he looking for me?"

"Yes. I came by your house and he was there."

"Well, he didn't find me, so he left town."

"Ah."

"Yeah. 'Ah.' And then I came home last night and found his mother sitting in my living room."

Lauren gasped, while Isabelle muttered "No fucking way."

Sophie felt a brief moment of vindication. That she wasn't the bad one. That that woman was seriously wrong in so many ways. But then she felt guilty. "Guys, I think she's truly unwell. She was confused. She thought I was my mom. She asked where her husband was."

"Oh, no," Lauren sighed.

"Yeah. I think maybe it's something more than just meanness on her part. I guess time will tell. In the meantime, I expect to wake up to find the word *slut* spray-painted on my house any day now."

"Who doesn't?" Lauren offered with a sympathetic smile.

"Me," Isabelle chimed in.

Sophie laughed then. Really laughed. She realized that half her martini was gone and her friends were smiling at her and she didn't care who was looking. It really wasn't a big deal in the grand scheme of things.

It wasn't a community disaster or even a personal one. At this point, twenty-five years removed from that awful day when two parents had gone missing, it was really just a sick old woman trying to work out her heartbreak however she could. She didn't want to be alone with her hurt. Sophie couldn't understand that, but maybe she could forgive it.

Isabelle took a swig of her beer and shook her head. "I can't believe you had sex with a hot guy with tattoos. I hate you, Sophie. I hate both of you."

Sophie patted her hand. "If you want a boyfriend, you need to get out and—"

"I don't want a boyfriend. I'm terrible with men. I'm awkward and inattentive and not feminine and cute like you. I'll be forty in a few years, for God's sake. I just want to be used like a cheap rag. Several times a month. Is there a service for that? Dark room? No talking? Big cock?"

Sophie laughed again. And this time she couldn't stop. She laid her head on her hands and laughed. Isabelle was so blunt about everything, but she'd never said anything like that before. But the laughter tipped over into tears. "Oh, God," Sophie sobbed.

"Hey." She felt Lauren's hand on her back. "Are you okay?"

Sophie only laughed harder, but she raised her head as she wiped the tears from her eyes.

"Oh, good. I thought the memory of big cock had finally broken you."

"He did come back last night," Sophie said when she could finally breathe.

"Oh, *speaking of...*" Isabelle muttered.

"That's not what I meant. We didn't *do* anything. Except argue."

"About his mom?"

"Kind of. I said he needed to stick around and take care of her. Make sure she's really okay. He said I needed to grow up and move out of here. Go somewhere new. As if I could just walk away from my dad. I told him to fuck off." She shook her head in exasperation, then noticed that her friends weren't giving quite the same look. "What?"

Lauren shrugged.

"What?" Sophie repeated.

"You've been here your whole life."

She bristled. "So? It's a great place. Ninety-nine percent of the people who live here moved from someplace else, because everyone loves Jackson."

Lauren didn't back down. "You don't love Jackson."

Sophie looked at Isabelle for support, but Isabelle shrugged. "What if you're meant to be somewhere else and you don't even know it?"

"You guys, my dad needs me."

"For what?" countered Lauren. "To cook and clean? I'm sure he can handle that just fine on his own. What's he going to do when you get married and you're too busy to help?"

Sophie didn't say what she was thinking, because

she was thinking that she'd never expected to get married. She couldn't. Because she needed to take care of her dad. And because she was just like her mom. Her friends wouldn't want to hear that even if it was the truth. "I take care of the books, too. All of the bills and accounting and—"

"Sophie," Isabelle interrupted. "There must be a thousand men his age in Wyoming who take care of that for their own ranches. Or they hire an accountant. I bet if you asked your dad he'd say he doesn't need you."

Sophie gulped the last of her martini. How could she say that? What if it were actually true?

"I'll get you another," Isabelle volunteered, setting off for the bar again.

"That's terrible," Sophie whispered once she was gone.

"What's terrible?" Lauren asked.

"Everyone keeps saying that he doesn't need me. That I should leave. But what is family for? We need each other. We take care of each other."

"I love my son to pieces, but he's off at college now and I'm fine. If he ends up back here at some point, I'd love that, but if he's happier somewhere else that's where I'd want him to be."

"You're a lot younger than my dad, Lauren."

"He's not the issue, Sophie. You've hung around here way too long. You want to travel, right? You always talk about it, but you never do it."

"I'll travel," she said defensively.

"Sure," Lauren said, but her smile was too sympathetic. It wasn't pity for what had happened to Sophie yesterday; it was pity for what happened every single day.

"You have the same life," Sophie insisted. "We live in the same place and work at the same library. If it's fine for you, why isn't that enough for me?"

"Because I think you want more. And I think you're afraid to take that chance."

Sophie stared down into her empty glass. Did everyone think that?

"Hey, I might be wrong. But think about it. You don't need to make any life-changing decisions. You could just try a road trip. Take a vacation. Spend a couple of weeks somewhere else."

But Lauren didn't understand. If she left for two weeks, her dad really could realize he didn't need her.

A new drink appeared. Sophie took it from Isabelle's hand and drank it quickly. "Sure," she eventually said. "I'll take a vacation."

But she knew she wouldn't. There might not be a place for her when she got back.

ALEX WANTED TO run. He wanted to get on his bike and tear out of town and never look back. But he tightened his hold on his mother's fingers as a nurse tried for the fourth time to get an IV needle into her other hand.

"I'm sorry," the nurse said. "She's really dehydrated."

Alex nodded and let his mom squeeze harder.

"There we go. All done. Just let me get this taped up. You did great, Mrs. Bishop."

His mom whimpered like a scared child just as she had with every blood draw they'd done over the past few hours.

Sophie had been right. Something was really wrong.

The doctor came in, squinting from behind oversize glasses. "My suspicions were correct. A severe vitamin B12 deficiency."

"A what?" Alex asked. "She needs vitamins?"

"Essentially, although it's not as benign as it sounds. Oftentimes, when seniors become malnourished, the lack of B12 can severely complicate their health."

Alex looked at Shane, who seemed just as confused as Alex felt. "Malnourished? What do you mean? She's not starving."

"Has she lost a lot of weight recently?"

Shane shook his head. "I don't know. I haven't seen her like this." He tipped his chin toward her, her naked limbs unprotected by the flimsy hospital gown. She looked shockingly thin without the protection of the layers and thick sweaters she always seemed to be wearing. "She's definitely thinner than she was a few years ago."

The doctor nodded. "I work over in the senior center, and this isn't uncommon, especially when older people get stressed. They stop eating. They start to lose weight, then their appetite just seems to fade."

Alex nodded. "So she's weakened. She just needs food and vitamins."

But the doctor didn't look reassured. "She'll be in the hospital for at least a few days. Likely a week. We'll slowly rehydrate her and renourish her. But the B12 deficiency will take at least a couple of weeks to reverse. It's not just about strength. She's had some erratic behavior?"

"You could say that," Alex muttered.

"B12 deficiency often has psychiatric manifestations. Depression, paranoia, even hallucinations."

"From vitamin deficiency?" Shane barked.

"Yes. Confusion, aggression, anger."

Shane and Alex looked at each other in shock.

"She's been having trouble for a couple of months now," Shane said. "We thought it was due to her mood disorder."

The doctor nodded. "Probably made it worse. And if she's on any medication, there's a good chance she hasn't been taking it."

"I'll ask her doctor."

"Sure. I just want to assure you that this is very reversible. But someone will have to be sure she's taking better care of herself. She also has very high levels of C-reactive protein. It could be an infection, but considering her lack of fever, I suspect it's arthritis. We can run some X-rays tomorrow to check. Has she complained of any pain?"

Shane looked at Alex, but Alex wouldn't know. Shane answered. "She hasn't complained much, but I notice she's had a little trouble walking. That started this summer."

"Well, don't worry. We'll figure it out, and she'll be able to answer more questions in a day or two. Right now she needs rest and fluids. We've got both of your numbers if we need to be in touch. I'll be on rounds starting tomorrow at nine."

"Thank you," Shane said.

Then they were alone. They both watched their mother for a long time before Alex spoke. "Sophie was right. She said there was something really wrong. I didn't buy it."

Shane blew air out on a long sigh. "I don't know how I missed it."

"It must have been gradual. And she's always been temperamental."

"Yeah." But Shane didn't look convinced. "But the messy house and the escalating behavior. Shit, I should've at least noticed the weight loss."

Alex hadn't been around to notice anything, so he'd never say a word against Shane. "You did notice. You said she'd been getting better and then she wasn't. You just didn't know what it meant. I've never heard of this B12 shit. Have you?"

Shane shook his head. They stared at their sleeping mother for a long minute. Finally, Shane cleared his throat. "I've got to call Merry. She's worried sick."

"Go on. Go see her. I'll stay with Mom."

"You don't need to do that. The nurse said she'd probably sleep through."

"It's fine. You stayed with her last night."

"Well, fuck," Shane sighed. "I didn't do a very good job of that."

"You're the one who's been here for her for years. I don't want to hear a word about it. Go see Merry and get some sleep. I'll stay for another couple of days so you don't have to take care of this on your own."

Shane met his gaze, a frown gathering between his eyes as if he wanted to say something. But in the end, he only said, "Okay. Thanks."

Alex felt shame roll through him at that. That his brother would feel a need to thank him for hanging around to help for a day or two. "I'll text you if anything comes up," he murmured.

It was quiet after Shane left. Even if his mom had been awake, Alex wouldn't have known what to say to her. But compared to some remote flights he'd caught on cargo planes, this hospital room was a luxury. He went to the vending machine and managed to make a three-course meal of chips, meat sticks and a candy bar, then he settled into the recliner and waited.

He wanted to call Sophie, or at least text her, but after what his family had put her through, she deserved a night free of chaos. Not that she'd necessarily take his call. He'd tried to help last night, but she hadn't wanted that.

He never knew what to say to women when they were upset. He didn't know how to comfort them. He'd spent his whole childhood blocking out his mother's pain and then running away from it.

According to his ex, and other women before her, he was insensitive and a jerk and heartless. Most of the time that was when he was really trying, which only left him more confused.

No, he'd fucked it up again, and what did it matter anyway? What was he going to do? Tell her how amazing she was, make her life better, and then wave goodbye on his way out of town? That probably wasn't what women meant by a "good listener."

He'd be in town for a couple more days now, but that wouldn't be enough. It wouldn't be enough for... whatever it was that he wanted. Some time with her. Easy time where nobody else needed anything from her. Time where they could talk about things that had nothing to do with their families or this place. Time when he could learn every kind of touch that made her sigh or scream or shake.

Two or three days wouldn't be enough for all that. A few days would only make it worse. But some part of him wanted to bring on the pain. And Alex wasn't sure he could take it.

CHAPTER EIGHTEEN

"DADDY?" THE SCREEN DOOR banged behind Sophie when she walked in. It was early, only 8:00 a.m., but she had to be at work in two hours, even if she was only presenting herself to be sacked.

The kitchen was quiet, but the steaming coffeepot beckoned. Despite her four martinis the night before, she hadn't fallen into bed and passed out. She'd tossed and turned for hours, thinking about her family and this place and what she wanted most in life. Now she was exhausted and hollow, and she still had no idea what to say to her father.

Her momentary relief of not finding him in the kitchen was cowardly. She knew it was, but she couldn't stop the feeling.

Sophie poured herself a tall mug of coffee and added sugar. After a few sips, she gathered up the breakfast dishes and set them in the sink, then she wiped down the table. She knew that she was comforting herself, that being useful was her Xanax, but it still helped. And someone had to clean the kitchen. It wasn't wasted work.

And what if this was the last time?

"Sweetheart? Is that you?" he called from deeper in the house.

"I'm in the kitchen, Dad!" Her heart pounded hard, but she resisted the urge to turn on the faucet and start washing plates.

"I was just about to head out. Is everything all right, princess?"

She nodded and gave him a hug. His big hand patted her back the way it always had. Three light pats and then a stronger hug. "I just wanted to check on you," she said.

"I'm good. Your brother is better. In fact, I was going to call you today. He's withdrawing the lawsuit."

"Just like that?"

"We had a talk. He seemed reassured, but I insisted we go ahead with the testing. Did you know you can order a kit online? The world is weird these days. But I think just getting it out in the open helped him feel better."

"He's an idiot."

"Don't talk that way about your brother."

She nodded, but she didn't apologize. Her dad might forgive such a thing easily, but she wouldn't.

"How are you doing, sweetie?" he asked. "I know Mrs. Bishop hasn't been kind to you. And after this..."

"It's fine," she said, not mentioning the little breaking-and-entering incident. "I'm fine. But I've been thinking...."

"I hope you don't want a DNA test, too," he said.

She laughed at his dry delivery. Sometimes it took people a while to realize when he was joking, but she always heard his wry humor.

She sat down with her coffee and her dad joined her. "You always took such good care of me."

"Of course I did. You're my little girl."

Tears sprang instantly to her eyes at those simple words. Her throat closed. She tried her best to swallow the tears.

"Dad, you never gave me any reason to feel this way, but when Mom vanished, I was so scared. I thought you wouldn't want me anymore. You weren't my real dad and you had no reason to keep me—"

"Sophie," he scolded.

"I know. I know you didn't feel that way, but I was so little, and I knew Mom had done something wrong. I wasn't sure what, but I knew it was bad, and I didn't want to be bad. I didn't want to be like her. I just wanted to stay with you."

He reached out and took her hand and the tears were back.

She breathed deeply, slowly, trying to get control.

"I took care of you and David. I wanted to. Because I wanted you to be happy and I *needed* you to be happy with me."

"Sophie, I adopted you so you wouldn't ever feel that way."

She nodded. "I know. But that was two years later.

And really, I just took it as proof that I had taken the right tack. That I was earning my keep."

"Oh, Sophie. You were my daughter from the moment I laid eyes on you. You didn't have to earn a damn thing."

"I know," she repeated, a sob breaking free when she spoke. She wiped her eyes with a rough swipe and sniffed hard. "I know that, but I was scared, Daddy. She just disappeared and suddenly everything was in question. Anyone could leave, even me."

He squeezed her hand hard. "I guess I should've been smarter about it. I should've gotten you some counseling at school, or something."

A watery laugh escaped her at the idea of old Mrs. Simmons in the school counselor's office doing anything to help. "Maybe. But we did the best we could. Both of us."

"We did," he said.

"I'm only telling you now, because I need to find a way to stop feeling that way. I…I just never got past it. I need to feel like you *need* me, because if you don't…" Her voice cracked but she forced herself to continue. "If you don't need me, then why would you love me?"

"Girl," he said, his fingers digging into hers now. "You know that's not true. I love you like crazy. I always have and I always will. There's nothing you can do to end that. *Nothing.*"

She nodded, but she couldn't speak now. She was

choking on tears. Her dad pulled his chair closer to hers and put his arms around her.

"I'm sorry," he said. "I'm sorry I didn't make that clear to you. I thought it would be easier if we went on as if things were normal. I thought that would be better for you."

She nodded. She needed to tell him it wasn't his fault, that he hadn't known, but all she did was weep into his shoulder.

"Shh," he murmured. "You're fine."

And she was fine. She knew that. She'd be fine if she could just stop crying all the time.

"I don't know if I should tell you this, Sophie, but I haven't actually needed you for a long time."

She nodded, but she frowned into his shoulder.

"When David was little, you took care of all the things I never would've thought of. You gave this place a woman's touch. But after that, I just assumed this was how you liked to spend your time. When you moved to your uncle's house, I was hoping you'd start forgetting about us."

"What?" What the hell? Was everyone crazy except her?

"You need to get out and start your own life, Sophie. You always wanted to travel. When are you going to do that?"

She slapped a hand to her mouth, half laughing and half crying. "Have you been talking to my friends?" she gasped through her fingers.

"Why? They been telling you the same thing?"

She shrugged.

"Then I guess I should've set you straight a long time ago. Cut the apron strings."

"I'm the one with all the aprons!"

"And you're too young for that. Go on. Stop hanging out with your old dad."

She pulled a napkin from the holder and mopped her face.

"I hope you and your brother are done with confessions. I can't take any more. At least space them a few years apart."

"All right. I'll save the next one up for a while."

He nodded. "You want to come out with me today? I'm just riding the fence. You loved that when you were little."

"I can't. I've got work." She'd have to reconstruct her face again and try to look dignified for her visit to Jean-Marie's office. If she could've stayed and rode the fence with her dad, she'd have been the happiest girl in the world. But she wasn't a girl anymore. She was far past it. She had to start facing up to that.

She gave her dad a long hug, then watched as he took on her role and found a portable mug to pour her coffee into. He even wrapped up one of the rolls she'd made the week before and stored in the fridge.

"Thanks, Daddy," she whispered as she took her care package. Just this small thing was different. A signal to her that he didn't need her.

He didn't need her.

She said it to herself as she got in her car and headed back to town.

It felt awful, but it was the truth. She'd tried to make herself indispensable and she'd failed. But if she'd failed, and he'd still loved her for all these years, then...

Sophie took a deep breath and let it out slowly.

She'd wanted this her whole life. To know that he loved her no matter what. And to be free to fly and know he'd be there if she fell.

Oh, God. She could do that. She could leave and it would be okay, because he said it would be.

And sometime in the past two days, she'd finally realized something important. She didn't have to fear turning into her mother. Not in that way. Her mother had never meant to leave at all.

So now what? She could walk into work without fear of being fired, because she could move on. Move away. Do something different. Her relief was braided up with fear, but she felt a little stronger already. A little more herself.

If she ever saw Alex Bishop again, she'd have to thank him. He'd hurt her, but he'd told her the truth, at least. He was the first one to see through her so clearly.

CHAPTER NINETEEN

ALEX'S MOTORCYCLE WAS in his mother's driveway.

A long day on her best behavior at the library had left Sophie feeling too exhausted to care about anything, or so she'd thought, but at the sight of that bike, she slowed her car and stared.

He was still in Jackson.

She saw his shadow move past the front windows and put her foot to the gas to scoot by before he saw her. She'd told him to fuck off. That was a fairly definitive declaration. She couldn't sit outside his house and moon over him now.

But she felt guilty as she pulled into her carport. She'd judged him and thrown his flaws at him like weapons. She'd tried to hurt him for hurting her. But she was just as screwed up as he was. Just as damaged by everything they'd lived through. Maybe more so, because as she'd made her way through her day, she'd realized that she'd spent her whole life making up for something her mother hadn't even done. Worse, she'd known that for a year now. That her mother hadn't walked out, she hadn't abandoned anyone, she'd just *died*.

So what was Sophie trying to prove?

Alex's experiences had been real, not imaginary. He hadn't woven his fears out of thin air, they'd been drummed into him by his own mother.

Sophie could talk to him about it. She could apologize for her anger. But what would be the point? There was no reason to try to improve their relationship when he'd leave tomorrow or the next day and she'd never see him again.

She dropped her purse on a chair and kicked off her heels and tried to pretend the idea didn't make her want to cry. She felt so close to him, so *connected,* but there was so much she didn't know about him and never would. His favorite movies, his favorite foods, what he was like to come home to after a long day. She just wanted a few of those things with him. Moments that would make him more real when he was gone.

Maybe she would call him when she made it to California. Because she would make it. Soon.

A soft knock broke through her thoughts. She swung around and stared at the door. It could be him. But it wasn't. He'd never knocked like that before. He didn't know how to be tentative. She told herself to stop hoping and went to open the door.

"Hi," Alex said. He held the gray kitten carefully to his chest.

She swallowed and didn't speak. He looked tired, but the dark shadows beneath his eyes and the stubble that covered his jaw only made him look sexier.

When she didn't say hello, he wrapped his fingers around the kitten's paw and waved it. "Pastel says hello, too."

Jesus. Was he trying to kill her?

"Please don't ask me to steal your mom's cat again." She had to fold her arms to keep from reaching for Pastel when she meowed plaintively.

"I'm sorry," he said, "that was a mistake, but I'm hoping you can take Pastel for a few more days."

She shook her head.

"You were right, Sophie. There was something wrong. My mom will be in the hospital for a while."

Sophie gasped and took the kitten from him, then backed quickly away so Alex could come inside. "What happened?"

"She collapsed. We took her to the hospital yesterday. Apparently she hasn't been taking care of herself. She hasn't been eating."

"Oh, no!"

"She's got a vitamin B deficiency, which can cause psychological problems. Have you ever heard of that?"

She shook her head.

"Well, you were right. She really didn't know who you were that day you found her here. And her behavior for the past few weeks… That was probably because of the vitamin issue, too."

"Wow," she breathed. "She doesn't really hate me?"

"Oh, I wouldn't get attached to that idea."

"Ha." She shook her head and snuggled the kitten as it curled against her chest and began to purr. "Are you okay?"

"Yeah. I'm tired. I spent the night at the hospital with her, and then spent part of the day trying to find the things she wanted me to bring to her hospital room. But the kitten… Do you think you could watch her for a little while longer?"

Sophie tucked her face into the warm fur. "I guess so," she said, resisting the impulse to cry, "You'll never take her from me!"

"Thank you," he said quietly. "And thanks for worrying about my mom. If it weren't for you, I'd have already been three states away."

She nodded. "What are you going to do?"

He sighed and rubbed a hand over his eyes. "I don't know."

Sophie tipped her head toward the couch without even thinking about it. "Want a beer?"

"Fuck yes."

She handed the kitten over and went to the fridge to get them both beers. Then she grabbed two more. She didn't know about him, but she thought she might down her first in one long draw. Her mouth watered at the thought.

"Thanks," he said when she handed him a beer. The kitten curled up on his lap. Sophie wished she could forget everything else and do the same.

"I need to apologize," she said. "For the other night. I shouldn't have yelled at you."

"I deserved it."

"No. You were right. I talked to my dad. He doesn't need me, he just thought I needed him. I guess I did." She finally tasted her beer, hoping to swallow her welling tears away. By the time she was halfway through the beer, she felt better.

Alex's hand touched her knee. "I shouldn't have said it the way I did. I'm not very good at helping out. But I guess you know that."

"You're helping your mom right now."

He shook his head. "I have no idea what I'm doing."

"That doesn't matter. You're trying. And you were trying the other night. I just didn't want to hear it."

"So we were both right? Just not about ourselves?"

She smiled. "Maybe that's how most people are."

"Most fucked-up people anyway."

He opened his second beer and finally relaxed into the couch, his head dropping back, eyes closing.

"What's going to happen with your mom? Will she be okay?" Sophie asked.

"I think so. She's already doing better today with some hydration and supplements. But she's got arthritis, too. I think that's why she stopped using the second level of her house. The first floor is a mess."

"But she'll get better?"

"Yes. She'll be able to go home in a few days. I don't know what will happen then. Her place needs work."

She watched him. Studying the blunt eyelashes

against his cheek, and the shape of his nearly smooth skull, and his wide mouth. "When are you leaving?" she asked, hating the way her voice went rough at the idea.

"I don't know," he rasped. "I have to be in Alaska in three weeks. I can't stay."

"You could stay for a little while."

His eyes opened. He turned his head to watch her, but didn't say a word.

"You could just help until she's better."

He still didn't say anything, and Sophie felt like squirming. Could he hear the selfish thread wound into her words? That *she* wanted him to stay? Even if he didn't want to?

He sat up a little and took a swig from his beer, then he kept his eyes on the bottle. "I don't know them, Sophie."

"Who?"

"My mom. My brother. They're family. I'm supposed to know them better than anyone in the world, but they're strangers. I don't remember my mom any way except sick. And my brother... We both grew up after I left. I don't know what kind of man he is. He doesn't know me. I feel like I just met him."

"So stay," she whispered. "Stay and get to know them."

He frowned at the bottle, not looking convinced.

"I'll make you a deal," she said.

That caught his interest. He turned to meet her gaze.

"If you stay here for three weeks, if you get to know your family again and stop running so far and fast…I'll plan my first trip."

His eyebrow rose.

"A big one," she said. "California. The coast. Maybe I'll even go all the way up to Seattle."

"Yeah?"

She smiled at the surprise in that one word. "Yeah," she answered. "You learn how to stay, and I'll learn how to go, and maybe we'll actually figure out how to deal with life."

"That seems like a big leap."

Sophie laughed. "I guess I'm a dreamer."

"It also sounds like we'd be moving in opposite directions."

Did he say that because it would bother him? "I won't be leaving right away."

"But I'm going to Alaska afterward. I'd miss your California trip, and I already promised to show you my favorite cove."

Relief made her eyes sting. "Maybe I could wait a little longer, then. Until you're back from Alaska. If you wanted that."

"Shit, Sophie." He reached out to touch his fingers to her jaw. His thumb brushed her cheek and she felt the wetness there. "Yes, I want that. I'd love to see the ocean with you."

Her smile was a little wobbly. "I thought I was never going to see you again."

"I can't imagine not seeing you again," he whispered, then he leaned slowly toward her.

Sophie closed her eyes and waited for his kiss. When it came, it was gentle and slow and sweet. The hand on her face didn't hold her still or pull her closer, it just touched her, his fingertips sliding over her jaw and then her neck until she shivered and pulled back.

The kitten jumped down and shot them a look of irritation before walking toward the bedroom.

"She's jealous," Sophie said.

"But I've been cuddling her all day."

"Now I'm jealous."

He chuckled as she got up on her knees to straddle his lap. She kissed his smile and felt his hands settle on her hips. She took her time tasting him, first his lips, then the seam of his mouth, then his tongue. His hands tightened. She eased her hips back, just to force him to pull her closer.

Yes. She liked that. When she tried to pull back again, he held her tight to him, his fingers digging into her. Sophie's heart sped as she kissed him more deeply and ran her hands down his arms, feeling his hard muscles flex as he held her still.

He moved one hand lower on her hip and pushed her black skirt up until he could slide his fingers around her hip and under her panties. She was almost innocent today. Cotton panties and no stockings. But he didn't let that fool him. This time, when she tried to slide back, his whole hand cupped her ass cheek and gripped her.

"Oh," she gasped into his mouth. She needed this so much. His other hand pushed into her panties and slipped between her legs to touch her. She jerked against him and tore her mouth from his to cry out.

"Why do you like to make me rough, Sophie?"

Oh, God. She shook her head. She didn't want to say it. She just wanted him to do it.

"You want me rough?"

She nodded.

"Tell me why."

"No," she breathed. "No."

The fingers that had been stroking her shoved deep inside her body.

"Tell me," he insisted. "Do you want to be punished?" His other hand rose to twist into her hair. Hard. "For wanting it so much?"

She tried to nod, but he twisted her hair harder. "Yes!" she finally cried out. "Yes." His fingers eased their hold, and his other hand slipped free of her body to stroke her clit.

"Oh, God," she breathed, working herself against his fingers. She was so turned on. So wet and swollen for him already.

"I'll punish you, Sophie," he murmured close to her ear. She shivered as his mouth brushed her neck. "I'll treat you like a whore."

She could barely control her breath now. Yes. That was just what she wanted.

"I'll fuck you hard. Is that what you want?"

She nodded.

"Tell me."

"Yes." She could barely get the word past her tight throat. "I want it hard. Please."

His hands were on her blouse then. He gripped both sides and ripped it open, tearing the fabric and sending buttons scattering. She cried out and her heart pumped so hard it shook, and suddenly she was turning, falling. Her back hit the couch and he was over her, shoving up her bra. His mouth was on her breast, then his teeth on her nipple.

"Yes," she said, gripping his head, feeling the rough stubble beneath her hands and against the sensitive skin of her breast.

He shoved her skirt up to her waist, then tore her panties down as he knelt on the floor between her legs. Books slipped off the coffee table when he shoved it aside. Alex got a condom from his pocket. Sophie squirmed in anticipation.

She didn't have to wait long. The head of his cock slipped along her pussy, making her groan with need. He fisted himself and she felt him begin to push inside. Her body resisted, but he was merciless and she was so damn wet. The pressure of it made her cry out, but he seemed to take it as encouragement. He pulled back a little, easing the tightness, and then he plunged deep.

Sophie screamed with pleasure. God, she loved the way he fucked. She loved the way he treated her gently in every way except this. He was right. She needed it rough. Wanted to be punished. His cock filling her so deep and tight was real and good and everything she wanted.

She stared up at him, heat sweeping through her whole body at the sight of him above her. He looked so dangerous. Furious. His teeth bared in a snarl as he began to fuck her. His hands slid up to her breasts. When he pinched her nipples she bucked against him in shock, then stretched out with a broken moan. Yes. His fingers twisted as he sank his cock deep and she tipped her hips up for more.

God, he was perfect. His big hands bringing her just the right amount of pain, his muscles pressing against inked skin, and his cock a steady, invading force. She wanted him naked, but she liked him like this, too. Jeans unbuckled and unzipped, because he couldn't wait to fuck her, he didn't have time to strip down before he got into her pussy.

"You need it like this, don't you?" he growled.

"Yes," she whispered, eagerly meeting each of his ruthless thrusts.

"Is this what makes you come, Sophie? Being fucked like an animal?" His fingers squeezed her nipples hard. "Being hurt?"

"Yes," she cried, arching up into his rough hands.

"Good. Because I love fucking you just like this. Like you're my personal whore."

Suddenly, one of his hands was on her belly, and

his thumb flicked at her clit. Sophie whimpered, the pleasure so good it almost scared her.

Her thighs began to shake. "Please," she begged. His other hand braced her hip and he fucked her harder. "Please," she said again, over and over. She needed it. She needed to come for him. She whispered his name.

His thumb circled her faster, harder as he matched each stroke of his cock. She loved his body inside hers. Loved his voice telling her what to feel. Loved the way he was so big and strong and in control and she could still break him with her own pleasure. That was what he wanted. Her orgasm. Her need. Her body taking him in.

"Please," she said again, so close to the edge. "Please. Alex." And then she came, screaming, arching up, her nails digging into his arms, trying to bring him with her. Another wave rolled through her, pushing another scream from her throat. She heard him curse. He fucked her harder. And then his hips were tight against hers as he grunted. His cock jerked inside her. She was floating.

She had no idea how long they were frozen like that, bodies still joined and brains not working, but he eventually leaned in to lay his weight on her. He kissed her neck, her shoulder.

"I love hearing my name when you come," he murmured.

"Ha. Narcissist." But when she curled her arms around his back, he sighed and melted into her. He liked to be held after he treated her like a whore. Sophie smiled into his skin. She wouldn't tease him about that. Yet.

"Can you spend the night?" she asked.

"Yeah. I was actually hoping you'd take me in. The kitten was just a ploy."

"Okay, but I'm taking you in for your shots tomorrow."

His laughter rumbled through her. "Fine. But for now… Let's order a pizza from bed."

"Perfect. I don't suppose you like veggie?"

"I should've known." He scooped her up and carried her down the hall. "Though after tonight, I might have guessed meat lover's."

Her shrieks echoed against the wood floors. With all the screaming she'd done tonight, her poor neighbors were going to believe everything they read about her in the paper. But it would be worth it.

CHAPTER TWENTY

"LAST ONE," SHANE SAID, before the drill screamed. He stood and stretched. "Shit. I should've let you have the honor. This is your first big project."

"All I did was lift and hammer and saw exactly what you told me to. This was your deal." Alex stood shoulder to shoulder with Shane and looked over the ramp they'd installed to the front door of their mom's house. It had taken two full weeks, but thanks to Shane, it was solid as hell and could still be easily removed if her rental contract on the house ever came up.

"Maybe it's too much," Shane said, eyeing the ramp with an overly critical eye for the hundredth time since they'd started.

"We're heading into winter soon. The doctor said her stiffness may get worse. She'll need the scooter more, and that temporary metal ramp was crap."

"Right." But Shane still frowned at the ramp. Ironic, considering he'd carved each corner post with a relief of pine trees. It was probably the nicest wheelchair ramp in the state. "Well, I'm glad we got it finished before you leave. When are you going?"

"In three days."

"You leaving the bike here?"

"Yeah. Mom said I could store it in her garage until I get back."

"Good. That means you'll have to come back."

"Yes, but then I'm off again." He grinned and Shane shook his head.

"You're in a bad way."

"Fuck off," Alex grumbled, but then he spotted the source of his trouble walking down the sidewalk and he felt a weakness he couldn't deny.

"Did you see it?" she called out, waving her phone.

"See what?"

"Your mom wrote to the paper again."

"Oh, shit," Alex groaned. She'd been so much better. She'd been almost *normal* for a whole week now. "Tell me you're kidding."

"I'm not," Sophie said. "Is she around?"

"No, she drove her new scooter to the store to pick up a cake."

Sophie smiled and handed him her phone. "Here. It's only in the online edition."

Alex glared down at the phone, but as he scrolled, his worry started to ease.

I'm the woman who wrote a few weeks ago to complain about my son's new girlfriend [Strumpet on My Street]. At the time, I did not appreciate your response, but I've since realized you were partially right. I was suffering from a serious medical condition at the time and I was not seeing everything rationally. I'd like to publicly apologize to my son for the harsh words I wrote. He's an adult and can make his own decisions.

I've gotten the medical help I needed and am now looking forward to a new relationship with my family. My life has been too lonely for too long.

Veronica says: At least I was partially right! I'm glad you've gotten the help you needed to ensure that you and your family are healthy and happy in the future.

"Well." Alex handed the phone off to Shane. "That was progress. But no apology for Sophie yet."

Sophie grinned. "It's okay. I'd say that's pretty amazing progress. And she speaks to me now. We'll get there."

"Maybe. But she still needs to make up for all the crap she spread around town."

Sophie shrugged. "You know what? I'm a big girl. I can handle it. And I managed to hold on to my job with just one tiny warning for stepping out on my shift that day. I couldn't keep up my perfect record forever." She leaned closer. "I'm a very bad girl, after all."

Oh, Jesus, she was a bad girl, even if she was

wearing his very favorite good-girl dress. He traced a thumb over the demure neckline. He loved the bright red of the fabric.

Shane handed him back the phone. "Quite a turnaround," he said.

"Come on." Alex tipped his head toward the front door. "Let's set the table." His mother was hosting a dinner to celebrate her cleaned and updated new kitchen.

Sophie headed into the kitchen to hang out with Merry while Shane and Alex got plates and silverware from the sideboard. The cabinet hadn't been in their family home, but Alex recognized the silverware. He traced a thumb over the checked pattern of the handles. Another thing he'd forgotten.

"Hey, look," Shane said. "It's my Christmas plate."

Alex glanced over at the red-rimmed plastic plate. He snatched it. "That's my Christmas plate!"

"No, yours was green with a Christmas tree in the middle. Mine is the one with Santa." He snatched it back. Suddenly Alex could remember this exact argument, back when he and Shane were young boys. He'd felt that Shane had always gotten the best of everything, because Shane had been older, but he'd also thought everything Shane had was better, simply because it belonged to his big brother.

Alex found the green plate in the same drawer and traced a finger over the chipped edge. "I'm glad you brought me back here," he said quietly.

"Wow. Are you sure? It wasn't quite what I'd envisioned when I asked you to come home for a few days."

"You mean the lawsuit, becoming a town scandal, Mom's hospitalization and three weeks spent fixing up her house?"

Shane quirked an eyebrow. "That about covers it."

"Strangely enough, it's been worth it."

"Sophie?" Shane asked.

Alex shrugged. "That's part of it. But it's more than that. I was so angry at you when I left home. Even angrier than I was at Mom. I felt like you'd betrayed me. We were supposed to be in it together."

Shane shook his head. "No. I was your big brother. I was supposed to protect you."

"I guess I thought that, too. But I was wrong, Shane. We were kids. Both of us. You were only a year older than me. How the hell were you supposed to handle all that bullshit any better than I could?"

"I don't know, but I should have."

"We were both mixed up," Alex insisted. "Both confused."

Sophie stepped into the room, then stopped in the doorway of the kitchen. He met her eyes. "And we were scared," he said.

She watched him for a moment longer, understanding in her soft brown eyes, then she turned and retreated back to the kitchen.

"We were scared, and I reacted with anger and frustration, and you tried to fix it with hope. Neither of us was wrong. I'm sorry it took me so long to forgive you."

"Shit," Shane muttered. "You don't need to apologize."

"Well, neither do you." He set down the plate and grabbed his brother in a quick hug. "I'm going to miss you."

"I'll miss you, too." Shane's arms pulled him tighter for a brief moment. "But I have a feeling you'll be back more often now."

Alex laughed. "Maybe."

Sophie entered again a few moments later, bringing in a big vase of flowers to set on the table. "I still can't believe how much work you boys got done in less than three weeks. The house looks great."

It did look great. They'd cleaned out the whole place, boxing up all the documents she wanted to keep and moving them upstairs. Then they'd moved her real bedroom furniture downstairs to the den, so she didn't have to use the stairs at all unless she wanted to. The house was set up for one-level living, the ramp was installed, the kitchen cleaned and the carpets all replaced with hardwood. He and Shane had worked their asses off. Alex had loved it.

The kitten loved it, too. She careened around the corner and slid across the wood. Alex watched her roll into the baseboard and tried not to frown. Sophie missed the kitten. So did he. But they'd both be traveling a lot now. Pastel was better off here, oddly enough.

Alex shook his head and finished the last place setting. He'd still be gone to distant places too often to have a pet. But maybe, just maybe…not too often to have a woman to love.

"How long until dinner?" he asked Shane.

"Another hour."

"Great. I wanted to fit in another lesson with Sophie before dark. She's getting pretty solid on the bike."

"Can she ride in that dress?"

"If she wants to. She's damn amazing."

Shane shook his head again, as if he were exasperated by the stars in Alex's eyes. Alex wasn't bothered by them himself. He couldn't see the stars, after all. All he could see was Sophie as she wandered into the dining room again.

"Ready for a lesson?" he asked.

For a moment, her face turned wicked and her lips parted, but then she paused and glanced at Shane and decided to play it straight. "Sure!" she finally chirped. Alex grinned as her cheeks turned pink. "I'll just grab my jacket."

She raced from the house, leaving Shane and Alex alone with just the faint sound of Merry singing in the kitchen.

"I guess you're a good teacher," Shane drawled.

"Ha. Maybe. Hey, do you remember when Dad taught us how to use the lawn mower?"

Shane frowned.

"The riding mower."

"Oh." His face cleared and he nodded. "I think I do. That old John Deere mower."

"I thought of that a few weeks ago, right before the dedication. He was a good teacher. Patient. That's what I was going to talk about at the ceremony. The summer he died, he taught me how to use the mower, and I can still feel it. The engine roaring, the sun hot on my arms, and him telling me what a natural I was."

"Maybe that's why you loved bikes so much. You brought your first one home at fourteen. Scared the hell out of me."

"Hmm." Alex frowned down at his hands, so big and blunt like his dad's. He could remember those big hands closing over his little ones on the mower, keeping the wheel steady. "You think?" The smell of gas and the deafening engine and the sun on his face…

Sophie's knock interrupted his thoughts. "Are you coming?" she called from the doorway. His frown disappeared at the sight of her wearing black jeans beneath her dress. She didn't trust herself not to tip the bike over.

"Show me what you've got," he said as he stepped outside and gestured toward his bike.

She looked nervous, the way she always did as she approached the motorcycle, but she swung a leg over, tucked her skirt under her thighs and set her foot to the shift.

"How are you feeling about shifting these days?" he asked.

She only nodded and sent him a quick glance before she turned the fuel cutoff and pulled the choke. She hit the starter switch, then grabbed the clutch and eased the throttle up, making the engine roar. She was getting better. Up until today, she'd gone over every step of starting it before she'd dared.

"I want to see you taking those curves a little faster this time," he said.

She gave him a thumbs-up, then kicked up the stand and balanced on her toes. Alex backed away and she took off.

He felt the strange mix of alarm and joy he always felt when she rode. He wished he could wrap her in a bubble and still let her enjoy her freedom. But he couldn't, and the freedom meant so much to her.

He'd been sure that he wasn't right for her, wasn't right for anyone. He drifted, he moved, he walked away. But he didn't feel any urge to walk away from Sophie, and she didn't seem afraid that he'd go. She hadn't once complained that he had to head to Alaska soon. She'd never pouted or asked him not to go. Either she trusted that he'd come back or knew she'd be fine if he didn't. After all, she'd survived worse.

And he'd been wrong about what she wanted from life. Once she'd started letting go, she'd bloomed. She was teaching her brother how to do the books for the ranch and teaching her dad to cook his favorite meals. She wasn't hanging on. She wasn't afraid.

He watched as she took a corner at a speed that

didn't make him terrified she'd fall over. "Much better," he whispered to himself. She had her permit. She knew what she was doing. Still, he felt his jaw clench as she drove out of sight. He could still hear her though, as she drove down the cross street, then took another turn. She wasn't going far. Thank God.

The Triumph wasn't a huge bike, so it was good handling for her, even if she had asked several times if she shouldn't be learning on a smaller bike. She'd look cute on a smaller bike, but he loved her on his.

Even as he thought it, the engine noise grew from a faint sputter to a steady purr and she turned the next corner with ease. He wouldn't even mention that there'd been a stop sign there because her smile was wide and happy as she drove toward him.

She sped past, kicking up briefly to third gear just to show him she could before slowing the bike and easing into a wide turn in the middle of the street.

Her eyes danced with life when she finally pulled next to him and killed the engine. "That was great," he said immediately.

Her smile grew even wider. "It felt good. Almost natural."

"It looked even better," he said, leaning close to kiss her. Her face looked so small in the helmet. It made him want to take her home and kiss her until she went breathless.

A strange thought. But it matched the even stranger feeling in his chest.

He didn't want to go.

"I'M SORRY I have to leave." Alex loomed over her, the sun and the roar of small jets behind him. "If I could…"

"It's okay." Sophie leaned up to give him another quick kiss. "You'll be back soon."

"I will," he rumbled.

"And I need a little time to recover. You've been pretty thorough the past few days."

"I had to get my fill," he answered.

She slipped a hand up the nape of his neck to his smooth scalp. She'd shaved him this morning in the shower. "So did you get your fill?"

"Jesus, Sophie." He stared down at her for a moment before cupping her head and holding her still for a hard kiss. "I'm not sure that's possible," he murmured against her mouth.

Her chest felt tight and hot at the words.

He kissed her more softly before he let her go. "My brother said you're free to come to brunch tomorrow. They're trying to make sure Mom doesn't get down about me leaving. Changes like that trigger her, I guess."

"I can't. We're finally burying my mom's ashes out near a little spring about a half mile from the house. It was a spot she loved."

"Good. Good for you."

"Yeah." She didn't want to let go of him, but she could feel the minutes ticking away.

"I love you, Sophie." His words were almost lost in the roar of a jet ascending. She stared up at him in shock for a long moment, that strange feeling taking her over again.

"Oh, Alex," she sighed. "I think I love you, too."

He smiled, his whole face going from dangerous to sweet with that one small thing. "You think?"

She nodded and kissed him one last time. "It's scary," she whispered into his ear.

"I know. I'm going to miss you."

"I'll miss you, too. But I'll see you soon."

He stood straight and slung his big bag over his shoulder as she smiled up at him. "Maybe you're not going to miss me enough. You look pretty cheerful."

"That's because we're leaving for California as soon as you get back."

"All right. But try to miss me a little. Okay?"

She grinned. "Okay. Just a little." She could see the mild confusion on his face, but he kissed her one last time, and then turned. He felt like he was hurting people each time he left, but he wasn't hurting her.

He glanced at the car. "You can practice on my bike while I'm gone. Just be careful."

"I won't hurt your bike. I promise."

"I'm not worried about the damn bike."

"I'll be fine, Alex. You're a good teacher."

"All right. And when I get back, I'll take you anywhere you want on that thing. I promise." He stole one last kiss and then he left, walking toward the tiny airport terminal.

"Send me lots of pictures!" she called.

He turned and walked backward. "Deal. I'll call you tonight."

She got in her car and pulled away, returning one last wave as she left. She'd enjoyed the way he watched her with such puzzlement, wondering why she wasn't crying and clinging. But she wasn't worried about him leaving. He was coming back. And then she'd go with him.

Plus, she had bigger things to think about.

After so many years without a life, she had plenty of vacation days saved up for her two-week trip to California. But she also had quite a bit of cash and a plan she hadn't mentioned to Alex yet. If she liked the trip to California, if she liked life on the road, she might make it permanent. For a year or two anyway. She had a lot of savings, an offer to help with curation for an online research library, and a brand-new motorcycle permit burning a hole in her pocket. Two more weeks, and she'd have her license.

If things went well with Alex in California… He'd mentioned his next gig was in Texas. And she so wanted to see Texas. And every state in between.

It'd be hard to leave her family, but she'd have the perfect distraction. She smiled all the way home, then raced into her house to see if her last email had been answered.

Yes. It was hers. A black-and-red 1982 Triumph Bonneville that ran like a dream and only needed a little polishing up. It was hers. She could pick it up in Idaho Falls as soon as she had her license.

Alex had no idea. He thought she'd be riding with him. But she'd be riding all on her own.

She didn't think he'd mind, especially considering her next purchase.

Sophie opened the page she'd bookmarked and stared lustfully at the leather cycling outfit. It was skintight and black leather, with a wide pink stripe that wrapped around the chest of the jacket. The helmet she'd picked out was black as well, with pink flames rising up the sides.

Sophie grinned. She loved it. And Alex would love it, too. Especially when she paired it with the new pink bra and panties she'd bought. Those didn't have flames on them, but they were hot enough.

When Alex got back from Alaska, she'd be waiting with her new bike and her new leathers and a new plan for her life. Nobody needed her, but Alex Bishop loved her.

So many adventures just around the corner. She couldn't wait.

* * * * *

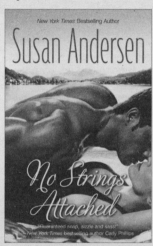

New York Times Bestselling Author

JULIE KENNER

Bookstore owner Veronica Archer is eager to oblige when sexy detective Jack Parker shows up at her shop, seeking help on the stalking case he's working. Verses from Victorian erotica are being left for the victims, and Jack needs to interpret the clues—before someone gets hurt. Thankfully, Ronnie's an expert on naughty turn-of-the-century prose, but if she's going to play teacher, Jack will have to be a dedicated student….

With her own love life stuck in Neutral, Ronnie's sensual studies have piqued her curiosity, and she wonders if reality can be as stimulating as fiction. She agrees to help Jack with his case if he'll satisfy her wildest, most scandalous desires—a request Jack has no problem accommodating. But the closer they get to each other, the closer the stalker circles in, leaving Jack to question if Ronnie is merely a very skilled scholar—or the key to something far more sinister….

Available now wherever books are sold!

Be sure to connect with us at:

Harlequin.com/Newsletters
Facebook.com/HarlequinBooks
Twitter.com/HarlequinBooks

HARLEQUIN® HQN™
www.Harlequin.com

PHJK926

REQUEST YOUR FREE BOOKS!

2 FREE NOVELS
FROM THE ROMANCE COLLECTION
PLUS 2 FREE GIFTS!

YES! Please send me 2 FREE novels from the Romance Collection and my 2 FREE gifts (gifts are worth about $10). After receiving them, if I don't wish to receive any more books, I can return the shipping statement marked "cancel." If I don't cancel, I will receive 4 brand-new novels every month and be billed just $6.24 per book in the U.S. or $6.74 per book in Canada. That's a savings of at least 22% off the cover price. It's quite a bargain! Shipping and handling is just 50¢ per book in the U.S. and 75¢ per book in Canada.* I understand that accepting the 2 free books and gifts places me under no obligation to buy anything. I can always return a shipment and cancel at any time. Even if I never buy another book, the two free books and gifts are mine to keep forever.

194/394 MDN F4XY

Name _____ (PLEASE PRINT) _____

Address _____ Apt. # _____

City _____ State/Prov. _____ Zip/Postal Code _____

Signature (If under 18, a parent or guardian must sign)

Mail to the **Harlequin® Reader Service:**
IN U.S.A.: P.O. Box 1867, Buffalo, NY 14240-1867
IN CANADA: P.O. Box 609, Fort Erie, Ontario L2A 5X3

Want to try two free books from another line?
Call 1-800-873-8635 or visit www.ReaderService.com.

* Terms and prices subject to change without notice. Prices do not include applicable taxes. Sales tax applicable in N.Y. Canadian residents will be charged applicable taxes. Offer not valid in Quebec. This offer is limited to one order per household. Not valid for current subscribers to the Romance Collection or the Romance/Suspense Collection. All orders subject to credit approval. Credit or debit balances in a customer's account(s) may be offset by any other outstanding balance owed by or to the customer. Please allow 4 to 6 weeks for delivery. Offer available while quantities last.

Your Privacy—The Harlequin® Reader Service is committed to protecting your privacy. Our Privacy Policy is available online at www.ReaderService.com or upon request from the Harlequin Reader Service.

We make a portion of our mailing list available to reputable third parties that offer products we believe may interest you. If you prefer that we not exchange your name with third parties, or if you wish to clarify or modify your communication preferences, please visit us at www.ReaderService.com/consumerchoice or write to us at Harlequin Reader Service Preference Service, P.O. Box 9062, Buffalo, NY 14269. Include your complete name and address.

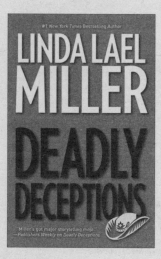

VICTORIA DAHL

(H) HARLEQUIN® HQN™

™ www.Harlequin.com